ONE STEP AWAY

CINDY KIRK

WAVERLY
HOUSE

ISBN: 978-0990716662

CHAPTER ONE

Tonight, Nell Ambrose would embrace the daring nature she normally kept hidden.

"I could have met you at the church." Nell slid into the passenger seat of Leo Pomeroy's BMW roadster.

The two-seater Z4 was an impractical car for northern Illinois, but that was part of the reason Nell enjoyed riding in it. Not that she availed herself of the opportunity very often. The last thing she wanted was for anyone in Hazel Green to think she and the mayor were "involved."

"Since we're both heading straight to the hotel after the wedding rehearsal, driving separately doesn't make sense." Leo, a handsome man with hair the color of rich Colombian coffee and vivid blue eyes, waggled his brows. "Shall I book us a room after we eat?"

Nell only laughed.

She might have agreed if the hotel was a large one in a city like Chicago, rather than an intimate ten-room vintage hotel owned by her best friend. After the rehearsal at the church, the dinner was being held at Matilda's, a farm-to-table restaurant inside the Inn at Hazel Green.

Leo put the car into first gear and pulled away from the curb. "You'll wound me eternally if you say you're not the least bit tempted." He hesitated for several seconds. "It's been a while, and I've missed...it."

Smart man. He'd learned not to say he missed *her*. And Nell was careful not to say words that would tie them together in any way other than physically.

"I am tempted." It had been several weeks since she and Leo had spent any time between the sheets. He'd been busy running the city. She'd been swamped with legal cases and with prepping for a platform performance as town matriarch Hazel Green. "But I won't sleep with you in the hotel owned by the bride."

Daring was one thing. Foolish quite another.

What Leo suggested would be terribly risky, especially since she was determined to keep her relationship with the mayor private.

Nell couldn't keep her lips from curving as a thought struck her. "What do you think about disguising ourselves one day soon and checking in under assumed names?"

It would be difficult since the staff at the inn were well acquainted with both of them. But if they could pull it off...

Escapades were her weakness. When she was young, she'd learned that being bad could be exciting and getting away with things could be addictive. Being very bad, well, that was thrilling.

Leo gave a good-natured chuckle. "Would you really do it?"

"Yes." She shot him a wink but could see he thought she was teasing.

She was dead serious. Which showed he didn't know her nearly as well as he thought he did. If he had any idea of the things she'd done before breaking free of her family...

Well, no matter. If she had anything to say about it, he'd never know all her secrets.

Because, if by some fluke, her past *did* catch up with her, the only house of cards she wanted tumbling down was hers. She would not let Leo, or any of her friends, be caught in the fallout.

"What's the matter?" He reached over, and before she knew what he planned to do, he brought her hand to his lips and pressed a kiss in the palm. "Cornelia Ambrose never looks stressed."

"True." For Nell, the importance of maintaining internal and external control had been drilled into her as soon as she'd been old enough to speak.

"It's been a busy week." She went on to tell him, in very general terms, about several of the cases she'd been working on and about a recent Hazel Green command performance.

"It was at the Palmer House?"

By his tone, you'd have thought she'd jetted off to Cairo instead of simply taking the train into Chicago.

Hazel Green was at the end of the Metra commuter rail. It had taken less than an hour for her to arrive at the front door of the turn-of-the-century elegant hotel off Michigan Avenue.

"It was a luncheon meeting of the Gold Coast Historical Society." Nell's brows pulled together when he turned into the church parking lot. How had they gotten here so quickly?

She enjoyed this alone time with Leo and wasn't ready for it to end.

They never went out together. Granted, there were a number of functions they both attended, but always separately. Tonight, as maid of honor and best man, it made sense for him to pick her up and for them to arrive and leave together.

She pushed open her door while he was rounding the front of the vehicle. "In doing research on their group's history, they discovered that Hazel Green once spoke to their society."

Leo stood next to the car. Even dressed simply in gray pants and a blue striped shirt, he looked every inch the successful businessman he'd been before running for elected office. Like her, the young mayor appeared in no hurry to rush inside.

Nell shut her eyes and lifted her face to the sun. When she opened her eyes, she found Leo staring. "I was remembering the meal. We had turtle timbales, kingfish and bonbons."

The flash of surprise that skittered across his face told Nell she wasn't the only one who found it an odd combination. "Lucinda Covert, the group's president, announced quite proudly that these same three items had been on the menu when Hazel Green originally spoke to the group."

Leo chuckled, seeming to find amusement in the comment. "I assume you gave the same speech to complete the déjà vu moment?"

His sharp mind was only one of the many things Nell liked about him.

"Hazel did a performance as Susan B. Anthony that day, so I spoke as her. Then I switched back to my Hazel Green persona and spoke about the importance of the arts."

"Two personas in one day." Leo appeared both awed and amused. "It's a wonder you can recall who you really are."

Nell wondered what he'd think if she told him she'd had a lot of practice playing different roles. Wondered what he'd think if he knew Cornelia Ambrose wasn't even her real name.

Though Nell knew she should hold back, tonight she didn't stop herself. After a quick glance to make sure they were alone, she gave in to temptation and brushed his lips with hers.

His lips were warm, and the citrus scent of his cologne teased her nostrils. Everything inside her yearned for the honest closeness she could never allow. "I'm enjoying being me this evening. Being me...with you."

"That's how I like it." His voice held a curious intensity.

The look in his vivid blue eyes had Nell shifting focus. She lifted a hand to his cheek and brushed her knuckles against the scruff.

Leo's tactile nature made him an amazing lover. The simple touch had the desired effect. Heat flared in his eyes.

"Are you growing a beard, Mr. Mayor?" Nell cocked her head and spoke in a teasing tone. "Or did you forget to shave this week?"

"That's two days' growth." His eyes never left her face. "I was thinking about letting it grow a little longer. What do you think?"

"Will it be scratchy?"

"If it is, I'll shave it off."

The coquettish smile she shot him was worthy of Hazel Green. "I don't mind it rough."

"Nell." Leo surprised her by taking her hand, tightening his fingers around hers. "Let me come home to you after the dinner tonight. We can—"

"I can't." Genuine regret filled her voice. "We're doing a girls' night at the hotel."

"I could rent a room." His tone turned persuasive. "You could sneak away and join—"

The sound of an approaching car had Nell jerking her hand free. A second later, a red sedan driven by a pretty blonde with a mass of curly hair rounded the corner and swung into the lot. "Looks like Jonah's sister is early, too."

"Think about my offer." Leo's devilish smile could tempt a nun to doff her habit.

Though she and Leo loved to banter, they were both conscious of their positions in the community. Or rather, *she* was conscious of Leo's position. Not only as mayor, but his position as part of what she thought of as the Pomeroy dynasty.

The Pomeroy family was one of Hazel Green's founding families. Jasper Pomeroy had been Richard Green's closest friend.

When Nell socialized with Leo in character as former town matriarch Hazel Green, it was as if she was part of the inner circle. Her lips curved at the thought.

"I can see you're tempted." Leo's low voice was a pleasant rumble.

She met his gaze, and her heart lurched. Truth was, she was

always tempted by Leo. Nell had learned from the best just how fun it could be to take what you wanted. But, like the toys of childhood, she'd done her best to leave that life behind her.

However, sometimes that past came calling, even when not welcomed. She narrowed her gaze at the black Land Rover pulling in beside Jackie's sedan.

What the heck was Dixon doing here?

Dixon Carlyle cut an imposing figure as he stepped from the ebony vehicle. From his stylishly cut hair—dark as a raven's wing —to the tips of his Italian loafers, everything about the man screamed wealth and privilege.

Thankfully, Nell had learned from an early age that appearances could be deceiving. In Dixon's case, she knew for a fact his persona as a successful wealth management adviser was a false front.

She knew his past.

Worse, he knew hers.

Nell still hadn't discovered the real reason Dixon had come to Hazel Green. He'd arrived out of the blue last fall and never left. Supposedly, he had an office in Chicago on Michigan Avenue, but that could be simply another lie he'd spun.

Ever since last month, when he'd taken an apartment in Hazel Green, Nell had done her best to keep her distance. She'd insisted he keep his—but he'd never been good at following orders.

"What's he doing here?" Annoyance laced Leo's words.

"I have no idea." Nell kept the irritation from her voice. Any sign of displeasure would indicate Dixon's presence mattered. *That* was definitely not the impression she wanted to convey.

When he walked over to Jackie and flashed his charismatic smile, Nell knew the groom's twin sister didn't stand a chance.

Jackie Rollins had arrived last week, surprising everyone by announcing she was moving to Hazel Green.

The blonde emitted a full-throated laugh. No doubt Dixon

was dazzling her with his charm. Something he possessed in abundance and knew how to use to his advantage.

She felt, rather than saw, Leo staring at her while her gaze was riveted on Dixon and Jackie.

Nell surprised Leo, and herself, by looping her hand through his arm. "We should say hello. Jackie doesn't know many people in town yet."

"Appears she's getting acquainted." Leo slanted a glance at her. "Tell me again how you know him."

"College friends." Nell kept her tone offhand. "Eons ago. Or at least it feels that way. Do you remember a lot from those days?"

"I remember some, but like you, it seems so long ago." An easy smile lifted Leo's lips. "Were you and Dixon ever romantically involved?"

"No." Nell nearly shuddered at the thought. "He never appealed to me in that way. Now, you, well, let's just say you captured my attention from day one."

"Good to know." He shot her a wink, and together they crossed the short distance to where the couple stood talking. Deep in conversation, Jackie and Dixon didn't turn immediately. When Dixon did look up, he glanced at the hand she rested on Leo's arm. One of his dark eyebrows rose imperceptibly.

Nell caught the gesture only because she knew him so well. Her chin inched up just enough to tell him she didn't care what he thought.

Irritation surged as amusement danced in Dixon's slate-gray eyes.

"Jackie." Nell greeted Jonah's sister, then made a great show of widening her eyes when they landed on Dixon. "And Dixon. This is a surprise. What are you doing here?"

"Frank Partridge came down with the stomach flu." Dixon pasted a sympathetic expression on his face. "I'd been consulting with Pastor Schmidt on several church financial matters. He knows I'm a pianist, and when Frank canceled, he asked me to step in."

Jackie smiled warmly at Dixon. "That was sweet of you."

"Frank Partridge?" Nell paused. "The mailman?"

"Postal carrier." Dixon's lips quirked. "That question tells me you don't attend services at Hazel Green Community. Frank is at the piano every Sunday."

Leo studied the man through curious eyes. "I didn't realize you played."

Dixon shrugged. "I'm not a classical pianist, but I'm accomplished."

"It was kind of you to step in and help." The grudging quality to Leo's compliment had Nell hiding a smile.

"What can I say?" Dixon winked at Jackie. "I'm a nice guy."

It took every ounce of control Nell had not to roll her eyes when Jackie giggled. Instead, she gestured carelessly with one hand toward the church doors. "We should go inside. I'm sure Abby and Jonah are wondering where we are."

Just before they reached the entrance, Henry Beaumont roared up on his Harley. Henry—known as Beau—groomsman and son of the editor of the *Hazel Green Chronicle*, would walk down the aisle with Jackie.

Nell knew the attorney-turned-trial-consultant superficially and had no intention of becoming better acquainted. From a young age, lawyers and police officials had been on her list of those to avoid.

Thankfully, because her practice specialized in child advocacy cases, her interaction with law enforcement was minimal. Her contact with other lawyers, well, that was often unavoidable.

Like now.

CHAPTER TWO

"Tomorrow, I get to scatter real rose petals." Eva Grace Fine, daughter of the bride and ecstatic flower girl, spun in a circle and favored Nell and Jackie with a blinding smile.

For tonight's rehearsal, Eva Grace had chosen to wear a red tulle skirt with a sparkly top covered in poppies. Her curly blonde hair was held back from her face by a thin red satin band.

"If I didn't know better," Nell said to Jackie, "I'd think you were her mother." When Nell had first seen Jonah's sister, she'd been shocked at the resemblance between Jackie and her young niece.

"That's quite a compliment." Jackie smiled. "Since I think Eva Grace is adorable."

Nell was careful who she let into her inner circle. Even those closest to her—such as Abigail Fine—were not privy to her secrets.

Still, she found herself cautiously liking Jackie Rollins. She sensed the woman hid her own secrets behind that sunny smile. Uprooting herself from Springfield, where she'd lived her entire life, to move to Hazel Green didn't make any sense.

Especially when, other than her brother and Abby, Jackie knew no one in town.

"I'm so happy you're both here." Abby stepped into the bride's waiting room and gave each of them a hug.

As was Abby's habit, she'd chosen a vintage dress for tonight's event. The sleeveless brown and white polka dot A-line dress with the white patent leather belt had been popular in the 1960s. It was perfect for someone with Abby's cute figure and big brown eyes.

"I love the dress." Jackie stepped forward and gave her future sister-in-law a hug. "You have such interesting clothes."

"As a merchant in a town that promotes itself as a place where history comes alive, it's practically a requirement." Abby jerked a finger in Nell's direction. "I'm still trying to convince that one to add more vintage to her closet."

"I'm an attorney, not a merchant." Nell ran her fingers through the blonde hair she was in the process of growing out. "I have quite enough vintage in my closet, thank you. Not to mention an entire Hazel Green wardrobe."

For a second, Jackie appeared confused. Then she laughed. "I keep forgetting that Hazel Green isn't just the name of the town. She was a real person."

"Wait until you see Nell in her Hazel Green persona." Pride filled Abby's voice. "You'd never guess it was Nell."

"The first time I saw her, I thought Mommy had made a new friend." Eva Grace quit twirling. "I asked Mommy who she was. When she told me it was Aunt Nell, I said, 'No way, Jose.' But it really was her."

Nell laughed, charmed by the childish chatter. No matter what persona she took on, it was a source of pride that she never broke character. Her mother had once dubbed her a chameleon, able to blend in no matter the surroundings.

"When do I get to walk down the aisle?" The six-year-old's pretty face pulled into a frown as she fixed her gaze on her mother. "Daddy told me if he knew I wouldn't have real flowers to toss, he'd have brought some for me."

"Daddy" was Eva Grace's biological father, Jonah Rollins. Abby had been a surrogate for Jonah and his then-wife, Veronica. When doctors warned the baby would likely be born with severe birth defects, Veronica pushed for an abortion. Abby stood firm and continued the pregnancy, breaking the surrogacy agreement. Eva Grace had challenges, especially during those early years, but none as severe as the doctors anticipated. Abby had spent the first five years of Eva Grace's life as a single parent before Jonah was back in the picture.

"Tossing real petals tonight would be a problem. Instead of leaving right after we finish rehearsing," Abby placed a hand on her daughter's shoulder, "we'd have to stay and pick each one up."

Eva Grace wrinkled her nose. "Oh."

"You're good at pretend." Abby smiled. "We'll see those petals even though they aren't there."

Nell knew the truth behind the statement. Most people saw what they wanted to see, not what was right in front of them. Perception, she'd learned from an early age, was everything.

Eva Grace appeared uncertain, but at that moment, Liz Canfield rushed into the room.

"I'm so sorry. The train was late and, well…" Liz paused. "Anyway, I'm here now."

Liz, who'd once been a reporter for one of Chicago's largest newspapers, was part of Nell and Abby's circle of friends. Nell liked the divorced mother of one, admired the strength she'd shown when her once happy life had unraveled.

Shortly after Liz's marriage had collapsed, her mother had been diagnosed with cancer and the newspaper had eliminated her position. The pretty brunette had appeared to take it all in stride. Cool confidence was the face Liz presented to the world.

"Jonah's parents are here. They walked through the door with me," Liz informed Abby in a low tone. "They stopped to speak with Jonah and Leo. I told them we'd be out momentarily."

Abby nodded and kept her voice equally soft. "I don't want Eva Grace too wound up before the practice."

Nell understood. This was exciting stuff for the six-year-old.

Liz nodded her approval. "It's important we all remain calm and focused."

The former reporter had taken on the task of wedding coordinator. A job she appeared to take seriously, if the directions she began barking out were any indication.

Twenty minutes later, Nell had to admit the woman had a talent for keeping everyone on task. Though it was only natural that Jonah's parents needed to be properly welcomed back to Hazel Green—even though they'd just been in town last week for a wedding shower—Liz cut the reunion short, announcing everyone could catch up at the rehearsal dinner.

This was Nell's first time as anyone's maid of honor. Unlike many young women her age, she'd never even been a bridesmaid. For most of her life, Nell had avoided close friendships.

Practically from the moment Abby had arrived in Hazel Green, she'd refused to let Nell keep her at arm's length. For that matter, neither had Liz. Or Rachel. Instead of no friends, Nell had a gaggle. She was truly mystified by how that had happened.

"Nell, listen up."

Blinking, Nell refocused on Liz, paying careful attention to the instructions on where to stand once she reached the front of the church. Huffing out a breath, Liz positioned her and Jackie at a slight angle.

"You are to remain evenly spaced. Never stand with your full back to the guests." Liz put her hands on Jackie's shoulders and made another slight adjustment in the bridesmaid's stance. "Bouquets are to be held in both hands in front of your body."

Liz scrutinized them with the intensity normally reserved for drill sergeants. Nell found herself holding her breath.

"Good." Liz gave a nod of approval. "We need to practice walking out. Remember, keep twenty feet between you and Abby."

Though Nell would be exiting the front with Leo, Liz insisted that she and Jackie get their parts perfect while the men watched from a nearby pew.

Leo smirked at her as she walked past. She couldn't help sticking her tongue out at him.

"Eyes forward, Nell," Liz called out.

Once the recessional was done to the drill sergeant's, er, to Liz's satisfaction, they moved on to the processional.

Abby and Jonah had chosen to follow the Midwest format where couples entered the ceremony in pairs. That suited Nell just fine.

After Jonah's mother had taken her seat at the front of the church, Jackie and Beau made their way down the aisle.

Liz nodded her approval at the pace.

Leo, standing at Nell's side, held out an arm to her. "Ready to do this?"

As Nell gazed into those clear, blue eyes, she had the odd sensation that she was about to step off solid ground onto shifting sand. Which, she told herself, was absolutely ridiculous.

She and Leo were practicing walking down a church aisle. Nothing more.

To the piano accompaniment of Pachelbel's "Canon in D Major," she started down the aisle.

Leo slanted a sideways glance at Nell. Per Liz's instructions, he was careful to keep the requisite twenty feet between them and Jackie and Beau. The truth was, he didn't feel the slightest urge to hurry. In fact, he'd like to prolong the moment.

It wasn't often he had a reason to be at Nell's side.

"You look amazing," he murmured, keeping his gaze focused ahead.

Out of the corner of his eye, he saw her red lips curve. She always took his compliments in stride, but he could tell he'd pleased her.

While he'd loved her hair when it had been spiky and platinum blonde, the golden strands brushing her shoulders gave her a softer, more approachable look.

The short silk dress with the geometric print she'd chosen to wear to the rehearsal flattered her figure and her endlessly long legs. The scent of amber perfume had his body on alert.

It might have been Nell's beauty that had originally caught his eye, but it was the intriguing woman inside who kept him coming back for more. She was smart and funny with a dry wit that often came from left field.

And while she'd deny it to her dying breath, she was kind. To her friends. To children like Eva Grace. To him.

All too soon, they reached the front of the sanctuary and were forced to separate.

He moved to the right.

She to the left.

Once in place, Leo turned and angled his body. He clasped his hands behind his back.

Jonah and Beau stood on either side of him, holding the same pose, as they watched Eva Grace stroll down the aisle, tossing pretend petals on the pretend aisle runner.

What would it be like to have a child? Leo wondered. In his twenties, a wife and child had been so far off his radar they didn't even register. Now, in his thirties, he could see himself as a dad.

Leo slanted another glance at Nell. As if she sensed his eyes on her, she shifted her gaze ever so slightly. Their eyes met and held.

When the music changed, Leo heard Jonah suck in a breath. Though Abby was wearing a dress with polka dots and not a wedding gown, her soon-to-be husband couldn't take his eyes off her.

Leo felt a stirring of something that felt an awful lot like envy. Though Jonah and Abby had gone through some tough times, it was obvious to Leo—and to anyone who knew them—how much they loved each other.

Jonah had told him that his relationship with Abby hadn't gained traction until the secrets in their past had been brought into the open. Only then had they started to see that a life together was possible.

There were no secrets in Leo's past, no skeletons in his closet. He couldn't say the same about Nell. He didn't know what went on in her head. Heck, she didn't even want to publicly date him.

Sleep with him, yes.

Date him, no.

Though her terms had seemed strange, he'd been okay with them when their relationship started. At the time, he had been newly elected as well as in the process of turning over his duties in the real estate development firm he and his brothers co-owned to them.

He didn't have time to date or build a relationship. Or so he told himself. The truth was, he wanted Nell so much he'd seen no choice but to agree.

Lately, he'd grown dissatisfied with the restrictions.

As Abby reached Jonah and the two hugged—totally off script —Leo wondered what Nell would say if he gave her an ultimatum.

Take their relationship public or break it off entirely.

The joyous sounds of the recessional filled the church. Jonah and Abby—with Eva Grace skipping between them—started down the aisle.

Leo met Nell in the middle and offered his arm. Her eyes danced with happiness, and when she slipped her hand around his arm, satisfaction surged.

She would be seated beside him at Matilda's, and they'd spend the rest of the evening together. The night ahead seemed practically perfect.

Until they reached the back of the church and Leo heard Abby invite Dixon to join them for dinner.

CHAPTER THREE

"I'm surprised Matilda has room for everyone."

Leo parked several blocks away, even though Nell had no doubt he could have found a spot closer to the inn. Then again, maybe not.

Memorial Day had been the launch of the tourist season, which was now in full swing. Tonight, another Jazz in June performance would fill the Green, a parklike area in the center of town. Attendees would be treated to amazing individual performances as well as multihorn harmonies paying tribute to the greats.

"Matilda closed the restaurant at five." Nell slowed her steps to match his turtle crawl.

Even though Friday nights were known for being one of the busiest for merchants, Matilda Lovejoy had willingly closed her restaurant for the evening. "The rehearsal dinner is her gift to Abby and Jonah."

"That was nice of her."

"She and Abby are good friends." Up ahead, Nell saw the green awning of the Inn at Hazel Green and slowed her steps even more.

The inn, which Abby had inherited several years earlier, was located in the middle of the town's historic district. Built in 1884, it had always been in the family. Abby's great-aunt had owned it until she'd passed away.

Leo's gaze narrowed. "Looks like Dixon and Jackie are getting along."

The dark-haired man and pretty blonde stood in the sunshine, as if enjoying the weather too much to go inside.

"They rode together."

Leo stopped and turned to her. "How do you know that?"

"I saw her get in his Land Rover." Nell spoke matter-of-factly. Like many other lessons she'd learned in childhood, being observant had been near the top of the list.

Puzzlement furrowed Leo's brow. "You were watching him?"

Not watching her. Not watching them. Watching *him*.

The subtle difference didn't escape her. She supposed another woman might have twisted the knife, fanned the flames of any jealousy. God knew, her mother had embraced such drama. But Nell genuinely liked Leo and had no desire for games.

"I'm simply observant." Okay, so maybe that wasn't quite accurate. But she certainly didn't have romantic feelings for Dixon.

Leo, whose arms had remained at his sides, surprised her by snaking one arm around her shoulders and giving her a squeeze.

Though a smile lifted her lips, she gazed pointedly at his hand, now toying with her hair.

Exhaling an audible breath, Leo released her. "By the way you act, you'd think one of us was married." His expression suddenly stilled, and he paled. "Tell me you aren't married."

If she had been, after nearly six months of intimacy, this was a strange time to ask.

Nell chuckled and shook her head. "No. I'm not married."

Like a quarterback seeing an opening in the line, Leo pressed forward. "Have you ever been married?"

Though this was the type of conversation she made every effort to avoid, the rehearsal had caused her to feel especially close to Leo. "No."

"Ever come close?"

They were standing three shops down from the inn. The mellow tones of a saxophone blended with a trumpet and a trombone as the scent of late-blooming lilacs teased her nostrils.

At one time, Nell had loved the sweet fragrance. Stanley's house had a lilac bush by the back terrace. It had been in bloom the night—

A chill traveled up her spine.

"Have you ever come close?" Leo repeated the question.

"No." Nell spoke more curtly than she'd intended. Her memories prior to coming to Hazel Green were not pleasant ones. They definitely weren't ones she wanted to revisit.

Leo studied her for a moment, then smiled.

How was it that a simple smile from him had the ability to ease the tension from her shoulders?

Impulsively, she reached over and touched his hand. His fingers wrapped around hers for barely a second.

"I wonder what's on the menu."

Nell pulled her hand casually away as Beau joined them. She hadn't jerked her hand or made any grand movement. But Beau had seen the gesture.

Though his expression remained implacable, he was sharp-eyed. Word in town was his father was pressuring him to take over the running of the newspaper. A move he was resisting.

Though, supposedly, Beau had shown great promise as an investigative reporter during his high school and college years, he hadn't pursued that career. Instead, he'd obtained a JD then a PhD in clinical psychology. He now worked as a trial consultant for a large Chicago law firm.

Being around the guy gave Nell an itch between her shoulder blades. She didn't let it show. Her mother had used trial consultants in the past, and Nell knew the importance of every gesture. Still, what did it matter if he thought there was something going on between her and Leo?

Attraction, even sexual relations, between two single, consenting adults wasn't a crime. Knowing Beau would likely find it suspicious if she ignored him, Nell flashed him a smile. "I haven't seen you around much. Not since you moved to Lincoln Park."

A look of puzzlement filled his gray eyes. "How do you know I live in Lincoln Park?"

Her stomach clenched. Nell made a great show of rolling her eyes. "There are no secrets in Hazel Green."

Beau chuckled. He was tall and broad-shouldered with muscular arms and a mop of hair that held shades of both blond and brown. Nell supposed he was handsome, if you liked guys who looked like Thor. That type held no appeal for her.

"Actually," she added when they neared the door to the inn, "Liz told me. Your father mentioned it to her."

"I'm surprised Dad didn't put it in the *Chronicle* as a news article." Beau reached the door ahead of Leo and held it open.

"Last Saturday's edition." Nell strolled past him. "Bottom of page two."

"Seriously?"

"Just kidding." With Leo's palm resting against the small of her back, Nell slipped into the comforting ambience of the inn.

While Nell had lived in numerous high-end residences over the years—nothing but the best for her mother—none of those houses had given her the warm feeling that wrapped around her each time she stepped through the door of the inn.

Nell likened it to the feel of a favorite sweater against your skin. As always, the place worked its magic, and she began to relax. Not completely. She wasn't a fool. But the hyperalertness that had been her constant companion since she'd been a child eased slightly.

The gleaming hardwood floor and the exposed brick in the entry radiated warmth and welcome. The hand-tooled maple banister leading to the second floor gleamed as if it had been freshly polished.

Iris Endicott, a young teacher and widow, manned the hotel desk this evening. Nell had heard that Iris and the doctor she'd been dating were no longer together.

Nell lifted a hand in greeting, but didn't interrupt since Iris was checking in a guest.

Leo leaned close. His warm breath fanned her face as they paused at the colonnade separating the lobby of the hotel from Matilda's. "Have you heard what's on tonight's menu?"

"Pizza, salad and breadsticks," Nell informed him without missing a beat.

Leo's eyes immediately lit up, then just as quickly turned suspicious. "Are you making that up?"

"Of course, she is." Beau's voice sounded from behind them. "You can tell because there was a change in her voice."

Everything inside Nell went cold, but she kept her composure, then turned to Beau with a smile. "I bet you were a real hit in high school when playing Truth or Dare."

"Actually, I never played that party game." Beau's voice remained even. "I was too busy with all my clubs."

A geek, Nell thought. Like Stanley. A smart guy from a nice family destined not to hit his prime until after high school.

"Even if I'd been invited to parties, it wouldn't have mattered." Beau's chuckle filled the awkward silence. "My observation skills were acquired after high school."

Leo smiled. "Nell is also observant."

She wanted to elbow him in the side. The less said about her to Beau, the better. Thankfully, Eva Grace burst into the hotel lobby like confetti tossed into the wind, her parents right behind.

Nell turned to greet her friend.

The party was definitely on now.

~

Nell made sure she and Leo sat at the other end of the table from Beau. That alone ensured she had a lovely time at the dinner.

If there was a downside, and it was a minor one, it was that Dixon somehow managed to snag the chair beside her. She told herself it could be worse. At least Dixon already knew her secrets.

"This pomegranate salmon is amazing." Abby raised her voice as her gaze sought out Matilda, who sat beside Beau at the far end of the table.

"It's always been one of your favorites." Matilda Lovejoy's skill with food and pastry had transformed the restaurant inside the small hotel into one that drew people from all over the region.

Several years ago, when the popularity of organic and farm-to-table restaurants had soared, Matilda had made significant changes to her menu. Now, most of the ingredients in her dishes came from suppliers within a fifty-mile radius of Hazel Green.

"It's a favorite of mine now, as well." Jonah stabbed the last bite on his plate with his fork.

Matilda appeared startled when Beau took her hand and looked into her eyes. "Marry me, Matilda."

Matilda let out a hearty laugh. She was a handsome woman with auburn hair and green eyes. Though Nell didn't know for certain, she'd place the woman's age somewhere in her mid to late thirties.

Like her, Matilda rarely spoke of her past.

"Excellent food and fabulous conversation." Dixon lifted his glass of wine and gave a little salute in her direction, or rather, in the direction of the bride and groom. "This has been a most enjoyable evening."

Dixon's comment appeared innocent and friendly, but Nell knew it held another message. This was the first time in years they'd sat at the same table and shared a meal.

"It was a wonderful dinner." Nell kept her tone light, but when her eyes met his, she knew he understood.

Dixon always understood.

But she couldn't forget he'd come to Hazel Green despite her express request that he keep his distance. Being in the same town together only increased the danger for both of them.

Nell still didn't know why he was here. They'd gone their separate ways years ago. Why show up now? She'd asked, but so far, Dixon had refused to give her a straight answer.

Expelling a breath, Nell schooled her expression, conscious of Leo's attention on her.

"It's been a long day," she said in answer to his unspoken question.

Abby and Jonah pushed back their chairs at the same time. Jonah took Abby's hand in his and brought her fingers to his lips for a kiss. The diamond on her left hand winked in the light.

"We want to thank you for all you've done to make the planning of our wedding a pleasure rather than a pain." Jonah smiled as laughter rippled around the table. "Having good friends to share this special time means a lot to Abby and me."

"Me, too." Eva Grace piped up, her mouth filled with a bite of mini lime cupcake.

"It means a lot to our daughter, too." Jonah offered the little girl an indulgent smile. "From the bottom of our hearts, thank you."

Along with everyone else at the table, Nell clapped.

"Does she feel hot to you?"

Nell jerked her head in Abby's direction. The back of her friend's hand was against her daughter's forehead.

While Nell watched, Jonah placed his hand on Eva Grace's flushed cheek.

He nodded, and worry filled his eyes. "How do you feel, sweetie?"

To Nell's inexperienced eyes, the child looked fine. But then, what she knew about kids could fit on the head of a pin.

"I feel good." Eva Grace smiled at Matilda. "My tummy is very happy."

Matilda smiled, but worry furrowed her brow.

Jonah's parents exchanged glances.

Abby shifted her gaze to Nell and Jackie. "I know we planned to get together this evening, but—"

"No worries." Nell waved her silent.

"You need to be with your daughter." Jackie shot Abby a reassuring smile. "I bet after a good night's rest, she'll be ready to toss those petals like a pro."

"Thank you for understanding." Abby expelled a shaky breath. "I love you both."

"Let's get our girl home." Jonah placed a hand against Abby's back.

"I don't want to go home yet." Eva Grace's lower lip trembled. Her voice stopped just short of a whine.

Jonah ruffled the girl's blonde curls. "Once you're in your pj's, we'll play a game of Sneaky Snacky Squirrel. Then we'll read not one, not two, but *three* stories."

Eva Grace's eyes widened. "Can I pick the books?"

"Of course." Abby smiled. "It's a special night."

Once the threesome left, Jonah's parents headed upstairs to their suite.

"Anyone up for checking out the action at Goose Island Grog?" Beau might have posed the question to the group, but his gaze was on Jackie. "They have karaoke on Friday nights."

Jackie tossed her head, sending her curls cascading down her back. "Sounds like fun."

"Count me in." Dixon finished off his glass of wine. "Matilda?"

"I'd love to join you, but my staff and I are handling the food for the reception." Even as she spoke, Matilda gestured to one of the servers to begin clearing the table. "I need to stay here and go over last-minute details."

Beside Nell, Leo remained silent, as if waiting to see what she had in mind. Though part of Nell wanted nothing more than to beg off, then meet him somewhere private, that would be wasting this opportunity.

If they went to Goose Island as part of a wedding party group, no one would think twice about them being together. Once they decided to call it a night, Leo could still come home with her.

"C'mon, Nell, it'll be fun." Dixon's urging had her reconsidering.

"It's been a long day." Her gaze shifted to Leo. "Would you mind terribly dropping me off at my place?"

The smile Leo flashed was bright, hot and filled with promise.

CHAPTER FOUR

On their way to the car, Leo and Nell maneuvered through side-walks filled with tourists. Many of the locals out for a fun Friday night were people Leo knew, or who knew him. Or knew Nell. Leo caught several guys giving her a second glance. He didn't blame them. Nell was a beautiful woman.

Leo resisted the urge to grab her hand. It wasn't just that he wanted to proclaim to the world that they were together—okay, that was part of it—but it wasn't the entirety. He liked physical contact. He liked her.

Heck, he could easily love her. Which was crazy when you considered he didn't know that much about her.

Leo told himself he knew enough. He'd witnessed her kind-ness and compassion, as well as her steely determination to right the wrongs done to children. She had a good heart.

But being friends with benefits was no longer enough.

Nell's hand brushed against his as they walked, as if she also found it difficult to keep from touching.

Leo recognized one of the two men coming toward them. Deep in conversation, oblivious to their surroundings, neither appeared to notice his and Nell's approach.

Leo punching Wells in the shoulder, perhaps a little harder than was necessary, had his eldest brother's head jerking up.

Wells's tight-set jaw released when he saw Leo. His gaze shifted momentarily to Nell before returning to his brother.

The older Wells got, the more he reminded Leo of their father. Wells had their dad's sandy-brown hair, hazel eyes and solid build. Leo and his middle brother, Mathis, had inherited their mother's blue eyes, dark hair and leaner frame.

"Jerome, this is my brother, Leo," Wells said. "And this is Cornelia Ambrose, a local attorney."

"You're Hazel Green." Jerome's eyes lit up. "My wife and I are huge fans."

"Thank you." Nell's smile was as gracious as her words. "It's a privilege to portray such an amazing woman."

"Jerome is considering investing in the warehouse over on Chandler Road," Wells told Leo.

If it was the one Leo was thinking of, the warehouse had been sitting empty for years. "That property has a lot of potential."

"I agree." Jerome nodded, then slanted a glance at Wells. "The price, well, that will need to be negotiated."

Wells only smiled and shifted his attention to Leo. "I thought you two were tied up at a wedding event tonight."

"We just got through with the rehearsal dinner at Matilda's." Leo kept his tone easy. "Eva Grace wasn't feeling well, so Abby and Jonah cut the evening short."

"Jonah." Jerome rubbed his chin. "That wouldn't by any chance be Jonah Rollins, the police chief?"

"That's him," Leo acknowledged. "Abby Fine, his fiancée, owns the Inn at Hazel Green."

Jerome's watch buzzed. His lips lifted in an apologetic smile. "I hate to rush off, but my wife and I are meeting at the Green Gateau. I promised not to keep her waiting."

After shaking hands with everyone, Jerome hurried down the street. Leo watched the man disappear into the crowd.

"I ran into Jerome on my way to Goose Island." Wells's gaze shifted briefly to Nell before returning to his brother. "It's an informal going-away party for Duane Hatcher in IT."

Leo pulled his brows together. "I didn't realize Duane was leaving."

"His wife got a job in Minneapolis." His brother's tone turned persuasive. "I know he'd love to see you before he leaves town."

Before Leo could respond, Nell touched his arm.

"Don't worry about me." She gestured vaguely with one hand. "I can find my own way home."

Leo gave his head a shake and turned to his brother. "Give Duane my best."

"Will do." Wells accepted his decision without arguing, then glanced at Nell. "I'll see you both tomorrow at the wedding. Enjoy your evening."

Nell's expression turned pensive. "I was surprised when Wells said he was headed to a party."

"Why?"

"You just don't see him much at social events. Or at least I don't run across him much," Nell amended.

"He's different since the helicopter crash." Leo expelled a heavy breath as he recalled the tragedy. "In one day, he lost his wife and our sister."

"I can't imagine how hard that must have been for him...and for you."

Leo gave only a jerky nod and changed the subject. "If Wells ends up unloading that old warehouse, we'll all party at Goose Island."

It didn't take them long to reach Greenbriar Place. Two months ago, Nell had entered into a short-term lease with the option to buy one of the spacious apartments.

Only a couple years old, units in the brick and stone building were highly sought after. The flats had ten-foot ceilings, a rooftop garden and sold for astronomically high prices.

When Leo had asked Nell how she could even consider buying, she'd alluded to some particularly lucrative stock purchases. One night, she'd shown him her portfolio. The woman might not be able to keep a plant alive, but she definitely knew how to invest.

Greenbriar Place, known for being one of the most secure buildings in Hazel Green, had a lobby concierge who doubled as a watchdog. Though discreet was the name of the game in this high-end building, until tonight Nell had preferred rendezvousing at Leo's house.

Before they reached the entrance, Leo took her hand and pulled her to sit with him on a bench under a large, leafy tree.

"What are you doing?"

Leo felt like a racehorse at the starting gate. His heart hammered against his chest. He told himself if you didn't enter the race, you never won. "We need to talk."

Nell's gaze turned watchful, but when she spoke, her tone was light and the smile remained on her lips. "Here I thought that was what we'd been doing all evening."

He angled his body toward her. "I want us to go public with our relationship."

Her eyes widened. Whatever she'd expected him to say, it wasn't this. "I don't—"

"Hear me out." Leo lifted a hand. "I think you and I could have a real future together. I'm ready for more, Nell. I'm asking you to give *us* a shot."

Instead of dismissing the suggestion, as she had the other times he'd pressed, Nell appeared to be considering the possibility. "Sneaking around *does* get old."

Leo waited for her to say more, but when the silence stretched and extended, he was the one to finally break it.

"Your silence tells me you have reservations about what I'm proposing." His gaze searched hers. "Tell me what they are."

When Leo had decided to pursue this discussion, he'd thought about what he'd do if she refused. As hard as losing her would be, if she truly didn't care enough to try to build a lasting relationship, he'd concluded it'd be best to walk away now.

"I care about you, Leo." Nell's fingers tightened around his hand. "I'd like more, too. What's between us is more than sex. Although, don't get me wrong, sex with you is exceptional."

He laughed.

"But I'm not prepared for the scrutiny that comes with being the mayor's girlfriend." Two lines furrowed Nell's brow. "I'm uncomfortable with all the public attention that would bring."

Of all the arguments he'd thought she might present, this one made the least sense. He'd never seen anyone more at ease in the public eye than Nell.

"Remember, I'm a small-town mayor, Nell, not a US senator like my father. Although, to be perfectly honest, I may run for higher office down the road." Leo offered her what he hoped was an encouraging smile. "I'm not discounting your worries, but I believe we can make this work. The thing is, I'm not sure how much longer I can go on with things the way they are now."

A startled look crossed her face. She jerked her hand from his. "What are you saying?"

Before Leo could respond, his phone buzzed. Pulling it out, he read the message and swore under his breath.

Nell lifted a brow.

"Family issue." He shot her an apologetic look. "I need to go."

"I hope everything is okay." She placed her palm against his chest, her blue eyes filled with concern.

Leo blew out a breath. The urgency of the text was disturbing. "Yeah, me, too."

Leo sat in the overstuffed chair in Wells's study. His brother Mathis, known as Matt to those close to him, had commandeered a nearby chair. Wells stood, one hand on the fireplace mantel, a glass of whiskey in the other.

"Dad and Steve have been friends for as far back as I can remember." Matt shook his head. "He's a good guy. Why would he do something like this?"

"I'm sure we'll get more details once we meet with Dad in person. I don't think he wanted to get into all the specifics on the phone." Wells's expression was grim. "I don't need to be a politician to realize the fallout could be the death knell for Dad's career."

"This whole situation pisses me off." Leo surged to his feet. "Dad trusted Steve, and *this* is how he repays him?"

"I couldn't believe it myself." Wells took another sip of whiskey. "Just from the little I know, it appears Steve has been lying to Dad for over a year."

Leo pressed his lips together and fought to bring the anger bubbling inside him under control.

Matt frowned. "He and Dad were best friends."

"Some best friend." Leo spat the title. "The man was lying to Dad every day of the last year when he pretended to be someone he wasn't."

Wells nodded. "With Dad up for reelection in November, this scandal couldn't have come at a worse time."

"You're acting like Dad did something wrong," Matt protested. "It was Steve who took the bribes."

"Steve was Dad's legislative director." Wells patiently pointed out something that should have been obvious. "In that position, it was Steve's job to advise Dad on key legislative decisions, including how to vote on issues."

"Which is why the bribery charge spills over onto Dad." Leo clenched his jaw so tight, the muscles jumped. "Not only does it look like our father didn't know what was going on in his own office, it makes all his votes suspect."

"Dad did the right thing in recusing himself from the vote on the trade deal." Wells's eyes remained as dark as his expression. "He couldn't vote for it, knowing Steve had taken money to secure a positive vote."

"The funny thing is he would have voted for it anyway." Leo's lips turned up in a humorless smile.

Sympathy filled Matt's eyes. "Steve is in a whole shitload of trouble."

"I don't feel sorry for him." Leo thought of his father, a good man who'd always tried to do his best for the state of Illinois. "It was Steve's choice to take the bribes. To lie to our father. To put Dad's entire political future at risk. Steve knew what he was doing was wrong, but he did it anyway."

"What about Karen?" Matt asked, referring to Steve's wife. "Has anyone reached out to her?"

Steve and Karen had been more like a favorite aunt and uncle than simply their parents' good friends.

For a long moment, no one spoke.

"It's best if we keep our distance from both Steve and Karen." Wells spoke as if the matter was settled. "Steve has been charged. Karen may be complicit. That hasn't been determined."

"I still can't believe it. This seems like a bad dream." Leo raked a hand through his hair. "Trusting Steve could end up torpedoing Dad's career."

"Is there anything we can do to help?" Matt asked.

"There is one thing. Dad doesn't need more bad publicity." Wells's gaze shifted between his two younger brothers. "Which means we need to make sure not to do—or say—anything that could make this worse for Dad."

Matt inclined his head. "Like what?"

"Nothing that would put any of us in the news in a negative way." Wells shifted to speak directly to Leo. "It goes without saying that some of your decisions as mayor may not be popular. I'm speaking more of our personal lives. And in our business"— Wells's gaze lingered on Matt—"we'll need to look at every aspect of our practices and the work done by each person we employ. I don't want us blindsided like Dad."

Leo thought of his relationship with Nell. Although they were both adults and single, how would it look if it came out that the mayor was having a secret, sexual relationship?

Perhaps, he should give her up…

The second the thought surfaced, Leo shoved it aside. The secrecy wouldn't be an issue much longer. Nell would agree to date him.

There was no other option.

CHAPTER FIVE

"Thank you, Anthony." Nell offered a smile to the man who held the elevator door open for her.

"I hope you had a pleasant evening." At six feet, Anthony Pugliesi had the lean, muscular build of a street brawler and the face of an Italian film star. The snake tat traveling up his right forearm added an element of danger to his polished appearance.

Anthony held the dual position of concierge and chief of building security.

"I had down you wouldn't be with us this evening." Anthony's cultured tone held no judgment.

"My plans changed." Nell stepped into the elevator. "Have a nice evening."

"You, too, ma'am."

The door slid silently shut before she could respond. *Ma'am?* Nell shuddered at the polite address. When had she made the leap from miss to ma'am?

Discarding the disturbing thought, she got out on the third floor. Leo had appeared disturbed by the text he'd received. She wondered about the family emergency. Though his parents lived in DC most of the year, and the boys were all in Hazel Green, the family remained tight-knit.

The text had come at precisely the right moment. Right before his phone buzzed, she'd had the feeling Leo was about to issue an ultimatum. Actually, in a way, wasn't that what he'd already done?

The panic she'd kept under wraps when with him rose to claw at her throat. Leo had brought up the possibility of going public with their relationship before, but had always backed down when she'd said no. This time felt different. She shoved the worries from her mind and changed out of her dress, pulling on silk lounging pajamas in a blue-gray shade.

After pouring herself a glass of wine, Nell took a seat on the sectional. To settle herself, she took out the journal written by Hazel Green that she'd purchased at auction recently and began to read.

Chautauqua, New York, 1900

My bosom friend Minnie Charles is betrothed. I am happy for her, truly I am, but sad because once she is married she will move with her husband to Philadelphia. Although we will correspond, she will be busy with her new life and I am certainly busy with mine. Still, the ache in my heart over losing her friendship tells me it is best not to form close attachments.

I have decided that I will be an independent woman like Miss Susan B. Anthony. I will go where I want and do as I please. I will fight for causes I believe in and inspire other women. I do not have to have a husband to be happy. I am content with my life.

H.

The ding of her cell phone had Nell's heart leaping as she put down the book. Perhaps Leo's family emergency had been a false alarm. As she read the text, that hope died. She frowned. How had Dixon gotten her phone number?

The minute the thought surfaced, she realized getting her phone number would be child's play to someone with his skills.

Reconsider joining us?

For one brief moment, Nell considered not replying. But Dixon would only text again. He knew the repeated text would irritate her, and tenacity was part of his nature.

Leo had a family thing. I'm staying home with a bottle of Merlot.

For a second, Nell almost added, thanks for thinking of me. But she wasn't glad he'd thought of her. Hadn't she made it clear she wanted him to leave her alone?

After hitting send, she tossed the phone on the end table and picked up her wineglass.

Less than fifteen minutes later, she jumped at the sound of a knock on her door.

Anthony hadn't alerted her she had a visitor, and the only way to the upper floors was through him.

Heart thudding, Nell crossed the room to peer through the peephole. Flipping the deadbolt, she jerked the door open. "What are you doing here?"

Dixon lifted a bottle of wine and smiled. "You deserve better than Merlot."

The ding of the elevator at the end of the hall had her hustling him inside.

"I thought you might be in the mood for company."

"I was enjoying the solitude."

She wondered if he heard her as he was already moving deeper into the room. He rocked back on his heels, his head turning as he assessed the luxurious, yet comfortable, interior.

"You always had a talent for making a place feel like home." His eyes went dark with memories. He laughed softly. "Except for the house in Vegas."

"Even I couldn't save that place from ostentatious ugliness." Nell's lips curved despite her efforts. "Especially when our mother embraced the over-the-top decadence."

For a second, his eyes locked with hers. This was the first time she'd mentioned their familial connection.

Dixon inclined his head. "I don't understand why you're so determined to keep a wall between us."

Guilt.

The word rose unbidden and was immediately shoved aside.

Nell realized two things. One, her brother wasn't going anywhere anytime soon. And two, he was right. It was time they talked.

She lifted the bottle from his hand and studied the label, then gestured to the sofa. "Thanks for this, but I have a bottle of Merlot already open. There's enough left for a couple of glasses."

Dixon waved away the suggestion. "Open the Joseph Phelps."

While Nell uncorked the Insignia 2012, a very fine vintage indeed, Dixon prowled the room, moving to the window to gaze out over Hazel Green. The lights of Chicago twinkled in the far distance.

Nell crossed the shiny hardwood and handed him a glass.

"You've got a nice place here, Suze. Good security."

"Nell," she reminded him. "I haven't been Susannah Lamphere for nearly fifteen years. It doesn't even feel like my name anymore."

She took a sip of the very excellent Bordeaux blend and felt some of her tension ease. It was just her and him. There was no harm, and plenty of benefit, to clearing the air. But first she had to ask. "Speaking of security, how did you get past Anthony? Not to mention the alarms?"

Dixon shot her a mocking glance. "I said the place has *good* security, not excellent. The guy at the desk doesn't even know I'm here. The hall security cameras, well, they're currently frozen."

By him.

"That's reassuring," Nell said dryly.

Dixon took a sip of wine. "Your security will keep out 99% of the riffraff."

"It didn't keep you out."

As if accepting a compliment, he dipped his head.

Nell glanced down into the inky dark hue in her glass. "Even when you were younger, you were the best."

"And you could charm your way in and out of any situation." Dixon swirled the wine in his glass. "We made a stellar team."

Nell remained silent for a long moment, sipping her wine as memories flooded back. Some pleasant. Others painful.

"What brought you to Hazel Green, Ky?"

The childhood nickname slipped out before she could stop it. A mocking smile lifted his lips. "Dixon," he reminded her. "Dixon Carlyle."

"Of course." Steadying herself, she asked again, "What brought you to Hazel Green, *Dixon*?"

"Took you long enough to ask."

"I kept hoping you'd go away."

"You know me better than that." He turned abruptly from the window and strode across the room. Setting down his glass of wine, he took a seat at the baby grand piano and began to play.

"I came here because I wanted to be near my sister." His long, artistic fingers caressed the keys. "I missed you."

While Nell had missed him, too, surely he realized having a relationship was impossible. The haunting melody of "Clair de Lune" only added to her melancholy. "Leo plays, you know. Better than you."

Dixon didn't look up, appearing lost in the beauty of the piece. "You like him."

"Leo?"

He nodded, his fingers drawing emotion from the keys.

She shrugged. "I hardly know him."

Her brother smirked. "Remember who you're speaking with."

"How could I forget?" Nell spoke almost to herself, but knew he'd heard.

"It's difficult not telling anyone who you really are or being able to talk about your past."

The honesty underlying his words touched Nell. When he stopped playing and looked at her, she found herself nodding.

"Us being in the same town is dangerous." For years, Nell had longed to see her brother, but the risk of having him close had never been worth the threat.

"I need family, Nell." His tone turned matter-of-fact as he rose. "Tonight was nice. It was…normal. Having dinner together and laughing with friends."

"Before I left, we talked about the need to keep our distance. Otherwise, if she tracks one of us down, she'll snare us both."

"You left home at seventeen."

"Remember Carmine? He crossed her when I was in kinder-garten. It took her ten years to exact her revenge. But she waited until the time was right." Simply thinking of her mother's brutality against the former lover who'd betrayed her had Nell's heart rate increasing. "Crazy people operate on their own timetable. That's why we need to be smart."

Dixon sipped his wine and raised a brow. "You think sleeping with the mayor is smart?"

Nell stiffened. "How do you know about that?"

Dixon took a seat on the sofa, his tone conversational. "I assume you think you're protecting him—and yourself—by all this undercover stuff."

"Leo is a mayor. His father is a senator." Though Nell's voice gave nothing away, she couldn't stop her fingers from tightening around the wineglass. "If Gloria should ever catch up to me, I don't want my past sins to touch him or his family."

"Well, if that's your goal, you're going about it all wrong."

Usually, Nell had no difficulty following her brother's logic. This time, he'd lost her. "What are you talking about?"

"Have you given a single thought to how it's going to look

when it comes out that you and Leo have a sex-only relationship?"

"It won't come out," she sputtered, wishing she felt more certain. "Besides, it's no one's business."

"Since when do people ever mind their own?" Dixon held up a hand when she started to respond. "Listen. Secret relationships always appear scandalous, even those between single, consenting adults. The smart thing is to have a relationship that's out in the open."

In the open.

Such lovely words.

Nell's lips curved, recalling how nice it had been to walk with Leo down the streets of Hazel Green. Would it really hurt to open the door just a crack? When Liz threw her next backyard barbecue, she and Leo could go together. She could even invite him up to her place for dinner without worrying someone might see him with her.

"We could date, but the relationship wouldn't be exclusive." Nell couldn't keep the excitement from her voice as her mind raced with possibilities. "I'd simply be one of the many women he dates. He'd just be one of the men I date."

"That's the spirit." Dixon gave her a sardonic smile. "There's the scam artist I know and love."

Nell shot him a look that had him lifting his hands, palms out. He chuckled. "No offense intended."

Could this really be the solution to her problem? Leo had said he wanted to date. While she knew dating around wouldn't give him *exactly* what he'd asked for, it would be a concession.

"Leo is pressing me to take our relationship to the next level." Nell tapped a finger against her lips. "This could work."

"No." Dixon shook his head. "It won't."

"How can you say that?" Her voice rose a full octave. "It was your suggestion."

"Actually, it was yours." Dixon drained his glass. "That pretend stuff might work in Chicago, but not in Hazel Green. Everyone knows everyone else in this town."

Her hopes plummeted, and the panic she'd felt earlier when Leo had issued his ultimatum returned.

"Besides," Dixon continued, "do you really think that if Leo is already telling you that he wants something serious, he'll tolerate you seeing other guys?"

"I get it." Nell barely stopped from snapping at her brother. She began to pace. It wasn't Dixon's fault she was against the wall and fresh out of options. "I need to think, to figure out what to do."

"What do you want to do?"

She whirled. "What do you mean?"

"If you knew for certain that our dear mother wouldn't come calling, would you date Leo?"

"Yes."

"Then I am the bearer of excellent news." He grinned. "Gloria is behind bars in California."

Despite her skepticism, Nell's heart gave an excited leap. "You're making that up."

Dixon's eyes never left hers. "I wouldn't kid about something this important."

It didn't surprise Nell that her mother had been caught. Crime was the woman's life. Still, Nell could count on one hand the number of nights Gloria had spent behind bars. "Is she really in jail? Or charged and out on bond?"

"She's in jail awaiting trial."

"How did you find this out?"

Dixon splashed more wine into his glass. "I like to check in every so often on Gloria."

"And?"

"I discovered that our beloved mama had been busy enjoying the high life in Palm Springs…as Ria Lamp."

One of her mother's many aliases. "Who was footing the bill this time?"

"A man by the name of Larry Whitestone." Dixon made a dismissive gesture with one hand. "The schmuck owns several high-end car dealerships. Apparently, she packed her bags, took some pricey *objet d'art* from his home and was on her way out of town with his Bentley when police stopped her."

"I'm surprised Mr. Car Dealer decided to prosecute." Seeing her mother being bailed out of whatever jam she'd gotten into had happened frequently during Nell's childhood. Gloria had a talent for sweet-talking boyfriends into forgiving almost any indiscretions. Even when the crime perpetrated had been against them. "They've always ridden to her rescue. Remember San Antonio?"

"How could I forget that yahoo?" Dixon chuckled. "She claimed verbal abuse and insisted she was only getting away for a few days—with his car—to clear her head. He ended up apologizing and dropping the theft charge."

"He even signed the Cadillac over to her." Nell rolled her eyes. "What went wrong this time?"

"Technology. Her real identity popped up before he had a chance to bail her out." Something in Dixon's eyes had Nell going on high alert. "The authorities saw she was wanted on an incident in Bakersfield."

"Bakersfield, California?"

He nodded.

"Who did she swindle there?"

"It was a couple of years before I left for good." Dixon abruptly pushed to his feet. "She'd cozied up to a city manager whose responsibilities included overseeing city funds."

"What did she do?"

"She embezzled money from one of the accounts he oversaw and framed him for it." Dixon moved to the window and stared out into the darkness. "I told her not to go for the frame, but she was pissed at the guy. It was a sloppy frame-up and didn't stick. When the police finally realized she was the culprit, we'd already left town."

"There is no statute of limitations in California on embezzlement of public funds." Nell briefly closed her eyes. What had Gloria been thinking? She focused on her brother. "What part did you play?"

He arched a brow. "Who said I played a part?"

Nell didn't press. The less she knew about his role, the better.

"Gloria was growing increasingly reckless. She was determined to prove we didn't need you." Dixon turned and rested his back against the sill. "She's canny and has a way of finding and exploiting weaknesses, but she relied on your insight more than I realized."

Nell only shook her head. Thinking about the cons she'd helped Gloria pull off made her sick inside.

"The detectives in Palm Springs are taking a hard look at previous crimes where she was a suspect."

"Standard procedure." Nell forced a reassuring tone. "Even if Gloria has gotten careless, she's still smart enough not to admit to anything."

"Which leaves you in the clear, in terms of the authorities." Dixon's lips twisted in a humorless smile. "I'm still in the hot seat. If they get too close to proving a case against her, she'll find a way to shift the blame onto me."

Nell knew that was exactly what would happen. The only loyalty their mother had was to herself.

"First, they'd have to find you," Nell pointed out. "That won't happen. Your skills are exceptional."

"True." Dixon agreed without a hint of modesty. "Which means, with Gloria now behind bars, we can finally live our lives without looking over our shoulders. And you can date Leo."

Nell couldn't sit. Not with her thoughts and emotions in such a tangled mess. She pushed to her feet. "Maybe. I don't know."

She'd always thought her mother would one day track her down and make her life, and the lives of anyone who mattered to her, a living hell. After all, that's what her mother had promised if she ever left.

But her mother was in jail and likely to stay there until the trial. Gloria's entire focus would be on her mounting legal troubles.

"There's nothing stopping you now." Her brother moved to her, and his tone turned persuasive. "You can finally have a normal life. The kind we dreamed about when we were kids. After everything you've been through, you deserve to be happy."

"Do I?"

"Of course you do."

"I did some bad things." Nell met his gaze. "And I wasn't there for you. I left you alone to deal with her when you were just a child."

"You *had* to go. We agreed."

"I should never have left you." A lump formed in Nell's throat, and she cleared it, conscious of his penetrating gaze on her. "Or I should have taken you with me."

He studied her for a long moment, then his eyes softened. "She'd have caught up to us in a week, and there would have been hell to pay."

"I left you with a monster."

"You had to get out." His tone was matter-of-fact. "Gloria was furious with you over the botched Britten job."

"She's the one who screwed up." Nell surged to her feet, and her voice rose. "She didn't need to torch the house. It was just lucky no one but Daisy was inside."

The entire Britten family had adored the sweet Maltese. Nell had loved the white fluff-ball, too. Each time Nell was at their house, Daisy would prance into the room and drop her red mini-tennis ball at Nell's feet.

Nell didn't need to close her eyes to see the images of the fire-fighters doing CPR and giving oxygen to the Maltese.

"The dog survived," Dixon reminded her.

"There was absolutely no reason for Gloria to set that fire." Nell whirled. "The safe was fireproof. Even with the house reduced to ashes, the investigators still knew money and jewels were missing."

"Gloria didn't set the fire." Dixon's tone turned mocking. "Remember?"

Nell took a swig of wine. Her mother never admitted to herself, or anyone else, that she was in any way involved with any of the crimes she'd perpetrated. Somehow, Gloria was always the victim.

"You had no choice but to leave. If you'd stayed, she'd have made you pay for not knowing the jewels in the safe were paste. Then, after punishing you, she'd have pulled you in so deep you'd never have gotten away."

"But you—"

"Hey, I think I've done pretty well for myself." Dixon held out his glass. "Enough about Gloria. Pour me some more wine and tell me what you've been up to all these years."

CHAPTER SIX

Nell paused in the doorway leading into the civic center ballroom, amazed by the transformation. Though Abby had initially said she'd be happy getting married at the courthouse, her future mother-in-law had seen past her weak protests. Over the past six months, she and Jonah's sister had helped Abby plan the wedding of her dreams.

The ceremony had gone off without a hitch. Nell wouldn't have been surprised to see cherubs singing overhead when Abby, looking amazingly beautiful in an A-line lace and tulle dress, first spotted Jonah in his dark tux at the front of the church.

The love in her eyes—and his—had brought tears to Nell's eyes.

Walking down the aisle with Leo had seemed surreal. Nell hadn't been able to quit thinking about her brother's comments the previous night.

"It's almost time to go in." Abby's voice shook as she clutched her daughter's hand and exchanged an excited glance with her new husband.

Eva Grace, fully recovered from last night's fever, stood between her parents. Abby wanted her daughter to be involved in every part of today's festivities. Jonah and Abby would spend tonight at the hotel before leaving on their honeymoon tomorrow. They had already arranged for his parents to stay with Eva Grace while they were gone.

From where she stood, Nell could see the ballroom had been transformed. Large urns of flowers were everywhere, and the candles on the linen-clad tables added a golden glow to the room.

In deference to Eva Grace and all the children in attendance, there was a designated kids zone. Instead of being topped with linen, tables in this area held sheets of paper with designs to color. The flowers and candles that centered the other tables had been replaced with containers holding a multitude of crayons.

Children were already hard at work. Romantic piano music filled the air. When Nell turned her head, she discovered Dixon was at the grand piano.

Nell frowned. "Surely he won't be expected to play all night."

Leo's eyes followed the direction of her gaze. "If I had to guess, I'd say through dinner. Once Jonah and Abby hit the dance floor, the band will take over."

"Once we can get away for a few minutes, we need to talk." Nell kept her voice low and the words vague, just in case anyone overheard.

"Is this about—?"

There was no chance for him to say more, because suddenly they were being introduced and entering the ballroom to the cheers of the guests.

It would be okay, Nell reassured herself. Leo would understand the parameters she would set.

Or he wouldn't.

Leo didn't have a chance to speak privately with Nell for several hours. At the head table, they were only inches away from the others. Even on the dance floor, there were so many people nearby that a private conversation couldn't be guaranteed.

Perhaps, before the conversation in his brother's study, Leo would have taken the chance and urged Nell to tell him what had put that worried look in her eyes. But she was a stickler about privacy, and right now, with his father in the spotlight, that was a good thing.

Setting aside his concerns, Leo let himself enjoy having her in his arms. "You're more beautiful than the bride."

The blue dress that hugged her lean figure showed curves in all the right places. Curves he knew intimately. It seemed so long since they'd been together...

We need to make sure not to do—or say—anything that could make this worse for Dad.

Leo tightened his hand around hers.

"Let's take a walk."

Her words had his head jerking up.

"I don't mean leave the building." She offered him an enticing smile. "We'll be back before anyone notices we've left."

Leo nodded to a couple he recognized and began steering Nell toward the edge of the dance floor. It took another ten minutes of stopping to talk with friends and acquaintances before they were able to lift two flutes of champagne off a passing waiter's tray and slip out of the ballroom.

Nell started down the hall that led to the front doors, but turned before getting that far. "This way."

He wasn't sure where she was taking him, but she'd spent as much time in the civic center as he had, so he had no doubt she knew her way.

Along this corridor were groupings of chairs and sofas, all of them currently unoccupied. Nell stopped at one, dropped onto a love seat and slipped off her heels.

Leo raised a brow.

"Taking off the heels gives the impression I couldn't walk another step and needed to stop and rest."

He took a seat in the adjacent chair, instead of beside her on the love seat.

Her approving nod had his unease ratcheting up a notch.

Leo assumed she'd launch right into whatever she needed to say, but her gaze swept the area, as if making sure they were indeed alone.

She took a sip of champagne. Several tendrils of hair that had been pulled back into an elegant mass of curls now lay in loose ringlets around her face. "I've been thinking about your suggestion."

Leo didn't like the suddenly serious look in her eyes. The *we need to talk* vibe put him instantly on alert.

"Like you, I believe it's time to make some changes."

Leo's fingers tightened around the stem of the flute he still held. She *was* breaking it off. His heart pounded an irregular beat against his ribs.

Outwardly, he remained calm, even taking a sip of champagne. Instead of asking for clarification, he lifted a questioning brow.

For a second, Nell hesitated, and he caught a glimpse of shadows behind the calm blue of her eyes. "You never wanted a purely sexual relationship."

"I honestly don't believe that was what you really wanted, either." When she started to protest, he lifted a hand. "Oh, it was what you said. The fact was, you didn't know if you could trust me."

"I went to bed with you," she pointed out, as if that negated his argument.

"You trusted me with your body, but not with your heart. Having a sex-only relationship was your way of keeping distance between us."

"That was probably part of it," she admitted. "Not all, but part anyway. I never knew my father. I don't even know his name. My mother had a series of boyfriends, and not one of those relationships was healthy."

"I'm sorry." His gaze searched her face. "That must have been difficult."

Nell lifted a shoulder and let it drop, her expression giving nothing away. "My mother ran hot and cold. I learned early the importance of not caring too much, of not expecting too much."

"I can't promise I'll never hurt you, because relationships always have that potential. I can promise I won't lie to you." Because his gaze was firmly fixed on her face, Leo saw the barely perceptible fluttering of her lashes. Obviously, lying was a hot button. "I hope by now you know that you can trust me and my word is good."

He lifted a hand, his fingers forming the Boy Scout salute.

A smile tugged at the corners of her lips.

Emboldened by the response, he moved to sit beside her. His hand cupped her cheek. "You can trust me, Nell."

"I know I can." The breath she expelled held a slight tremor. She took his hand and began making circles with her finger in his palm. "You realize if we suddenly show up as a couple, our friends will be shocked. Right now, they think we're social acquaintances, nothing more."

His heart gave a leap. It sounded as if she was agreeing to date him.

"I think they already suspect we're more than friends." Leo kept his tone even. "If we do start dating, I believe they'll be happy for us."

"You're probably right."

"I *am* right."

"And you're trustworthy."

"Don't forget sexy."

The smile she flashed arrowed straight to his heart. Then her expression sobered.

"Abby has a man who loves her. Her relationship with Jonah is solid. They don't play games." Nell met his gaze. "I don't want to play games with you."

"Are you saying you want to date me?"

"Yes."

He kept his tone as offhand as hers. "What changed your mind?"

"I realized that maybe, if I was open to the possibility, I could have more. It's a bit frightening." Her eyes took on a distant look before her gaze turned steady. "Now that I've made the decision, I'm excited."

He took her hand, finding her fingers ice cold. Regardless of how much she was trying to downplay her decision, he knew it was huge. "I'm excited, too."

"We should celebrate." She stood abruptly and slipped on her shoes. "You know, seal the deal and all that."

"There's lots of champagne in the ballroom." Leo slowly rose, his gaze settling on her mouth. "Or we could go to my place?"

Nell didn't hesitate. She wrapped her arms around his neck and lifted her face for a kiss. "I pick door number two."

"I thought we'd never get out of there." Nell cursed the breathlessness that crept into her voice while she waited for Leo to unlock his front door.

Mentioning her mother and alluding to the chaos in her childhood had been a first step toward total honesty. It hadn't been as difficult as she'd feared. Probably because Leo was someone she already trusted. At least, as much as she trusted anyone.

Baby steps, she told herself.

The door swung open, and he stepped inside, flicking on the lights.

Nell was once again struck by the beauty of his home. "I love the simplicity of the furnishings."

She didn't realize she'd spoken aloud until Leo turned and grinned. "That's good to know. If I can't wow you with my intellect or sexual prowess, I've got the house in my back pocket."

"You don't need the house." She wrapped her arms around his neck, enjoying the laughter in his eyes and the warmth of his touch. "You've got it all, mister. You're the total package."

"Funny." He kissed the tip of her nose. "That's what I think every time I'm with you."

Nell resisted the sudden insane urge to giggle. *Giggle.* She hadn't been that kind of girl even as a young teen. But then, her mother had always been lurking in the background.

As if sensing her sudden tenseness, Leo tightened his hold. "Thanks for telling me about your childhood. I'm sorry you had to go through it. I wished it had been different."

Nell sighed. "What doesn't kill us makes us stronger. Right?"

He laughed. A low, pleasant rumbling sound that pushed aside the coldness that wanted to take hold. "That's one way of looking at it. I prefer to think that those times make us who we are. Who you are is someone I like very much."

When his gaze met hers, Nell realized she wouldn't let the shadows of what had happened so long ago interfere tonight.

She twined her fingers into his hair, grazed her lips along his jaw. "I happen to like you, too."

The tenderness in his blue eyes told Nell that he was as happy as she was about this change in their relationship. A wave of longing rose up, nearly swamping her.

Had her brother been right? Could she recapture those dreams she'd discarded so long ago? Could she really have it all?

Leo flashed a smile that held a hint of devilment. "Now that we've established our mutual liking for each other, want to go to bed with me?"

No more game playing, Nell promised herself.

She would give this relationship her best effort.

"Yes."

The simple answer appeared to take him by surprise, but he quickly rallied. When they reached his bedroom, Leo pulled her to him. A second later, warm lips closed over hers for a long kiss that sent blood flowing like warm honey through her veins.

When the kiss ended, Leo leaned his forehead against hers. "I'm glad you said yes."

They both knew he wasn't talking about sex.

"I'm glad, too."

Nell undressed slowly, watching him as he did the same. Her skin prickled. Though they'd made love many times before, she couldn't recall ever feeling closer to him than she did now.

With those few sentences about her childhood, Nell had cracked open a door that had been firmly closed for as far back as she could remember. Only her brother had been privy to her hopes and fears.

Now, she had let in Leo.

His gaze traveled slowly over her. He studied her for several seconds, his steady gaze shooting tingles down her spine. "You look at me like you've never seen me before."

Nell closed the short distance between them. The citrus scent of his cologne wrapped around her senses as she gazed up at him through lowered lashes. "Just admiring my boyfriend."

"Boyfriend, eh?" The corner of his mouth twitched. "I like the sound of that."

Her cheeks heated with stinging color.

His hand cupped her cheek, his voice deep with reassurance. "I like it very much."

The look in his eyes had her heart stumbling. She saw her own desire reflected in Leo's dark blue depths.

Nell could feel her heart somersaulting as his gaze moved from her mouth to her breasts, then back up again.

Before she had a chance to breathe, his hands were everywhere and his mouth was voracious on hers. Hot riffs of sensations shot up her spine, sending Nell's world spinning out of control.

Need erupted.

The room shrank until it was only him. And her.

Giving herself up to the moment, Nell embraced the desire racing through her veins. No words were necessary. By her touch, by her kisses, by her response, she showed him just how much she cared.

When the world began to quake and the orgasm hit with breathtaking speed, Nell didn't hold back. She gave in to the shock waves of feeling coursing through her body and let herself fall, knowing she could trust Leo to catch her.

CHAPTER SEVEN

Nell couldn't believe it had been a week since Abby's wedding, which meant it had been seven days since she'd seen Leo.

They texted every day and had spoken on the phone one evening for nearly an hour, but this would be the first time she'd seen him. Work was crazy busy for her. And apparently for him as well.

She tried to hide her eagerness when the elevator door opened and she spotted Leo in the lobby.

Only the fact that Anthony watched from behind the desk kept her from flying into his arms for a welcoming kiss. They could easily have met at the park for the Shakespeare on the Green performance. For her, it was a short walk.

But when she'd offered the option, he'd told her this was a date and he would pick her up.

She held out both hands in greeting.

He took them, then leaned close to brush a kiss across her lips. "Beautiful, as always."

She thought she looked perfectly ordinary in white capris topped with a periwinkle-blue shirt and jazzed up by a pair of strappy sandals decorated with glittery gemstones.

Charcoal-colored chinos and a white shirt open at the collar appeared to be his idea of casual. He looked positively yummy.

Last week's lovemaking suddenly felt like a dinner eaten too long ago to still satisfy.

"You smell terrific," he murmured, his gaze never leaving her face.

"Thank you." She patted the bag slung over her shoulder. "I have a blanket in here, so we won't have to sit on the grass."

"Let me carry that." Before she could protest, he lifted the satchel from her shoulder.

Anthony was on his feet and at the door, holding it open by the time they reached it. "Enjoy the beautiful day."

"You, too." Nell looped her arm through Leo's as they stepped out into the sunshine.

"I like the red lipstick." He took her hand as they started down the sidewalk.

She smiled and let him swing their hands between them. How long had it been since she'd allowed herself the simple pleasure of walking down the sidewalk holding a man's hand?

"You had a busy week."

Nell thought about everything that had gone on and nodded.

"Anything you can talk about?"

She was used to keeping everything to herself, but weren't relationships about give-and-take? Nell decided there was no harm in discussing a couple of her cases as long as she kept the details general. "Two pro bono cases took most of my time. One is a child seeking emancipation."

"How old is this child?"

"Seventeen." Nell decided she was glad they were walking slowly, because when they came to a series of rosebushes beside the path, she took a moment to bend close and inhale the sweet scent. "Some of the varieties you get from floral shops look pretty, but have little to no scent."

"I take it you prefer the scented variety."

"Absolutely."

"I learned something new about you today."

She returned his smile and resumed walking. "Anyway, this child, who I'll refer to as Avery, which is—"

"Not his or her real name," Leo supplied.

"Exactly. Well, Avery lives in a functional but dysfunctional household."

"There's an oxymoron if I ever heard one."

Normally, his light teasing tone would have made Nell smile. But Avery's situation hit too close to home. "Both parents are in the home. The dad is willing to go along with the minor's request, but the mother is blocking it."

Nell pressed her lips together.

"Where does that leave Avery?"

"Among other factors, emancipation being granted rests on both parents giving their approval." Nell thought of her mother. Not only would Gloria never have agreed, she'd have made Nell's life miserable because she'd made the attempt.

"What do you think about this spot?"

Nell blinked and realized they were at the Green. Or nearly there. The area Leo pointed to was far enough off the path to be private. Most of those who'd come for the performance were seated closer to the stage.

The sound checks could be heard clearly, which meant they shouldn't have difficulty hearing the actors. Best of all, they were high enough to have an unobstructed view of the temporary stage. "I say we've got a winner."

Nell followed Leo across the grass and waited until he'd spread the blanket on the ground. Though her thoughts remained on Avery, she put aside her anger with the injustices in the child welfare system.

By shifting the focus to where they would sit, Leo had told her he was done with the discussion. Which was odd. Nell couldn't recall the last time he'd cut short a conversation.

After lifting a hand in greeting to a woman Nell recognized as being on the school board, Leo returned his attention to her. "Is there anything you can do to help Avery?"

Well, Nell thought, apparently he *was* still interested. "I'm not sure. I don't give up easily, even when the fight is uphill with twenty-pound weights strapped to each ankle."

"That's one of the things I like about you, Nell." He grinned. "You don't cut your losses and run. You're a scrapper."

She pulled a snack bag of green grapes from her purse and held it out to him. "Sometimes running is the only option."

Leo took a stem holding three or four grapes, broke off one and put it into his mouth. "Think Avery will run away?"

Nell thought for a moment, then shook her head. "I don't think so, although it's impossible to say for certain."

Leo munched on the grape. "Is what's going on at home something a counselor at school could help with? I know several of the counselors personally. I could speak—"

"No." Nell raised a hand and shook her head. "Thank you for offering, but what's going on is of a sensitive nature. I'm not sure the student will want it shared with anyone."

Leo's expression turned grave, his eyes searching hers. "Abuse?"

"Not physical or sexual, if that's what you're asking. That would need to be reported." Nell blew out a breath. "It's psychological."

Some people, Nell thought, should never be parents. She wondered if she fell into that category. She certainly hadn't had good role models.

"Situations like this make me realize how lucky I am to have the parents I do." Leo popped another grape into his mouth.

It was a perfect segue. Nell was still considering the best way to help Avery. Because she was bound by confidentiality, she couldn't give Leo any more information. In fact, she'd probably already given him more details than she should.

Now, they could move on to another topic. She reminded herself that this was her chance to find out more about Leo.

Nell reached into the bag of grapes, but the stem of the small grouping must have been wrapped around the others, because the rest tumbled out, rolling not on the blanket, but onto the ground.

"Oh, darn."

"No worries." Leo helped her put the grapes back into the bag, then held up the two remaining ones on his stem. "We can share."

The warmth in his eyes brought back memories of Stanley. Her last con had begun in the high school cafeteria when she'd deliberately dropped her lunch tray in front of him. Stanley had, of course, scurried to help her pick up the contents. Showing her vulnerability had been a way to gain his trust more quickly.

Her classmate had already known she was smart and popular. *Credibility before vulnerability.*

A lesson learned at her mother's knee. How to Use People for Your Own Gain 101.

The friendship she'd been ordered to forge had seemed innocent enough. Gloria hadn't told her how she planned to use Stanley, although Nell had known the boy was destined to play a role in one of her mother's schemes.

For several months, Nell had fostered a friendly relationship. As she was the popular senior and Stan a geeky junior, he'd been all for it.

Nell hadn't known then that the scheme Gloria had mapped out involving Stanley would ultimately lead her to take off and leave her little brother behind. If only she'd seen that her mother was spiraling out control.

"Nell." Leo's hand touched her arm. "It really is no big deal. If you're hungry, we can grab something at one of the food trucks."

Nell shoved memories of Stanley Britten aside.

"Good conversation and a grape are all I need." She smiled

and plucked one of the grapes still dangling from his fingers. "Oh, and this."

Impulsively, she kissed him on the mouth.

He grinned. "What was that for?"

"You shared your grapes."

His eyes danced with merriment. "I wish I had a dozen."

"I like grapes."

"I like kisses more."

The silly banter made her laugh.

He studied her for a long moment, a smile hovering on the edges of his lips. "You know, I enjoy dating you."

She brought the grape to her mouth and let her tongue swirl around it before taking it into her mouth.

His eyes darkened. But when he leaned forward to kiss her, she turned her head at the last second and gestured. "Isn't that your niece?"

Leo abruptly sat back. A second later, he called out, "Sophie."

The eleven-year-old had hair the color of winter wheat, and her eyes reminded Nell of violets.

She and Leo were standing by the time the girl made her way across the grass to their blanket. "Hi, Uncle Leo."

Leo gestured to Nell. "This is Nell Ambrose. Nell, this is my niece, Sophie."

"Pleased to meet you, Sophie."

The girl nodded. A tiny frown furrowed her brow as she studied the grapes covered in grass and dirt in the plastic bag.

Nell lifted her hands and offered a rueful smile. "I thought I was pulling out one, and the whole bunch dropped on the ground."

A smile tugged at the corners of the girl's lips. "That's happened to me, too."

Sophie turned to her uncle. "Daddy didn't tell me you'd be here."

Leo glanced around as if expecting Wells to suddenly appear. "Where's your father?"

"At home." Sophie shrugged. "He's not much for these kinds of things."

"Sit with us." Leo gestured to the blanket. "There's plenty of room, and the view is great."

"I would, but my friend Taylor is down there." Sophie pointed to an area thick with lawn chairs near the stage. "Her parents brought a chair for me."

"Maybe next time." Leo offered a reassuring smile. "I'll see you soon."

The girl inclined her head.

"I assume you'll be helping your dad get the cottage ready for Grandma and Grandpa's visit."

The child's face brightened. "Will you be there, too?"

"Of course." Leo gave her a wink. "Maybe we can slip off and bring pizza back for the others like we did last year."

Her smile blossomed, wide and full now, showing a mouthful of braces. "I'd like that very much."

He and Nell didn't sit until Sophie had reached her seat.

"She seems like a nice girl."

"Sophie is a sweetheart." Leo expelled a breath. "She reminds me so much of my sister."

There was a beat of silence.

"The sister who died in the helicopter crash."

"Yes, Kit died in the same crash that killed Danielle, Wells's wife." Leo's gaze shifted to a nearby tree, where a large bird cawed for no apparent reason. "Why is it starlings always sound as if they're shouting obscenities at you?"

Nell let her gaze linger on the beady-eyed bird with the shiny black feathers. "I kind of like the in-your-face attitude."

He grinned. "Now, why doesn't that surprise me?"

There was no time for further discussion, because *Much Ado*

About Nothing began. Lost in the performance, Nell barely noticed when Leo took her hand.

She identified with Beatrice, who despised love. Not that Nell despised love, but the thought of opening her heart fully to someone else was incredibly scary. She slanted a glance at Leo, who must have sensed her eyes on him.

He smiled and brought the hand he held to his lips before resting their entwined fingers back on the soft, plaid blanket.

Returning her attention to the play, Nell was intrigued by the way Beatrice and Benedick teased and insulted each other and denied they would ever marry anyone, much less each other.

Nell tightened her fingers around Leo's hand. She'd never thought that marriage could be in the cards for her. But something told her if it was, she wouldn't have to look far to find the perfect man.

After the performance ended, Leo wasn't in a hurry to take Nell home. They were strolling in the historic district when a man walking in the other direction bumped him.

"Sorry," the guy murmured, intent on continuing on his way.

The stranger would have been out of sight in seconds if Nell's hand hadn't closed around his arm.

"Hey," the guy protested, attempting to jerk free.

"Give it back." Nell's eyes were as hard and cold as her voice.

"I don't know what you mean." The man, skinny as a snake and with a pock-marked face, cast an imploring glance at Leo. "Tell her to let me go, man."

Surprisingly, they weren't drawing much attention, as the man kept his voice low.

Puzzled, Leo inclined his head. "Nell?"

Her gaze didn't leave the man's face. Her fingers must have dug in a little deeper, because the guy yelped.

"You're hurting me," he whined.

"Nell." Leo set his hand on her shoulder. "What's going on?"

"Give him back his wallet," Nell ordered. "Or I'll have someone get the police and—"

"Okay, okay." With his free hand, the man did a few gyrations, then pulled Leo's wallet from inside the camo jacket he wore and shoved it into his hand. "I found it on the ground."

"You slipped it out of his pocket when you bumped him." Nell released her hold. "I'm going to give your description to the police, just to make sure that you don't *happen* to find any other wallets."

Before she'd finished speaking, the man had disappeared into the crowd.

"I didn't even feel him take it." Leo gazed down at his wallet, then at Nell. "How did you know?"

She shrugged. "I guess my attention was on him at just the right time."

"Definitely the right time for me." He slipped the wallet back into his pocket. "Thank you."

"My actions were a bit self-serving."

"How so?"

"Now you have money to buy me an ice cream at Lily Belle's."

Minutes later, Leo held the door open to an ice cream shop that appeared to have been plucked out of the past and dropped into the twenty-first century. Red upholstered swivel barstools lined the counter. There was an onyx soda fountain from the 1893 World's Fair and a tin ceiling of richly patterned tiles with an eye-catching cornice.

But this store also embraced modern sensibilities. While Lily Belle's appealed to those who loved real ice cream sodas and sarsaparillas, it also provided a wide variety of vegan and organic selections.

Instead of taking a seat at the bar or one of the small, round ice cream tables, they stood in line and walked out seconds later with their cones.

Nell licked the mound of maple bacon and smiled.

Leo, who'd ordered the strawberry ice cream that the shop was known for, lifted a brow. "How is it?"

"It's really good." This time, she took a bite.

"What does it taste like?"

She thought for a moment. "Like a pancake. Actually, like the maple syrup you pour on the pancake. The bacon adds a nice crunch." Nell held out her cone. "Try it."

His mouth close over the top. "You're right. It's good."

"It's the salty surprise." Her tongue swirled around the top of her cone, and his mouth went dry.

Her eyes twinkled as if she realized exactly where his mind had gone.

Leo could have cheered when they made it to the edge of the historic district and the crowds thinned. Being jostled and unable to speak with Nell were two negatives about the popularity of this area.

Still, Leo felt pretty good about the direction the date was taking when he spotted Dixon and Liz coming toward them.

He slanted a sideways glance at Nell and found her studying the couple with a curious intentness.

"Liz. Dixon." Leo's tone gave no indication of his feelings.

Dixon's gaze shifted between him and Nell. What Leo thought of as a politician's smile lifted the man's lips as he held out a hand. "Leo. Good to see you."

When Dixon turned to Nell, she was already speaking to Liz and telling her about the ice cream flavor.

"Where are you two headed?" Dixon asked.

"Just taking a walk." Leo kept his tone equally offhand. "We went to see Shakespeare on the Green. If you have a chance to see a performance, I'd recommend it."

Before Dixon could speak, Leo continued, "I didn't realize you and Liz were dating."

"We're not." Dixon shot a fond smile in the woman's direction. "Liz wanted to pick my brain about some investments."

"That's right. Investments are your business." While Leo, or either of his brothers, could have given Liz advice, he had the feeling Liz's interest in Dixon was more personal than professional.

Liz shifted her attention from Nell to him and Dixon. "Please don't say he's been telling you one of those perfectly awful financial planner jokes."

Before Leo could reply, Nell piped up. "I want to hear one."

"Oh, Nell." Liz put her hand on Nell's shoulder. "You are so going to regret saying that."

"Let's hear it." Leo resisted the urge to add, *And make it quick.*

With a confident smile, Dixon began, "What's another name for a long-term investment?"

"No idea," Nell said.

Dixon smiled. "A failed short-term investment."

Nell's groan brought a smile to Dixon's lips.

"They're all bad," Liz confided. She might have said more, but her watch dinged. "Oops. I hate to rush, but I need to get home."

That's all it took. In less than a minute, Dixon and Liz had turned a corner and were out of sight.

"You never know who you will run into." Nell tossed the rest of her cone in a nearby trash can.

Without either of them saying a word, they continued walking.

"I know he's your friend, but I don't fully trust him."

"Dixon is okay."

As much as Leo would have liked to take the conversation in another direction, the closeness he sensed between Nell and the financial planner had him pressing for more. "You said you knew him back in college."

Nell nodded and slipped her arm through his.

"How did you meet?"

"Meet?" Nell inclined her head and appeared to consider the question. "I don't recall the exact moment. It feels as if I've always known him."

"There's a certain…something—I'm not quite sure how to describe it—between the two of you."

"Are you saying we're both snarky?" Her lips curved in a teasing smile. "While I'll admit we share the same sense of humor, I would never, ever regale you with bad lawyer jokes."

Leo laughed, but immediately steered the conversation back to Dixon. "I'm surprised you two never dated."

"Never crossed my mind." Nell wrinkled her nose. "I think of Dixon more as a brother. Trust me, I've never had any romantic feelings toward him."

"I believe you."

"Good. Because it's the truth."

Leo wondered what kinds of men she'd found appealing in the past. "Have you had many boyfriends? Has there been anyone you cared about?"

Though that slight smile remained fixed on her lips, the slight widening of her eyes told him the question surprised her.

"I've dated some, but like I said before, I've never let anyone get close." Nell's blue eyes pinned him. "Is there anyone special in your past?"

"One." The pain that had once tied his heart in knots when he thought of Heather was barely a twinge.

They'd reached the lake near the edge of town. Leo motioned to a bench and waited for Nell to sit before dropping down beside her. In the distance, a group composed of mostly seniors followed the movements of a tai chi instructor.

"What happened?" Nell shifted toward him, giving him her full attention.

Leo hesitated. Talking about Heather, a woman he'd once loved, felt uncomfortable, like a shoe that had once fit but no longer did.

"I don't mean to pry. It's just that you told me part of the reason you date someone is to get to know them better."

Leo knew she wouldn't press further. He could make some excuse or even change the subject and she wouldn't call him on it.

Was that really what he wanted? Heather was part of his history. In order for him and Nell to successfully take their relationship to the next level, they both needed to be honest and upfront about their pasts.

Clearing his throat, Leo took Nell's hand in his. "Heather and I were engaged."

CHAPTER EIGHT

For several long seconds, Nell kept her gaze fixed on Leo's face. She knew her expression gave nothing away. Inside, her stomach roiled.

Now that he mentioned it, she did recall reading about an engagement. But in all their months together, this was the first time Leo had mentioned the woman to her.

Nell immediately chided herself. There were many things she hadn't mentioned to him. Things that were a whole lot more significant than an ex-fiancée.

Nell shifted her gaze to the tai chi group to see a man kick with his right heel in slow motion and the rest of the group follow.

"You're probably wondering what happened." Leo's voice was raspy, like a dry hinge that hadn't been oiled in a long time.

"Don't tell me if you don't want to." After slipping her arm through his, she rested her head against his shoulder.

"I want to tell you."

She nodded.

"Heather and I met when we were seniors in college. We hit it off right away and began dating." His voice sounded like he was giving a report. "We became engaged. My brothers and I had launched the real estate development firm, and Heather was busy with her job being a PR spokesperson for a large Chicago health system."

"Sounds like she was your perfect match." Nell kept her tone light. "Were there any warning signs the relationship was in trouble?"

He stilled, as if the question surprised him.

The truth was, Nell wasn't sure where the question had come from. Maybe she asked because it just seemed to her that often people overlooked obvious signs, refusing to notice anything amiss until they're in too deep to get out.

"I don't believe so." He paused for a long moment. "We were both busy, but we both made time for each other. Then one of the hospital's ER physicians was accused of sexually assaulting a patient. That incident occurred during the time the hospital was still reeling from a nurse posting a picture on her social media of a prominent patient recovering from a car accident."

"Both PR nightmares."

Leo nodded. "Heather did a good job containing the fallout from both incidents, but it was difficult."

"Knowing how you are, I'm sure you were there for her."

"I was. She worked a lot of hours, and the hospital board was thrilled with her performance." His eyes took on a faraway gleam. "Then a position opened up doing PR for a large international corporation in Chicago. They needed someone with Heather's skill set. It was her dream job. She was over the moon when they called and offered her the position."

There was a wistful quality to his voice. "The next day, I received word there'd been a helicopter crash in the Grand Canyon caused by wind gusts. The pilot, along with my sister, Kit, and sister-in-law, Danielle, died in the crash. Wells had only minor injuries."

Nell straightened. "I'm so sorry," she said, her voice thick with sympathy.

"Thank you."

She squeezed his hand. "How did it happen?"

His eyes now held a sheen. "My sister had moved to Tucson to work for the university's athletic office. Even more than any of us boys, Kit ate and breathed sports."

"What about Danielle?" Nell didn't want to press, but she sensed Leo needed to talk.

"The complete opposite. Dani was quiet and not very athletic, but she was nice and one of those people who'd do anything for you." Leo raised his free hand and wiped it across his face. "Sophie was four. Dani and Wells had been trying for a second child, and Dani had finally gotten pregnant. Then she miscarried. I think Wells hoped the trip would cheer her up. They left Sophie with my parents. It was the first time they'd gone anywhere without her."

"Thank God they didn't take her with them."

Leo expelled a breath. "Wells told me Dani hadn't wanted to go on the helicopter ride. She was scared. She was always saying she didn't have an adventurous bone in her body. Wells and Kit convinced her it would be fun."

Nell felt his fingers tighten around hers.

"We were all devastated."

Nell wondered if "we" included Heather.

As if he'd heard the unspoken question, Leo continued. "Heather hadn't spent much time around Kit, and she and Dani were at far different places in their lives."

A picture formed. Leo grieving two women he'd loved and Heather attempting to be solicitous but failing to comprehend the magnitude of his grief.

"It was difficult for her to understand what you were going through."

"She tried," Leo said, as if trying to convince Nell. "But it was such a happy time in Heather's life. In the same way she wasn't there for me, I wasn't there for her."

"You're referring to the parties, the galas, the events where she wanted her handsome fiancé on her arm."

For a time, Gloria had been into art, or rather stealing art. Nell knew her way around galleries and the events they hosted.

"I tried." Leo's gaze shifted to the group of seniors doing tai chi. His lips lifted slightly. "Lilian is there. See? She's the one on the end."

Nell obligingly looked and spotted the elegant Lilian de Burgh, dressed in black stretchy pants and a blue cotton shirt. She watched as the woman did a left heel kick, then Nell turned back to Leo.

"Heather told me she understood what it was like to go through something horrible, but sometimes you just have to shake off the grief and move on."

Nell cocked her head. "She's lost family members?"

It was an important part of the story. Nell wondered why Leo had omitted it.

"She meant the PR fiasco at the hospital."

"Oh."

"Three months later, she gave me back the ring." Leo's tone turned matter-of-fact. "I wasn't moving on from my grief as quickly as she wanted—needed—me to. We parted friends. I was invited to her wedding the following summer."

"No wonder you were interested in a relationship with me that was just about sex."

"I agreed to that arrangement because it was the only option you gave me." His blue eyes met hers. "And because I understand what it's like to not be able to give another person everything they need at a specific moment in time."

He brought her hand to his mouth and placed a kiss on her knuckles. "I'm glad that's changed."

~

I'm glad that's changed.

The next morning, Leo's words still circled in Nell's head. She was back at Lily Belle's. Ice cream had always been her go-to food when she felt stressed.

The taste of chocolate and coffee ice cream came together on Nell's tongue. If the mocha mud pie didn't completely erase the tension in her shoulders, it came pretty darn close.

On her way back to her office from the courthouse, Nell had detoured to Lily Belle's. She was the only customer. Apparently, ten a.m. on a weekday wasn't a high-traffic time. Nell had taken her selection to one of the outside tables.

Her solitude ended less than five minutes later when Rachel Grabinski dropped into the seat opposite Nell. "Mocha pecan mud pie? It's ten in the morning."

Nell lifted a brow. "Your point?"

Rachel flashed a quicksilver smile. "That it's a fabulous idea and I'm going to join you. If I may?"

"You definitely may." Nell waved a spoon. "In fact, I insist."

Like a jack-in-the-box, Rachel sprang up and scurried inside.

Nell watched her go. Rachel was one of the group of friends she'd amassed since moving to Hazel Green. With her cream-colored hair—there really was no other way to describe the odd but natural shade—and dark eyes enhanced with amber-framed glasses, the food bank volunteer coordinator reminded her of the hot librarians in the porn videos her mother's boyfriends liked to watch.

Rachel was back in seconds with a tray containing her own mud pie and two cups of coffee. She placed one of the cups in front of Nell before settling into her seat. "They'd just brewed a fresh pot of Ethiopian blend. I seem to recall that's a favorite of yours."

"Thanks, Rachel." Nell found herself touched by the kindness, but not surprised.

Rachel was one of those people who thought of everyone else first. Probably because raising her younger siblings after their parents died had forced her to be a mother figure at an early age.

It suddenly struck Nell that Rachel's unexpected appearance had been fortuitous.

"I suppose you're wondering why I'm not at the food bank."

Actually, Nell hadn't given it a thought. But now that the woman mentioned it, it was strange.

"Okay, I'll bite." Nell took a sip of the steaming brew and smiled. "Why are you not at work?"

"Today's my birthday." Rachel's cheeks pinked. "I took the day off so I could do whatever I like."

"Your birthday is the eighteenth." Nell had it on her calendar. "I have your gift wrapped and ready to give to you tomorrow."

Rachel laughed. "Nell, honey, today is the eighteenth."

Nell pulled out her phone, glanced at the date and groaned. "You're right, and I'm a bad friend. Happy birthday, Rachel."

"Thank you, Nell." Rachel had brought out both a fork and a spoon. She studied them thoughtfully.

"I'll drop your gift by your house tonight."

"No worries." Rachel waved an airy hand, then picked up the fork.

"I'm glad we can celebrate by enjoying mud pie and coffee together," Nell said.

"I can't imagine anything better than spending time with a friend." Rachel dug the fork into the pie and took a big bite.

Spending time with a friend.

Nell's heart swelled. Friends hadn't been part of her life before coming to Hazel Green.

"I didn't roll out of bed until eight this morning," Rachel confided, dabbing chocolate from the corner of her mouth with a paper napkin. "After a leisurely shower, I decided to go for a walk. I'm having lunch with a couple of my sisters at Matilda's, then Marc and I are going out for dinner this evening. I'm not sure where. It's a surprise."

Up until Rachel mentioned her boyfriend, the day had sounded wonderful. Nell didn't like nor trust Marc Koenig. Especially with her friend's heart. "Sounds like you've got a wonderful day planned."

The gratitude in Rachel's eyes made Nell glad she'd held her tongue. Until she had enough information on Marc to bury him, she would continue to keep her mouth shut. Rachel was aware that none of her friends cared for Marc, but the only thing voicing those concerns had accomplished had been to drive the two closer together.

"You know, Rachel, I have a case that's troubling me. I'm hoping you might be able to help."

Rachel's eyes widened. "But I—"

"It's okay if you prefer not to talk business." Nell lifted a hand. "It *is* your birthday."

"I'm happy to do whatever I can. But I don't have a legal background, so I'm not sure how much help I can be."

"Let me be the judge of your expertise." Nell inclined her head. "When your parents died, you had to go to court to gain guardianship of your minor siblings."

Rachel nodded.

"I'm assuming there wasn't a provision in their wills nominating you to be their guardian."

Rachel sat back in her chair and expelled a breath. "They were young and healthy. I'm sure the thought of dying together never occurred to them."

A good estate attorney would have discussed the possibility with them and come up with a plan. But no purpose would come of mentioning that fact now.

"I also assume the probate court appointed a guardian to care for your siblings and a conservator to oversee the financial details of the guardianship."

"Aunt Jane, my mother's sister, came to Hazel Green after the car accident." Rachel's eyes grew distant with memories. "Initially, she was appointed both temporary guardian and conservator. But as much as she loved us, she was single and devoted to her career. She was willing to help out, but she had no desire to raise her sister's five minor children."

It struck Nell as odd that she'd heard the story of how, at eighteen, the girl had taken over the raising of her five younger siblings, but had not learned the specifics. "Were any other relatives interested?"

"Nope." Rachel dug into the mud pie with extra gusto. "Just me."

"They probably would have been split up and placed in foster care if you hadn't been willing."

"I could never let that happen." Rachel sighed and set down her fork. "You know how it is with siblings. You might fight, but there's always the love. I guess I've never asked, do you have brothers or sisters?"

Actually, Nell recalled, Rachel *had* asked in the past. Several times, in fact, but Nell had always skirted the question. "I have one brother."

"Well, you know how it is, then. The connection. The love. You'd do anything to protect them."

Nell thought of Dixon. They shared a special bond. Her and him against the world. More specifically, her and him against their psycho mother. The tie had been severed when Nell had taken off at seventeen and left him behind.

The lifesaving act of self-protection had come with a price. Dixon had been left behind to pay it. For years, Nell had tried to avoid thinking too hard about that fact.

Unlike Rachel, who'd taken on the care of multiple younger

siblings, Nell had left the only one she had behind. The situations weren't the same, but Nell still felt guilty.

"Tell me about your case."

Grateful for the reprieve, Nell blinked away the past and refocused on the present. She picked up her spoon, more to buy herself more time than a desire to eat.

While the mud pie was amazing, thoughts of Dixon had dampened her appetite. Perhaps she *was* as narcissistic as their mother. Recalling how Gloria had often referred to her as a Mini-Me—when she wasn't claiming they were sisters—torpedoed the rest of Nell's appetite.

"Does the case you're handling involve siblings?"

"It does." Nell glanced around, pleased to see that all the tables were still empty. She wouldn't give her friend any specifics, but she didn't want to be overheard. "While judges are supposed to rule in the best interests of the child—or in your case, children—some are more sympathetic to cases where an older sibling is attempting to gain custody of a younger one."

"Did the parents die?" Rachel pushed her own mud pie aside. She leaned forward, her brown eyes intently focused on Nell's face.

Nell resisted the urge to tell Rachel that wasn't the issue, that the only thing she needed from her was the name of a sympathetic judge. Since she'd been in Hazel Green, she'd been able to present before all the judges. But this was the first case of this type she'd handled.

"The father is unknown. The incarcerated mother's parental rights were recently terminated." Nell lowered her voice. "The minor female wants to live with her adult sister, who is willing to assume the responsibility."

"Does anyone else in the family want the child?"

Rachel's keen instincts—other than in regard to her current boyfriend—were one of the things Nell admired about her friend. "The mother's sister and her husband."

Though they looked good on paper, Nell didn't trust the couple's motives. She'd done her own digging into their background. Based on her own past, several red flags had popped. Unfortunately, nothing she could use in court.

"Judge Geoffrey Tomjack." Rachel leaned back and took a sip of coffee, punctuating the name with a decisive nod. "Though your case is different than mine in that there were no other family members interested in taking my siblings."

"I appreciate the name."

Rachel's sunny smile was back. "Happy to help."

Thankfully, Rachel didn't probe for more details as to why Nell didn't see the aunt and uncle as a good fit. Instead, they spent several minutes discussing the upcoming Fourth of July extravaganza, where Nell would be making an appearance as Hazel Green.

Rachel had just started telling Nell about her spa afternoon when she stopped talking and a smile lit her face.

Nell turned in her seat. Her own smile froze.

"Marc," Rachel called out as he approached. "What a nice surprise."

Apparently feeling quite dapper in his brown suit and blue tie, Marc sauntered over. Just seeing the guy had Nell wanting to wash her hands. He was about her age with pale blue eyes and a receding hairline. Nell had found him repulsive even before he'd asked her out on a date while he was still married.

Nell had mentioned that fact to Rachel, but Marc had already told his story first. He'd said Nell had *misunderstood* his question. He hadn't been asking her out on a date. He'd merely wanted to see if she'd represent him in a divorce.

"Happy birthday, sweetheart." While keeping those creepy eyes locked on Nell, he bent to brush a kiss across Rachel's cheek.

"Where are you headed this morning?"

Seeming to take Rachel's question as an invitation, Marc pulled out a chair and sat. "Just finished a meeting with Lilian."

Everyone knew Marc had been trying to get his hands on the rich widow's money since last year when Lilian had divested herself of some of her husband's extensive commercial holdings. According to Rachel, Marc simply wanted to ensure she made the most of those funds.

"I wasn't aware Lilian had chosen to work with you." Nell offered a pleasant smile. "Congratulations."

A muscle in Marc's jaw jumped. "We're still in the discussion phase."

There were so many ways Nell could have responded, but Rachel was her friend. This was Rachel's birthday, and she would not spoil it by being snarky. Still, she *really* wished she could do or say something to wipe that supercilious smile from his lips without it being obvious.

"Can anyone join this party?"

Nell looked up to find her brother gazing at the group with a friendly, polite smile. But there was an unmistakable gleam in his eyes that reminded her of a shark spotting its prey.

Unlike Marc, Dixon looked as if he'd be at home in a *Fortune* 500 boardroom in his hand-tailored dark suit with crisp white shirt and red tie.

"Please." Nell motioned for Dixon to take a seat. "Join us."

Out of the corner of her eye, she saw Marc scowl.

Mission accomplished.

CHAPTER NINE

"I could practically see the steam coming out of the top of Marc's chrome dome when you mentioned you were on your way to Lilian's house." This was Nell's first opportunity to speak with Dixon since their encounter at Lily Belle's on Monday.

When she'd texted him later that day, he'd responded with some cryptic comment about having business to take care of and he would be in touch when he got back. All week, it had been radio silence.

Then suddenly, here he was, at Liz Canfield's backyard barbecue. Nell didn't ask her brother where he'd been, just as she didn't ask why he hadn't contacted her once he was back in town.

"Marc is a putz." Dixon's gaze scanned the crowd, stopping where Liz was having an animated conversation with Beau. "Who'd have thought you and I would be socializing with a reporter and a trial consultant?"

Dixon had sidled up to her a second after Leo stepped away to answer a phone call. For now, they could speak privately.

"It's a backyard barbecue." She kept her voice equally low and her eyes focused on the group. "Innocent and wholesome."

"No such thing." Dixon brought the bottle of beer to his lips and took a sip. "Remember the story about the scorpion and the frog?"

"Of course." That particular story had been one of her mother's cautionary tales. The frog gave a ride across the river to the scorpion, who stung him once they reached the shore. "When the frog asks why the scorpion stung him, he says, 'It's my nature.'"

"Digging into things that are not their concern are in some people's nature." Dixon's gaze shifted from Beau to Liz before returning to her. "You like getting close to the flame. You always did."

"I believe you're thinking of yourself." Nell studied her brother from under lowered lashes. "You wouldn't even be here tonight if it wasn't for your new friend Liz."

He stuck out a tongue and grabbed a strand of her hair, giving it a hard tug.

"Hey, stop that." But she was laughing when she said it, the action taking her back to their interactions as children.

"As for why I'm here, I'm an investment adviser." His lips curved in a slight smile as he leaned close as if about to impart a secret. "These kinds of parties are prime feeding grounds."

"You better not—"

"Better not what?" Leo, who seemed to have appeared out of nowhere, raised a brow. "Hello, Dixon. I didn't realize you'd be here."

Dixon straightened. "That's the thing about me. You never know where I'll turn up. Oh, there's Liz. I need to say hello to our hostess." Dixon sauntered off with that same smug look in his eyes he'd displayed as a child when stirring up trouble. Nell wished she could give him a solid jab in the arm.

Leo looped an arm around her shoulders in a show of possession. "What did he want?"

"This is nice."

Leo inclined his head.

"Your arm around my shoulders." She gazed up at him. "It's like we're coming out of the shadows into the light tonight."

Liz, who loved to entertain, had dubbed this event her pre-Fourth of July backyard barbecue, complete with horseshoes, croquet and badminton.

His fingers played with a lock of her hair. "Are you telling me being with the mayor hasn't been as bad as you thought?"

"We haven't been together all that much." After their date to see *Much Ado About Nothing*, Nell hadn't seen much of Leo for the rest of the week. He'd been busy with his mayoral duties, and her caseload had exploded. In the evenings, she'd been fine-tuning the speech she planned to give during the Independence Day celebration.

Out of the corner of her eye, Nell saw Abby give her a thumbs-up. Her fears in the friend area had proven groundless. Everyone was treating them as if they'd always been a couple.

"How about a game of horseshoes?"

She angled her head. "Seriously?"

"They're a lot of fun."

Nell shot a doubtful glance toward an isolated area at the far back of the yard where stakes and horseshoes begged for attention.

While she was enjoying the party, she was also craving some alone time with Leo. Once they'd reached the party, they hadn't been alone. Not for one second.

"Sure."

Surprise flickered in his blue depths. "You'll do it?"

She looped her arm through his and started to walk, tugging him along.

"I may need a few pointers initially." Nell smiled up at him. "But I sense victory on the horizon."

∼

The horseshoe sailed through the air and dropped, wrapping around the stake with a clank.

Nell let out a whoop. With her face flushed and her blue eyes sparkling, she held up a hand for a high five.

Leo couldn't keep from smiling even as he shot her a suspicious look. "Are you certain you've never played before?"

She grinned at his teasing tone, her hair damp and curling around her cheeks in the hot afternoon sun.

"I'm athletically inclined." She rose up on tiptoes and brushed her lips across his mouth. "With, apparently, a talent for horseshoes. Who knew?"

Who knew, indeed? Leo found her good humor infectious. After he'd explained the rules of the game, they'd taken a few practice throws.

Nell had a keen eye and an ability to focus on the target. He caught her eyeing the foul line several times. Though she came close, and he could tell she was tempted, she never stepped over it.

"Want to play again?" she asked.

"All this pitching has made me hungry. Let's grab something to eat. Once we've got some food in us, we can come back and play another game."

When he turned to go, she grabbed his hand. "What's your rush?"

Curious, he turned. He thought she'd be eager to get back to the party, to her friends. Leo remembered that when he and Heather were together, it was all about socializing. Of course, they'd had alone time after the parties ended.

"I thought we could talk for a few minutes." Her smile was tentative, as she were navigating uncharted waters. "We haven't seen much of each other this week."

"I've missed you." He shoved his hands into his pockets and rocked back on his heels. The words had simply popped out, but now with those assessing eyes on him, he felt as awkward and gauche as he'd felt at sixteen. "I—"

"I've missed you, too."

Warmth rushed through Leo's body. He couldn't recall her ever saying those words to him.

"Tonight is Jazz in June." He gestured to the crowd. "If Liz wouldn't have thrown this party, I'd have asked you to go with me."

"There's always so much to do in Hazel Green." Nell's expression grew pensive. "I sometimes feel guilty about not taking advantage of all the town has to offer."

"How do you prefer to spend your Saturday nights?"

"This is going to sound so lame."

He waited.

She lifted a hand. "Don't get me wrong. I really love activities and events. But..."

"But..." he prompted.

"Sometimes, I like to stay in, get a pizza and watch a movie." She gave a little laugh. "Told you it sounded lame."

"With popcorn?"

"Of course."

Leo found her throaty chuckle incredibly sexy.

"I don't have to be entertained every weekend." Nell briefly brought a finger to her lips, the action drawing his attention to her perfectly sculpted mouth. "Being with you is enough."

Her comment arrowed straight to his heart. Leo cleared his throat. "Next Saturday. Pizza and beer at my place. Or yours."

"I'd like that very much." Her lips lifted in a sexy smile. "Pizza. Beer. Dessert. The trifecta."

Leo stepped to her. "What kind of dessert?"

Nell lifted a brow, an impish twinkle in the liquid blue depths. "Is there more than one kind?"

"Well, there's the cake and pie version." He trailed a finger down her bare arm and smiled at her quick intake of breath. "Then there's the version where I—"

"Someone told me I'd find you back here."

Leo slowly lowered his hand and turned. He tried to tell himself he had no cause to feel annoyed by the interruption. This was a barbecue. People mingled at these types of events. They didn't come here to think about getting their girlfriends naked.

Girlfriend.

He liked thinking of Nell like that. The term fit. As he faced Wells, Leo found himself smiling. "Liz didn't mention you were coming."

Since Dani's death, his eldest brother had shied away from social situations that didn't have a business component. Even then, he usually found a reason to leave early.

Leo was happy to see his brother venturing out.

Wells glanced at the horseshoe pit, then at Nell before returning his gaze to Leo. "I didn't realize you liked horseshoes."

"They're fun." Leo put a hand on Nell's shoulder in a deliberate gesture. "Nell is a horseshoe ace."

Wells's smile appeared forced. "Is that right?"

Nell reached up and brushed back a strand of hair, effectively dislodging Leo's hand. His irritation surged, but fell away when she reached over and gave that same hand a brief squeeze. "Rachel is waving to me. I'm going to go say hi."

Before Nell left, she shifted her attention to Wells. "It was nice seeing you. Hopefully, we'll have a chance to talk later."

Leo watched her go. She was headed toward a large group milling around the monster grill. Rachel might have been part of that crowd, though he couldn't pick her out from this distance.

Reluctantly, Leo refocused on his brother. He gestured toward the horseshoes. "Want to give them a try?"

Wells shook his head. "It isn't a game that interests me."

Leo chuckled. "I wasn't sure it interested me, either. But surprisingly, I enjoyed playing."

Wells studied him for a long moment. "Are you sure it wasn't the woman you were competing against that made it fun?"

Leo grinned. "A beautiful woman with a horseshoe in her hand, well, you have to admit it's a sexy sight."

"Nell is beautiful and obviously intelligent," Wells agreed. His brow furrowed. "But..."

"But what?"

Wells scrubbed a hand across his face. "I saw her earlier cozied up to Dixon. They were laughing and seemed, I don't know, close."

"They're friends. That's all." Leo lifted his chin, daring his brother to disagree. "Nell and Dixon went to college together."

"I wanted to speak with you about your, ah, your relationship with Nell." Wells shifted from one foot to the other. "Look, I'm going to just come out and say it. With everything going on with our father, we can't afford for anything to make Dad look worse. You're going to have to stop screwing Nell."

For a second, Leo was sure he hadn't heard correctly. "What did you say?"

If Wells heard the warning in his voice, he chose to ignore it. "I get the appeal of the no-strings thing, I do. Don't think I'm judging you, because I'm not. As far as I'm concerned, you can sleep with a different woman every night. But right now isn't a good time for casual sex."

"You're wrong." Leo's tone was ice. "Nell isn't just some woman I'm sleeping with. We're in a legitimate relationship. I care about her."

"If it's so legitimate, why keep it a secret?"

"We aren't keeping it a secret. Not anymore."

"I don't buy it." Wells lifted his hands and shook his head. "How well do you know this woman? What if she wants to keep it private because she's hiding a husband or something?"

Leo stared at his brother, then shook his head. "You've been alone too long if those are the kinds of stories you're concocting in your head."

"I just don't want to see your, or our father's, reputation sullied."

"You don't have to worry about that." Making an effort to rein in his irritation, Leo forced a reasonable tone. "Why does the idea of my dating Nell bother you so much?"

Wells blew out a breath. "Forget I said anything."

For the first time, Leo noticed the lines of worry bracketing Wells's eyes. He grabbed his brother's arm. "What's wrong? Tell me."

"I heard from Dad." Though Wells kept his voice low, he glanced around as if making sure no one stood nearby.

Leo did the same, feeling like a hunting dog suddenly on high alert.

"FBI agents raided Steve's home and found a hundred thousand in cash in his freezer. The serial numbers matched the ones on the bills given by the FBI to their informant."

"Steve really is guilty." Leo pressed his lips together as a sick feeling filled the pit of his stomach. This was the man who'd taught him how to throw a slider. The guy with the infectious laugh that came all the way from his belly was a liar and a thief. "It wasn't just a one-time thing."

Wells shook his head. "This has been going on for a while."

Leo had all sorts of questions, but wasn't sure he wanted to hear the answers. There was one he had to ask. "Dad is in the clear?"

"Our father would not take a bribe." Wells shifted into a fighting stance, his hands clenched into fists at his sides. "If you think—"

"I don't think," Leo snapped, his nerves now as tightly wound as his older brother's.

"Oh." Wells expelled a ragged breath. "Sorry. Hearing that agents executed a search warrant in Dad's Senate office…"

"A search warrant?" Leo voice started to rise, but he pulled it down. "When? Why?"

"They didn't find anything implicating Dad."

"Of course not. He's clean." Even as Leo said the words, he knew it wasn't that simple. Good men were often sucked into the messes that others had made.

Wells nodded, suddenly looking much older than his thirty-six years. "The FBI claims it uncovered six schemes where Steve sought money for favors."

Leo thought of Steve's wife, Karen, and their children. Had his wife suspected something was wrong? Or maybe she was involved.

"It's all over the media." Wells gave a little laugh. "Whoever said there is no such thing as bad publicity was obviously never embroiled in this kind of scandal."

"What happens now?" Out of the corner of his eye, Leo saw Marc headed their way, a phony-ass smile on his face.

"The media circus is only beginning." Wells's eyes flashed a warning as he turned. "Marc. How's it going?"

"Probably better for me than for you." Marc's expression of faux sympathy missed the mark by a mile. "I heard about your father. I was shocked."

Wells should have been a politician, Leo thought. His placid expression gave nothing away. "I believe you're referring to the situation involving Steve Olssen, a staff member in my father's office. At this point, I don't know enough to comment on the situation."

"Everything I've read indicates he and your father are close." Marc's eerily blue eyes glowed with malevolent glee.

Though to a casual observer, Wells appeared in perfect control, Leo could tell his normally mild-mannered brother wanted to punch the guy.

Leo understood. He wanted to wipe the smirk off Marc's face, too. But getting the guy to walk away seemed a more prudent option.

Before Leo could say anything, Nell appeared and tapped Marc on the shoulder. "Rachel is looking for you."

"I'm busy now." Marc gestured with one hand toward Leo and Wells. "I don't know if you heard, but—"

"It was something about Lilian." Nell lifted a shoulder. "No worries. I'm sure Dixon can answer her questions." Her gaze slid to Leo for only a second before returning to Marc. "What were you discussing?"

The investment counselor had already started stepping away from the small group, his gaze now focused on the white-haired woman.

"Leo and Wells can tell you about the scandal." Marc turned, his feet moving so fast Leo expected him to trip and tumble to the ground any second.

Leo arched a brow. "Rachel was looking for him?"

"She's always looking for him." Nell rolled her eyes, but there was affection in her tone. "And Marc is always looking for Lilian."

"Now you've sicced him on the poor woman," Wells remarked.

"Lilian is more than capable of handling a worm like Marc." Nell narrowed her gaze. "Would you rather he remained with you and your brother until one of you punched him?"

"We wouldn't have hit him," Wells protested.

"You wanted to." Nell's tone turned cheerful. "I recognized the signs because it's how I feel every time he comes close."

Leo laughed, swung an arm around her shoulders and planted a noisy kiss on her cheek. "I'm grateful."

"I am, too," Wells said grudgingly.

Nell glanced from him to Wells. When her gaze returned to him, Leo braced himself for questions.

Instead, she picked up a horseshoe. "Anyone up for a game?"

CHAPTER TEN

Leo played another game of horseshoes, but Nell could see his heart wasn't in it.

"What's wrong?" She didn't bother to ask if he wanted another game.

It hadn't been just Leo who looked grim when she'd walked up. Though both brothers hid it well, something was definitely troubling them. For a second, Nell had thought it had to do with Marc. But the man was more of a troublesome gnat, easily swatted away.

"It's my dad." For a second, his voice broke.

"What about him?" Nell gripped his arm. "Is he okay?"

"Physically, he's fine." The eyes that Leo settled on Nell were bleak. "But, no, he's not okay."

Nell released her hold, but didn't retreat. "What's going on, Leo?"

"I need to hold you. Just for a second."

They might be in the far reaches of Liz's yard, but anyone who chose to glance in this direction would see them.

Nell knew she had to do this—for his sake—whether she was comfortable with the public show of affection or not. She moved close, and he enfolded her in his arms. When she lifted her face, his lips covered hers for a brief moment. As he stepped back, his hand lingering on hers for a few seconds longer, she felt him steady.

"Dad's legislative director has been charged with taking bribes." Leo's expression darkened. "Wells informed me that FBI agents raided Steve's home."

"Steve is your father's legislative director." Nell knew the power of that position. Whoever held it had the responsibility for drafting legislation and making voting recommendations.

Leo nodded. "Steve was also my dad's friend for as far back as I can recall. He and his wife, Karen, are—were—like family."

She wondered if Leo realized he was already speaking of the lifelong relationships in the past tense.

"Maybe he's not guilty." Even as she spoke the words, Nell knew it wasn't likely. Not if the FBI had grounds to obtain a search warrant.

"The agents found a hundred thousand in cash in Steve's freezer. The serial numbers matched the ones on the bills given by the FBI to their informant."

Nell's mouth went dry. "Doesn't sound good."

"It wasn't even a one-time thing." Distaste flickered across his expression, then disappeared. "Though I couldn't excuse even that."

A shiver traveled up Nell's spine.

"So far, the FBI claims it has uncovered six schemes where Steve sought money for favors." His face tightened, and the disgust in Leo's voice was so interwoven with pain that it was difficult for Nell to tell where one ended and the other began. "He pretended to be my dad's friend. All the while, he was lying to him."

Nell's heart pounded. "This has to be incredibly difficult for everyone in your family."

She thought of Stanley. Beginning with the dropped tray in

the cafeteria, everything about their "friendship" had been a lie. Even the relationship she'd forged with his parents had been built on deceit. Her conscience had reminded her many times that what she was doing was wrong, but she'd silenced the nagging voice.

At the time, Nell had seen no choice but to do her mother's bidding. But seeing no way out didn't excuse her actions and the hurt and pain she'd caused. "Perhaps Steve has a good reason for doing what he did."

The incredulous look Leo shot her had Nell rushing her next words. "I mean, you don't have all the details. There could be some reason to explain his actions, even if you can't understand it."

"Steve and my dad were like brothers. He and Karen were family." Leo's hands clenched and unclenched at his sides. "I don't care why he did it. There's never a good reason for betraying someone you love."

Abby slanted Nell a sideways glance. "You never wear jeans."

"I knew painting was on the agenda today." Nell held the paint roller in one hand.

"That's why I wore my oldest shirt." Rachel gestured to her sleeveless tee that was already splattered with paint.

"This is one of Cohen's," Liz remarked, referring to her ex-husband, a pro baseball player-turned-sportscaster. "I like getting it messy. It's small of me, but there it is."

The four friends were all members of the Green Machine.

The organization had purchased, and was in the process of renovating, a cottage in the town's Gingerbread Village, a collection of small houses built between 1890 and 1910. The colorful cottages had been the brainstorm of Hazel Green, who'd once seen something similar in the Martha's Vineyard area.

Most of the homes in Gingerbread Village were privately owned and had been used during summers by the same families for generations. The majority were in remarkably good repair. But this small cottage, neglected for years, had become an eyesore.

After the city purchased the house, the outside had been tackled first. Shingles were stripped and new ones put on. The porch had been shored up, and the broken gingerbread on the eaves replaced. Other volunteers had scraped and painted the exterior, while those knowledgeable in landscaping had added sod and a nice assortment of bushes and flowering plants.

Floors were on tap to be sanded and refinished as soon as the interior painting was completed. Plumbers had been working in the kitchen and bathroom when Nell and her friends had arrived, but they had already left for the day.

Once the living room was done, another set of volunteers would descend on the house and continue their work.

"If we didn't have to cut around all this white trim, we'd have been done at noon." Abby straightened and put a hand to the small of her back.

"It will be worth it in the end." Nell stared in satisfaction at the wall she'd just finished. "This shade of blue pops against the white trim."

"I love spending time with you guys." Rachel carefully cut around a piece of trim with her brush.

"I still can't believe you got time off from the food bank," Nell commented.

Rachel shrugged. "I think it's because this is a Green Machine project. My boss is a huge supporter."

"Speaking of Leo," Abby began.

Nell frowned. "We weren't speaking of Leo."

"We weren't?" Abby's innocent expression didn't fool anyone in the room, least of all Nell. "Oh, well, we are now."

Liz pointed a paint rag in Nell's direction. "After that kiss in my backyard, you had to know this was coming."

"I did," Nell admitted. "I just wonder what took you so long to bring it up."

"You and the mayor." Rachel expelled a breath, a dreamy look on her face. "Even if he hadn't kissed you in front of everyone—"

"We were hardly in front of everyone," Nell protested.

"Puh-leeze." Abby waved a dismissive hand. "We all saw it."

"When did this all start?" Liz asked, the reporter in her evident.

"There's been this attraction between us for a while now."

"I think he's in love with you," Rachel said. "You can tell by the way he looks at you. He gets this dreamy look in his eyes. Marc doesn't look at me that way."

An uncomfortable silence descended over the room.

Abby cocked her head. "Would you like being a politician's wife?"

"Wife?" Nell laughed, a short, nervous burst of air. "Leo and I just started dating."

"You'd be an asset to him in his rise up the political ladder." Liz's gaze narrowed on Nell. "You're smart and accomplished and beautiful."

"Jonah told me Leo has his sights set on higher office." Done painting for the day, Abby dipped her brush in the pail of soapy water. While keeping her gaze on Nell, she began to work the paint free of the bristles with her fingers. "Everyone knows being mayor of Hazel Green is just a first step for him."

Though Nell kept her expression impassive, her heart stopped, then began again. Why hadn't she taken into account Leo's political aspirations before agreeing to date him?

"I think he'll go far." Liz's gaze grew thoughtful. "He's got this squeaky-clean image. And so far, he's done everything right."

"This thing with his father could really mess things up for him," Rachel announced in a matter-of-fact tone. "Marc says—"

"Marc should keep his mouth shut," Abby retorted, casting a worried glance in Nell's direction.

Rachel froze and high red blotches appeared on her cheeks. "Everyone at the picnic was talking about Senator Pomeroy. Marc didn't make it up. It's been on the news."

"It's okay, Rachel." Nell kept her tone easy in an attempt to soothe her friend's obvious agitation. "What we need to remember is that no one, including the FBI, is alleging that Tim Pomeroy did anything wrong. It's his legislative director who's being investigated."

"Marc says he and the guy were friends and that will hurt him." To her credit, Rachel appeared distressed at the thought.

"Marc," Nell spoke the name through gritted teeth, "has a right to his opinion. I just don't happen to share it."

"I sincerely hope this whole matter doesn't affect the senator's reelection chances." Liz sounded as if she had her doubts. "He's done a lot of good for Illinois."

"I'm sure the senator will be doing everything he can to distance himself from the scandal." Abby's positive comment went straight to Nell's heart.

Was this what would happen if news of her past came out? Would those closest to her be forever tainted by their association with her? And Leo—she couldn't imagine being responsible for destroying his political future.

Nell glanced at the faces of her friends, so familiar and so dear. They were her rocks. Would they abandon her if the news of her past misdeeds came out?

Breathing suddenly became difficult. Tears stung the backs of her eyes.

Suddenly, Abby was at her side. "Nell? Are you okay?"

Nell blinked and gazed into Abby's brown eyes. The look in her friend's gaze was as steady as the clasp of a hand.

"You're as white as a ghost."

Brushing a stray piece of hair out of her face with the back of her hand, Nell managed a smile. "It's hot in here."

"Don't let—" Abby began.

"Wow. This looks amazing." Leo's deep voice filled the room.

Nell turned, and there he was, looking more handsome than a man had a right to look in cargo pants and a T-shirt.

As if a light had been switched on, her world suddenly became a whole lot brighter.

Until she remembered what she should have never forgotten —her past had the power to rock his entire world.

"I like the blue." Though Leo spoke to everyone, his gaze remained focused on Nell.

"Original color." Nell kept her voice easy and pleasant. "We're trying to stay as true to the original cottage as possible."

"Hence the pink and white exterior." Leo's grin had her heart rate quickening.

"Yes, hence the pink and white exterior." Nell heaved a sigh. "I realize some people may not like all the bright colors—wait until you see the purple bathroom cabinet—but I find it cheery and uplifting."

"This one," Liz pointed her paint brush at Nell, "is not only a world-class horseshoe thrower, she's one hard worker."

"And so pretty." Abby waggled her eyebrows.

Nell groaned. "Stop it. All of you."

"I happen to agree." Leo surprised Nell by crossing the room and pressing his mouth against hers. "She's also a great kisser."

Nell caught Rachel's not-so-subtle *I told you so* look.

"Are you here to work?" Nell asked Leo when she finally found her voice.

"He isn't on the schedule." In addition to her work as volunteer coordinator for the town's food bank, Rachel had taken on the Herculean task of coordinating the volunteers on the Pfister cottage.

"I saw Nell's car outside and thought I'd say hello." Leo gestured toward the doorway. "Our cottage is down the block."

Something else she didn't know about this man she was dating. "Your family has a cottage?"

"You should stop by and see it when you're done," Leo urged. "I'm headed over there now. My parents are arriving on Saturday. Wells is hoping they'll stay with him, but they may prefer the privacy of the cottage."

Though everything inside her told Nell to keep her distance, she smiled. "If you're still there when I get through here, I'd love a tour."

After giving her the address, Leo didn't stick around. It was another thirty minutes before they finished the cleanup.

Nell stood back, hands on hips, and surveyed the room. Okay, so maybe the blue was a little bright, but it wasn't gaudy. Certainly nowhere near her mother's decorating attempts. For someone who always looked picture-perfect, Gloria had atrocious taste in home decor.

"I'm picturing a gray sectional with blue and white pillows. Perhaps a blue and white plaid sofa." Nell tapped her lips with a finger. "Once the rugs and furniture are in and the artwork hung, this is going to be one cozy room."

Abby stretched, then pulled her hair from the band and let the dark strands tumble loose. "It will be nice. But right now, I'm all done."

Rachel scooped her bag up from the floor and slung it over her shoulder. "I need to scoot. Marc is taking me out to dinner."

"Where are you going?" Liz asked.

"I was hoping for Thai, but Marc wants a burger." Rachel lifted a shoulder. "I like burgers, too."

Rachel waited until they were outside before flicking off the lights and locking the door.

After hugs and goodbyes, Nell left her car where it was parked to stroll down the picturesque street. She'd gone only a few feet before she saw Leo walking toward her.

Her heart flip-flopped. "Hey, are you headed home?"

"Actually, I thought I'd walk you to the cottage." He slid such an appreciative gaze over her jeans and top that she felt as if she were wearing a designer original.

"You're quite the gentleman."

He flashed a smile. "I try."

This guy had it all.

Liz's words about Leo having his life in perfect order punched like a fist.

Still, Nell slipped her arm through the one he offered. The late summer sun shone down through the trees that lined the block. A light breeze carried the scents of the flowers that added splashes of color to the front yards and porches.

"I love all the different colors." The house, er, cottage they were in front of now had weathered cedar shingles for siding and bright orange trim around the doors and windows.

"The variations in color and style are what gives the area its charm." Leo greeted an older couple headed in the opposite direction.

After they encountered two other couples, Nell realized everyone they met was going the other way. It felt as if she and Leo were swimming upstream.

"Where is everyone headed?"

"The Pavilion."

The Pavilion was an open-sided building that Richard Green had designed. It had been the site of several early-twentieth-century Chautauqua performances. "Why?"

Leo slid his hand down to lock his fingers with hers. Monday is Pie and Ice Cream Night at the Pavilion."

Nell inclined her head. "It's only six o'clock."

Leo grinned. "Most of the owners are older and prefer the earlier start time."

"I have to remind myself that most people in Hazel Green eat early. Not like Chicago or New York, where dinner at nine is the norm."

"This isn't even Hazel Green."

Nell shot him a curious glance.

"Okay. It's technically part of Hazel Green, but Gingerbread Village is a section of town, a community, with its own unique flavor."

"From what I understand, most of the residents only live here during the summer."

"Some are year-round." Leo gestured to a pretty cottage, much larger than the one they were renovating. "This one belongs to Jocelyn Valentine, the owner of the Hat Box."

The milliner's home had a blue roof, a wraparound porch and three main paint colors—fuchsia, blue and cream. It was bright, bold and eye-popping, and Nell felt as if she was looking at the cover of a storybook.

Leo's family cottage next door was equally colorful.

The color in the living room they entered came from the chartreuse chairs and a teal love seat with white stripes, not from the walls. The walls and the ceiling in this large open room had been painted a pristine white.

Grouped for conversation near a large stone fireplace, the furniture invited her to have a seat and kick off her shoes. Colorful Chinese lanterns hung from one of the white beams in front of the window.

"This is lovely." Nell glanced around.

Leo smiled. "Let me give you the five-minute tour. Not because I want to rush you, but that's all the time it will take. None of these cottages are particularly large."

He showed her the modern kitchen, large enough to hold a table for eight, and a bathroom with a claw-foot tub. Nell pictured herself soaking in the deep tub up to her chin in bubbles.

The downstairs bedrooms might be small, but each retained its own flavor, with the master having French doors with stained-glass borders and the guest bedroom being a pale lavender with white filmy curtains.

At the top of the stairs was another bedroom under the eaves, this one decorated in a nautical theme.

"This is so cute." Nell glanced around. Why was it her condo in Greenbriar Place—which she hoped to buy—suddenly seemed sterile and cold?

"Lots of good memories. We spent a lot of time here as a family when I was growing up." Leo's lips lifted as if he was looking back. "Once my parents decided to live in DC year-round, my sister, Kit, lived here for a while before moving to Arizona."

Nell thought about the houses she'd lived in prior to leaving home at seventeen. None of them had felt like a home or held pleasant memories.

"Thank you for showing this to me."

He winked. "My pleasure."

When Leo's arm slid around her shoulders, Nell was seized with a longing so intense she couldn't say another word. The moment Dixon had told her Gloria was in jail, Nell had thought happiness was within reach. Was she only fooling herself?

"My parents had a lot of friends in this neighborhood," Leo murmured, almost to himself.

Nell had seen the couple from a distance the few times they'd been back in Hazel Green, but had kept her distance.

"My mother and Jocelyn's mom were very close when we were younger." A distant look filled Leo's eyes. "In the summer, the kids would run back and forth between each other's houses. It was an open-door policy. No knocking required."

"Sounds like fun."

Though Gloria had a couple of women she called friends, they weren't really her friends, merely weaker women she could manipulate and use for her own gain.

Even if their constantly moving lifestyle would have allowed it, Nell and Dixon had been encouraged to keep their distance from other kids. Unless, of course, Gloria saw some purpose in a relationship.

"I hope their friends will stand by my dad." Leo looked away, but not before she saw the worry in his eyes. "Everything might be different now."

"I'm sure it will be fine," Nell said with more certainty than she felt. "After all, it wasn't your father who broke the law."

A muscle in Leo's jaw jumped. "No. It wasn't. It was someone he trusted."

Nell placed a hand on his arm. "How about we check out the Pavilion?"

"Speaking of the Pavilion. My parents get into town on the thirtieth. My father has been asked to speak. It's a political thing, but mostly a way for them to greet old friends and meet new. I'd like you to come with me."

Nell mentally checked her calendar. "Is the thirtieth this Saturday?"

Leo nodded.

"I was already planning to attend. I've been invited to say a few words as Hazel Green."

"Can you do that?" Leo arched a brow. "I thought Hazel Green was apolitical."

"Hazel spoke a lot about honor and integrity. I'll be giving one of those speeches."

"Great. We can go together." Leo reached out and took her hand. "You can meet my parents."

Nell told herself to pull her hand back, to put some distance between them. The problem was, Leo was hurting. Steve's duplicity had hit him hard. Nell knew what it was like to need a friend.

"Normally, Hazel never attends a function with a date." Nell reached up and kissed his cheek. "She'll make an exception for you."

CHAPTER ELEVEN

"You and Leo came together." Abby kept her voice low. She appeared to be making a concerted effort not to smile. "You never come to events like these with a date."

Nell—or, really, she needed to think of herself as Hazel this evening—resisted the urge to squirm. "Leo asked, and I didn't see what it would hurt."

"Has he introduced you to his parents yet?" Abby picked up a flute of champagne off the silver tray held out by a passing waiter.

Nell lifted her gloved hand and waved the waiter off with an elegant gesture. "I'm here as Hazel."

"You're here with their son." Abby's determined expression told Nell she was unlikely to back off.

Still, Nell had to try. "What do you think of my new dress?"

For tonight's event, Nell wore a silk dress with chemise detailing. The ivory silk and embroidered fringe shawl provided a nice contrast to the dark blue of the dress. A large hat with ostrich feathers rested on her dark wig.

"It's gorgeous." Abby's jaw set in a firm tilt. "You and Leo are exclusive."

It was more statement than question.

Nell nodded. She saw no need to mention she had no desire not to be. She could barely juggle one man, let alone more.

"You only want to date him, nothing more."

Nell smiled at a passing couple, hoping they'd stop to chat and distract Abby. But after a wave of acknowledgment, they continued on.

"I know what it's like to want someone you're not sure you should want." Abby's dark eyes met Nell's. "It does no good to run from the issue."

"There is no issue—"

"Is it because his father is—"

"It doesn't have a thing to do with his father's current situation." Nell spoke firmly.

"Then why don't you want to get serious? It's obvious, at least to me, how much you like Leo."

Nell resisted the urge to sigh. Being evasive with her friends was the part of the new life she'd built that she hated the most.

"Can't you tell me, Nell?" Abby's soft voice and pleading expression wrapped around Nell's heart.

Maybe it was time, Nell thought, to not only be honest with Leo, but with her close friends, as well. "My childhood was a mess, Abby, filled with turmoil and chaos. There were things I did in my adolescence that I very much regret."

Even as her heart twisted, Nell kept her expression serene. She knew anyone looking at her would likely think they were discussing fashion or the weather, or something else equally inane.

"You don't think you're good enough for him."

"I'm not." Though it hurt Nell to admit she was lacking, it felt good to be honest.

Abby inclined her head. "Have you told Leo about your teenage escapades?"

"Not yet." Nell swallowed against the sudden dryness in her

throat, desperately wishing she'd taken the glass of champagne. What she'd done back then went far beyond escapades.

"Before you cut him loose—" Abby met her gaze. "Don't give me that look. I know that's exactly what you've been considering. Before you just walk away, tell Leo all your secrets, then decide."

Nell hesitated for a moment, then nodded.

Abby put a hand on her gloved forearm. "Promise me. Say the words."

"I promise." Nell lifted her arm and Abby released her grip. "I need to get ready for my speech. We'll talk later."

As Nell hurried away, she let the Hazel Green persona settle over her. Apparently, people found her more approachable when she was alone. Every few steps, someone stopped her, either to discuss something related to town history or to take a photo with her.

Nell didn't mind these pictures making their way onto the internet. The expert use of stage makeup had added nearly a decade to her face. Specialty putty changed the shape of her nose, and a mouthpiece transformed her lower jaw. Emerald-green contacts completed the transformation. Nell was confident she wouldn't set off any facial-recognition alarms.

Was this why, she wondered, she felt more comfortable in Hazel's skin than she did in her own? Perhaps, she thought, as she posed for another selfie, it was because she didn't have to worry about keeping secrets. Hazel's life was an open book.

Nell thought of Hazel's diary. If she was home, she'd be reading it now.

Later, she promised herself. Once she gave her speech, she could leave.

When an older man and his granddaughter stopped her, Nell realized she was as much an attraction as the senator and his wife. Leo's parents stood across the large Pavilion, where they'd been greeting friends and constituents for the past hour.

Wells was beside his parents, along with Sophie. Leo was

there, too. She didn't see Matt. Up until now, Nell had done her best to steer clear of the area. Eventually, Leo would introduce her, but tonight it would be as Hazel Green, not Nell Ambrose.

Several minutes later, she was signaled to move closer to the stage. Senator Pomeroy would say a few words. Then Nell, or rather, Hazel, would take the platform.

Once on stage, Hazel would speak on her efforts to help women secure the right to vote in the early-twentieth century and mention the connection between the Chautauqua movement and the feminist movement.

The speech she planned to give was one Nell had composed herself, taking bits and pieces from several speeches Hazel had given prior to Congress ratifying the Nineteenth Amendment in 1920. She was immensely proud of the women of that time, women who had fought for what was right and just.

Women who had been everything her mother was not. Nell, who'd once been headed down that same path, wondered if she'd have stayed if not for the Britten incident.

"Ms. Ambrose."

There was authority in the deep voice. It was a voice that commanded, rather than requested.

Nell slowly turned and found herself face-to-face with Leo's father.

Timothy Pomeroy was a fit, striking man in his late fifties with thick, sandy-brown hair peppered with gray. He reminded her of an older version of Wells.

Tim's warm smile, well, that reminded Nell so much of Leo that she found herself offering a genuine smile back.

She extended her hand. "Hazel Green. It's a pleasure to meet you, Senator."

Surprise flickered momentarily in his eyes before the senator took her hand in a firm grip.

"When Nell attends an event as Hazel Green, it's total immersion." Admiration ran through Leo's words.

"Mr. Mayor."

"Please." Before she realized what he meant to do, Leo had taken her gloved hand and brought it to his lips. "I think we know each other well enough for you to call me Leo."

The senator's gaze grew sharp and assessing.

It was a good thing, Nell thought, she'd never been a woman who blushed. If she were, her cheeks would be bright pink.

"Mayor Pomeroy." Nell added a hint of chiding to the cadence favored by Hazel in several audio recordings she'd studied. "You know Richard prefers me to address gentlemen of my acquaintance in more formal terms."

Leo burst into laughter, drawing the attention of those nearby.

A startled look crossed the senator's face before he brought his expression under control. "I'm confused."

"She's speaking of Richard Green." Leo's laughing eyes had her relaxing. God, he was gorgeous.

"You're referring to the architect who founded this town."

"We're speaking of my husband, the world-renowned architect," Nell clarified, then saw that the senator was being called to the stage. "Again, a pleasure to make your acquaintance, sir."

"You as well, Mrs. Green." The senator climbed the steps to the dais with a self-assuredness that was undoubtedly second nature.

Leo stepped closer. "You confused him. That doesn't happen often."

Nell simply smiled.

"He'll remember you."

Likely, the comment was meant as a compliment, but Nell cringed inside. She hoped if the senator from Illinois remembered her, it would be as Hazel Green.

Though the scent of Leo's citrus cologne was distracting, Nell kept her attention on the stage. She liked to study other speakers, especially the experienced ones.

The senator waited for the audience to quiet, his gaze sweeping the crowd. He began his speech with an anecdote that had the crowd laughing.

As the senator continued, he kept his message clear and simple. He was proud to represent the citizens of Illinois and to do what he could to make their lives better. A thread running through the talk was he'd never forgotten his roots.

"In *The Adventures of Tom Sawyer*, Tom tells Huck, 'Everybody does it that way.' What does Huck say?" Tim paused for dramatic effect. "'I am not everybody.' Like Huck, I am not everybody. If a fellow politician or someone in my office chooses to go down a wrong path, that doesn't mean Tim Pomeroy will follow along."

The senator placed his hands on either side of the lectern and leaned slightly forward, his gaze panning the audience. "I am my own man. I follow my own path. I am not everybody. I am myself. You are why I do this job. I will do my best for you. I am not everybody."

"There's the sound bite." Nell spoke softly, the words for Leo's ears only.

The immediate and enthusiastic applause had the senator waving to the crowd.

Beside her, Leo said nothing. She hated the concern in his eyes, but didn't have time to ask if there had been more news on the Steve front before she was called to the stage.

Like the senator, she was a pro at giving speeches. Sometimes, she wondered how she'd been lucky enough to land the role of Hazel. As herself, she could have never stood in the public eye. Portraying Hazel afforded her the opportunity to speak on a variety of topics that interested her.

Once the introduction had been completed, Nell stepped to the microphone.

"It's lovely to listen to a fine orator who speaks from the heart." She gestured with one gloved hand toward the senator, and the crowd cheered again.

Nell realized she'd nearly given the man an endorsement, something she hadn't done before. But Hazel *had* supported fellow platform speaker William Jennings Bryan during his various runs for the presidency. There was precedent. Besides, Tim was Leo's father, and she would do what she could to ease Leo's worries.

"I'm going to speak from the heart today, too." Though Nell had planned to use an amusing anecdote to kick off her speech, Tim had used that tactic and also taken some of her time, so she got straight to the point. "As Independence Day approaches, we need to consider that since 1848, women such as Elizabeth Cady Stanton, Lucretia Mott and Susan B. Anthony have fought for the rights of women to vote."

Nell continued, doing as the senator had done, keeping her message simple. She thanked the good people of Illinois, which had been one of the first states to ratify the Nineteenth Amendment.

Applause followed, as it always did after she'd spoken. She noticed Liz taking pictures, undoubtedly doing freelance work for the *Hazel Green Chronicle*. Nell smiled broadly, feeling secure in her disguise.

Liz could take as many pictures as she wanted, could interview and quote her. The one thing Nell never allowed was for her name to be mentioned in any of the articles.

She was representing Hazel Green, that was the story. Focusing on who was behind the woman was another story altogether, and a not very interesting one.

Nell stepped from the stage. Instead of being grateful the speech was over, she felt exhilarated. Being in front of an audience was a far more potent upper than any drug.

"Mrs. Green." Leo was waiting for her at the bottom of the steps. "If you have a moment, I'd like to introduce you to my mother."

Nell was struck again by how strange it was that until today she'd never met either of Leo's parents. While his father was a handsome man with a commanding presence, Leo's mother could be described in one word—average. Average height. Average weight. Average looks.

Her straight, dark brown hair brushed her shoulders in a stylish bob. Her features were pleasant but nondescript. But her eyes...

The blue was quite extraordinary. It wasn't just the color that drew Nell's attention, it was the warmth residing there. The woman radiated kindness and acceptance.

"It's a pleasure to meet you, Mrs. Green." Leo's mother's lips quirked upward. "May I call you Hazel?"

Nell took the woman's outstretched hand. "I'd like that."

"And you may call me Marty."

"Well, Marty," Nell said, a genuine smile lifting her lips, "what did you think of the speech?"

"Yours?" Marty lifted a brow, good humor dancing in her eyes. "Or my husband's?"

"Mine, of course."

Out of the corner of her eye, Nell saw Leo's gaze shift between her and his mother, a look of puzzlement on his face. If he didn't expect her to converse with his mother, why introduce them?

"Leo," Wells called out. "Do you have a minute?"

Leo lifted a hand, acknowledging his brother before turning back to Nell. His easy smile had her relaxing. "I won't be long."

"Take all the time you need." Nell gestured to Marty. "I'll keep your mother company."

"My son likes you." Marty spoke softly as Leo headed toward his brother.

"Leo is a great guy."

"Yes, he is." Marty looped her arm through Nell's. "Let's take a little walk, and you can tell me about all the work you've been doing for disadvantaged children."

"That's Nell Ambrose's work," Nell insisted, but let herself be drawn through the crowd, with Marty scattering smiles like fairy dust over the crowd.

"I imagine it can be difficult to know where Hazel's life ends and your own begins." Marty's tone was conversational, but thankfully, the woman didn't appear to expect an answer.

While they strolled, Nell realized Marty had done her homework on Cornelia Ambrose. Leo's mother was familiar with most of the child-advocacy work Nell had done in the past.

As the crowd around them thinned and they entered the streets of Gingerbread Village, the slight tightness around the woman's mouth relaxed.

Nell realized suddenly that while Marty presented a good front, she wasn't completely comfortable in the public eye even after all these years.

"How long have you and my son been seeing each other?"

"We've known each other since I moved to Hazel Green five years ago." Nell smiled, remembering the first time she'd seen Leo. He'd been striding down the sidewalk toward her, and their eyes had met. "Since then, Leo and I have become good friends."

"Just good friends?" Marty simply continued to walk, not speaking again for several long moments. "Is that because you don't feel my son is the right man for you?"

There were plenty of ways to answer the question, but Nell chose the most direct and the most honest. "Leo has a brilliant political future in front of him. I'm not sure I'm the right woman for him. I'm sure that doesn't make sense, but—"

"On the contrary, I can very much identify with your feelings." Marty gestured to her cottage. "Let's sit on the porch. We can enjoy the quiet and this beautiful day for a few minutes."

"We'll have to go back." Even as she spoke, Nell took a seat in one of the rockers.

"Of course, but not for a little while." Marty leaned her head against the back of the rocker and sighed. "I've always loved the relaxing pace of Hazel Green, but Tim wanted more."

Nell's eyes widened. Had she just seen a firefly light up? Could it be a sign? She shook aside the fanciful thought and refocused on Marty. "Some senators maintain homes in two locations."

"We did for a while, but it's difficult when you have a family. Sacrifices must be made." Marty's blue eyes settled on Nell. "When Tim and I were dating, I wasn't convinced I was the right woman for him. Even as a young man, well before he dipped his toes into politics, he had high aspirations. I'm a homebody. I never wanted a fast-paced lifestyle."

"Yet, you married a man destined for bigger and better."

"I loved him too much to let him go." Marty began to slowly rock back and forth, the chair creaking in a soothing rhythm. "I spoke with Tim about my fears. He promised he'd only ask me to participate in events when absolutely necessary. He also agreed that we would spend as much time as possible in Hazel Green."

Nell fought a pang of envy. "Why are you telling me all this?"

"To let you know that sometimes if love is deep enough—and if both parties are willing to make sacrifices—what appears impossible can work." Marty gave a little laugh. "The road isn't always easy. For me, it's been well worth the effort."

If only what stood between her and Leo was as simple as compromising on public events or where to live. If only she could count on Dixon's assurances that he'd covered her tracks so thoroughly that her past and her mother would never catch up to her.

If only—

"I wondered where you two had disappeared to."

Nell's heart flip-flopped as Leo strode up to the porch.

He winked at Nell before shifting his gaze to his mother. "Dad is looking for you. Something about a photo op."

Marty pushed herself up from the chair. "I'd best get back."

When Nell started to rise, Marty waved a hand. "You and Leo enjoy a few moments of quiet."

Nell settled back into the chair while Leo walked Marty to the sidewalk.

Leo stopped, and Marty gave her son a hug.

"I like her," his mother told him in a voice that carried easily on the breeze.

Nell felt a rush of warmth. Until this moment, she hadn't realized just how much having Marty's approval meant.

"I like her, too." Leo brushed his lips against Marty's cheek. "Very much."

"I want you to be happy."

Nell doubted the two realized she could hear every word they spoke.

Leo slanted a look back at Nell before assuring his mother, "I couldn't be happier."

But for how much longer? Nell wondered.

Would Leo still be happy with her...once he knew all her secrets?

CHAPTER TWELVE

The memory of Nell's smile when he'd left her apartment buoyed Leo's mood on the short walk back to the cottage. He'd been willing to wait while she got out of her Hazel garb and removed the gunk from her face, but she'd sent him on his way.

Nell insisted his parents would be in town only a short while, and this was his opportunity to spend some one-to-one time with them. Though she told him she was perfectly comfortable walking to the cottage alone, he'd made her promise to call him as soon as she was ready to leave.

"It's me," Leo called out as he stepped inside the cottage.

"Out in a minute," his mother responded from the bedroom.

He wondered if she, like Nell, was changing into something more comfortable.

Leo had just grabbed a beer from the refrigerator and dropped down on the sofa when his father entered the cottage from the backyard.

The senator still wore the suit and tie he'd had on this afternoon. The only concession he'd made once he was out of the public eye had been to loosen his tie.

"That didn't take long." Tim took a seat in the chair next to the sofa.

"She doesn't live far. It takes a while for her to change from Hazel back to Nell, so she'll text me when she's ready." Leo lifted the bottle of his father's favorite craft beer and took a long sip. "Like I said, it isn't a great distance, but I don't want her to walk here alone."

When she'd accepted his invitation to spend the evening with his family, Leo had known she was serious about giving their relationship a chance.

"Nell is a lovely woman." His mother appeared from the bedroom, only to detour into the kitchen to get a beer for his dad.

Marty handed Tim a beer, then perched on the arm of his father's chair.

"Nell is the total package." Just thinking of her made Leo smile. "When Heather and I split, I wondered if I'd ever find someone I could love again. I'm starting to believe Nell is that someone."

"Sounds serious." His father lifted the bottle of pale lager and studied him over the top.

"The potential is there." Leo leaned against the back of the sofa. The windows were open, and the sounds of crickets chirping brought memories of long-ago summers flooding back.

"Does she have family around here?" his mother asked.

"No." Leo hoped that was accurate. He assumed Nell would have told him if she had family nearby.

"Where did she grow up?" his mother pressed, more, he knew, out of genuine interest rather than a desire to pry.

"I'm not exactly sure where she would call home. She moved a lot when she was younger."

Tim cocked his head. "Does she have a parent in the military?"

"She never knew her father. Her mother doesn't sound like the type for military service." Leo didn't want to break any confidences, so he would tread carefully. "From what she's told me, her childhood wasn't a happy one. But she's done well for herself. She went to college at Madison and got her JD from Marquette."

Of that, he was certain. He'd seen the diplomas on her office wall.

"How did she end up in Hazel Green?" His father took a sip of beer and loosened his tie even further.

"She decided this would be a good place to set up her law practice." Leo hoped his dad would let it go at that, but when his father opened his mouth, Leo knew he wouldn't be that lucky.

"Why here?"

His mother spoke up. "I got the feeling from our talk that she likes the sense of community. It's how I've always felt about Hazel Green."

Tim's brows pulled together. "She doesn't like big-city life?"

"Why so many questions, Dad?" Leo asked curiously.

"My own career might be damaged beyond repair, but you've got a bright future in politics."

"You didn't do anything wrong," Leo asserted. "You'll be fine."

"You and I both know innocence doesn't always matter. Those around us can bring us down just as easily as our own actions." A bleakness filled Tim's eyes. "Look what happened with Steve. If you don't know who you're in bed with—figuratively and literally—then you're rolling the dice with your future."

"Surely you're not saying you think me being with Nell could damage my reputation." It took great effort for Leo to keep his tone even.

"I honestly don't know. She seems like a lovely woman, but I don't know her." Tim expelled a breath. "I'm not sure you even know her."

"You knew Steve for forty years," Leo pointed out. "He was like a brother to you."

"Exactly. And because I had a friendship with him, I let

emotion override diligence. I didn't question him like I should have. I trusted, but didn't verify."

"Fine, you had too much confidence in Steve. This isn't the same. Nell doesn't work for me—"

"No, but she could be angling for a position much closer. She wouldn't be the first woman to try and trap—"

"Tim." Marty slapped a hand against her husband's arm.

"Nell isn't angling for anything." Leo felt a muscle in his jaw jump. He didn't add that it had taken a lot of convincing just to get Nell to agree to date him. "She's not like that. Like you said, you don't know her."

"And do you, son? Do you really know this woman you're falling in love with?"

Leo took a calming breath. "Look, I understand you feel betrayed, but on this you need to trust my judgment. The way I see it, if someone you care about betrays your trust, you deal with it then."

"It doesn't always work that way."

When Leo's gaze turned puzzled, Tim continued, "If you run for reelection as mayor, or decide to seek a seat at the state level, you can bet your opponents will try to destroy your reputation."

"I understand that—" Leo began.

"All I'm asking is that you be practical. Before you get in too deep with Nell, take time to get to know her. Sometimes, we see in a person what we want to see. Or what they want us to see." When Leo opened his mouth again, his father held up a hand. "You've wanted to be in politics since you ran for student council in middle school. I only ask that you make sure you know the person you may be trusting with your future."

~

The wig came off first. Then the dress and underbust corset and brassiere. Finally free of the corset's constraints, Nell inhaled fully.

She reveled in being able to draw a deep breath for the first time in hours. Nell pulled on cotton pants and a faded Marquette tee, then sat down to clear all traces of Hazel from her face. Once she looked like herself again, she'd pull on a dress and call Leo.

Tonight, she'd spend the evening getting to know Leo's family.

Though Tim seemed like a nice man, the look in his eyes when he'd studied her made Nell uneasy. She'd seen that same look on the faces of countless detectives and police officers in the years she lived with her mother.

Concern. Suspicion. Disapproval.

The authorities had rarely been able to prove their suspicions, and their frustration had been evident. Gloria had spun her lies— lies she fully believed—while Nell and her brother had done as she demanded and kept their mouths shut.

Nell had learned early on what happened when you spoke up. She'd been fourteen when she added what she thought was a helpful comment supporting her mother's lies. It had been the first, and the last, time she made that mistake. After the cops left, her mother had beaten her viciously. Ky--er Dixon--had attempted to intervene, but he'd been only ten and no match for the woman's fury and strength.

The next day, Gloria was all solicitous, telling Nell she was her best girl and so smart. Just remembering had Nell's hands shaking as she applied moisturizer to her now clean face.

Leo seemed confident his father would weather this latest crisis. Nell wished she could be so certain. Even though up until the scandal, his father had enjoyed a stellar reputation, Nell knew there were people who loved keeping things stirred up.

Her mother had ruined many lives and reputations with a few well-placed lies. Sometimes—many times—there had been nothing in it for her. She'd done it simply for the fun of seeing someone she envied—or detested—squirm.

It would be the same for Tim Pomeroy. Some people would fan the fires of the scandal, hoping he'd get scorched simply because he'd been close to the source, or because they had political aspirations he could thwart in some way. Or simply because they enjoyed seeing a good man fall.

A buzz pulled Nell from her reverie. She set down the mascara brush and saw Anthony's name on the screen. "Ms. Ambrose, Leo Pomeroy is here."

"Send him up." Nell padded across the floor and opened her door.

Several seconds later, the elevator dinged and Leo strode off.

When he reached her, Nell moved to the side and made a sweeping gesture for him to step inside.

He looked so yummy in his cargo shorts and graphic T-shirt, Nell felt desire surge as the door to her apartment clicked shut.

"I couldn't wait." Leo wasted no time in kissing her soundly.

"You smell wonderful." Nell slid her fingers into his hair and savored the taste of him.

She felt his mouth curve as Leo continued pressing his lips lightly to hers, teasingly. Finally, with one hand, he pushed Nell's hair back from her face. It was such a tender gesture that her heart lurched.

His gaze searched her face. "You look amazing."

"Yeah, right." She gave a little laugh. "I was just about to put on some makeup."

"Not necessary." Leo touched her cheek, one finger trailing slowly along her skin, leaving heat in its wake. "You're beautiful without it."

The words pleased her more than he knew. Her mother had always insisted she had to be perfectly put together to even meet minimum standards.

"I think you might be just a bit prejudiced," she teased.

"Guilty."

With a quiet laugh, she gazed up at him. "I wish we could stay in tonight."

"My parents are eager to get to know you better, but I promise we won't stay long." The desire shimmering in his eyes wrapped around Nell like a caress.

For a second, she imagined the touch of his strong hands on her bare skin, and her pulse jumped.

"Screw it," he said abruptly, as if fighting his own desperate ache. Leo pulled the phone from his pocket. "I'll call and tell them something came up."

"We need to be there." Nell shoved aside temptation and placed a staying hand on his phone. "Whether he admits it or not, your father needs you. As a politician, you, more than your brothers, understand what he's going through."

"This scandal has been hard on him." Leo expelled a heavy breath. "The funny thing is, he seems more worried how all this will affect my political future than he is about his."

"It's a valid concern." As much as she wanted to reassure him, they both knew his father's worries were realistic. "Actually, everyone around him will likely be impacted to some degree once all this goes down."

"I told him he doesn't have to worry about me. Let them dig into my background, into the decisions I've made since taking office." Pride filled Leo's voice. "I have nothing to hide."

He might not, but she did. Though the odds were low of her background coming out, Leo should know. Then he could decide if being with her was worth the risk of her past one day affecting his career.

"There's something I need to tell you. When I was a child…" Nell tried to say more, but nothing came out.

Don't do it. Don't do it. The self-preservation instinct that had been her constant companion since she'd been old enough to talk blocked the words poised on the tip of her tongue.

"Nell?" Leo stepped to her. He ran his palms up and down her bare arms, but the warmth didn't touch the chill that invaded her body. "What's wrong?"

She cleared her throat, realizing it wasn't self-preservation that had her pausing, it was painful memories. "When I was a child, my mother—"

"Sweetheart, you're shaking."

Before she could respond, he pulled her tight against him, pressing her head against his shoulder. His arms were strong, and she let herself lean on him for just a moment.

Nell steeled her spine. She could do this.

"My childhood was awful." Despite the matter-of-fact words, her voice wavered. "Even after all these years, it's difficult for me to speak of that time. You've had questions that I haven't answered. I need to be honest with you. I—"

"We don't need to discuss this now." He wiped the tears slipping down her cheeks with the pads of his thumbs.

"If I crossed my mother in any way, if she *thought* I crossed her, she'd make me pay. One time, she beat me with a lamp." Nell gave a nervous laugh. "A lamp, of all things. She normally avoided the face, but the cord caught my cheekbone."

Her fingers rose to the scar normally carefully hidden with makeup.

"The woman is a monster." A muscle in his jaw jumped. "And that wasn't the only time she hit you. I've seen the scars on your body."

He'd asked about the scars several times, but Nell always changed the subject.

"It wasn't just physical abuse." She coughed in an attempt to dislodge the lump clogging her throat. "I was the spawn of Satan one day and her little princess the next. I ran away from home at seventeen and never looked back."

"You did what you had to do to survive."

Leo didn't realize he'd spoken the words she'd repeated over and over to herself in an attempt to assuage her guilt.

"I did all sorts of horrible things. Sometimes, I even thought they were fun." She refused to present herself as some sort of martyr. "I lied and cheated, and then when things got so bad, I ran. I left my little brother in her clutches. He had no one."

"I'm sure you did the best—"

"He had no one." Nell fisted a hand against her heart. "Dixon had no one to protect him."

"Dixon." Leo cocked his head. "Dixon Carlyle is your brother?"

Nell met his gaze. She could say it was a different person, maybe even make him believe it was true. But she couldn't lie. Not with those blue eyes firmly fixed on her, asking only for the truth. "Yes. Dixon is the brother I left behind all those years ago."

"You don't have the same last name." It was an inane remark, but it appeared Leo's brain was having difficulty processing.

"We don't have the same last name." She didn't elaborate. "When he showed up in Hazel Green last fall, that was the first time I'd seen him since I was seventeen."

She could almost see the puzzle pieces falling into place in Leo's head.

"Why the secrecy? Why not just tell everyone he's your brother?" Puzzlement filled Leo's eyes. "It would likely help his business for people to know that he's got a family connection to someone in Hazel Green. Especially someone like you, who's so well regarded."

"Dixon and I are in the process of mending fences." Nell cleared her throat and kept to the truth. "He's a reminder of a time I've tried so hard to forget. I wasn't certain he'd stick. I wasn't sure I wanted him to stick."

"You didn't mean to tell me."

"It just slipped out," she admitted.

"You could have lied and told me the Dixon I know isn't your brother."

"I don't want to lie to you."

The tears began to fall in earnest now. For years, she'd kept her emotions locked down, refusing to feel too much. Despite having still so much to say, so much to tell him, she let the floodgates open.

After several long moments, Nell sniffled and lifted her head. She would get through this. He needed *all* the facts.

"When I was growing up"—more moisture filled Nell's eyes, but she determinedly blinked it away—"I wasn't a good person. If you'd known me then, you wouldn't have liked who I was. I don't like who I was."

"I would have liked you, even then," he murmured, stroking her hair in an attempt to comfort.

He was honest and good and sincere. She was a cheat and a liar. She was a con artist who'd viewed stealing as a game. Thoughts of all she'd done had the self-loathing she normally kept at bay surging. "Let me tell you—"

"Shhh." He pulled her against him, pressing her head to his chest. "You've told me enough for now. We can talk more another time. I'm always ready to listen. But I don't need to know who you were then, because I know who you are now. And who you are now is incredible."

She, who had never clung to anyone in her life, clung to him, wanting desperately to believe that, despite her past, they could make what was building between them work.

When he felt her steady, he stepped back, his gaze traveling slowly over her. "Better?"

Nell flushed. "I'm sorry. I lost control for a minute."

His gaze was steady on hers. "You don't ever have to apologize to me for showing your emotions. I feel honored that you trusted me enough to let down your shield."

She gave a watery laugh and swiped at her eyes. "My shield?"

"I understand more and more why it's been so hard for you to let me get close." Sympathy shimmered in his blue eyes. "I'm sorry you had to go through that abuse as a child. And I'm sorry those memories still have the power to hurt you."

"I've moved past it." When she spoke this time, there wasn't the slightest quiver in her voice.

"You're a strong, remarkable woman, but you don't have to hide your scars—or your pain—from me." He placed a hand on her shoulder. "I'm proud of you, Nell. Proud of what you've accomplished and of the warm, caring person you've become."

Had anyone ever said those words to her before? Nell felt the depths of his regard all the way to the tips of her toes. He truly cared about her. And in that moment, she realized something else.

She loved Leo Pomeroy. With every fiber of her being, she loved this wonderful man.

Her gaze locked with his, and desire surged. She suddenly had trouble catching her breath.

"I told my parents it might be a while before we returned." His glittering blue eyes never left her face.

"Which means there is no reason to rush."

The despair and pain that had consumed her only minutes ago disappeared. Her lips curved. "It seems, Mr. Pomeroy, that for the next hour, you're all mine."

Needing the reassurance that things were okay between them, Nell wound her arms around his neck and lifted her face.

His mouth closed over hers. It felt amazingly good to hold him. To taste him. To touch him. She stroked the back of his neck, twining her fingers in his hair.

How, she wondered, could such a simple gesture feel so intimate and erotic?

"Let me take you to bed." Need had his voice sounding raspy. "Let me make love to you."

She nodded, planting a kiss at the hollow of his throat to seal the decision.

They walked hand-in-hand to her bedroom. When he turned toward her, Nell stepped into his arms. Despite the raw need she saw in his eyes, Leo appeared determined to take this slow.

Tonight, there would be nothing—and no one—between them. Despite being together for months and making love more times than she could count, this felt like the first time.

"I understand there might be things in your past you prefer to keep to yourself." Leo's gaze searched her face. "I want you to know there isn't anything you can't tell me. Nothing you can say will change the way I feel about you."

She stroked his hair, her heart a warm, sweet mass.

His fingers weren't quite steady as they touched the curve of her cheek, trailed along the line of her jaw. "I'm here for you. I'll always be here for you."

Then, as if deciding the time for talking was over, Leo pressed his mouth to hers.

CHAPTER THIRTEEN

Searching fingers found their way under her shirt, and Leo made a sound of pleasure when he discovered she wasn't wearing a bra. When his hands closed over her breasts and his thumbs brushed against her sensitive tips, Nell moaned.

She wanted him. Wanted to show him how much he meant to her. In a single fluid movement, her shirt was off. Her drawstring pants quickly followed.

Not to be outdone, his clothes hit the floor beside hers.

After six months, she knew his body as well as she knew her own. The broad shoulders and the dusting of dark hair across the chest. The flat abdomen, slender hips and muscular legs. The clever hands that could make her alternately sigh or moan with pleasure. And that incredible mouth.

Nell gave in to the erotic sensations, letting hands and lips that knew all her sensitive spots stroke, caress and arouse.

He wasn't the only one who knew little secrets. She knew what Leo Pomeroy liked. She knew what he liked, and she gave it to him, warmly, willingly, without reservation.

There had been times when sex had been quick and fast,

sometimes even rough, when the need had been great. But not tonight.

The edge, the brink, was kept just out of reach as they showed the depths of their feelings for each other. When he backed off slightly, she begged for more, even though she didn't want this to ever end.

He gave her what she asked for, edging her higher and higher with words and kisses. Long, lingering kisses that had her drunk on the taste of him.

Her heart swelled with emotion. She could kiss him for hours, and it would never be enough.

"I love...kissing you." The words came out on a breath.

"I love kissing you, too." Leo scattered little love bites up her neck.

Craving his touch, she moaned and leaned back, giving him greater access to the sensitive area he knew so well behind her ear.

The gentleness of his caresses, the sweet but intoxicating kisses he continued to bestow on every part of her body touched the part of her heart she'd once kept closed off.

As those clever hands and mouth pushed her closer and closer to the edge, Nell fought to hold on to control. Remaining in control was a habit, a lesson learned early on and ruthlessly enforced.

But Leo wouldn't let her hold back and wouldn't take his own pleasure without first seeing her satisfied. Even as she fought to not feel too much, to not love too much, he continued to stroke and caress and kiss, while rhythmically pumping deep inside her.

She could hold on no longer. The orgasm hit suddenly, and love for him exploded inside her. She cried out his name, her nails clawing his back as sensation after sensation pummeled her.

Leo held tight to her, kissing and murmuring sweet words until he was satisfied he'd wrung the last ounce of pleasure from her body. Only when the tremors settled, did he take his own release, plunging deep and shuddering.

He lay there for the longest time on top of her, their bodies still joined. Nell wrapped her arms around him, gently sliding the pads of her fingers up and down his back.

"I'm crushing you," he murmured, but didn't appear to have the strength—or the desire—to move off of her.

"You're fine where you are." Nell kissed him lightly on the lips.

His mouth curved when the kiss ended.

"What's that smile about?"

"I was just thinking I could lie here forever and be happy." Leo pushed himself to his forearms and gazed down at her. "As long as I'm with you."

What could she do but smile back?

When he rolled off of her, he pulled her to him.

Relaxing in the afterglow, Nell smiled.

Her mother was in jail.

Dixon had covered their tracks.

She was with the man she loved.

Life was good.

The streetlights flickered on as she and Leo strolled down the sidewalk toward the cottage. The bed had been so comfortable and he'd been so warm that when Leo offered to text his parents that they couldn't make it, Nell had been seriously tempted.

Her eyes were red and swollen from crying, and she knew it would take all her makeup skills to conceal the ravages of the tears. Although sex with Leo had given her a boost, she still felt drained.

But his family wouldn't be in town long, and she knew they wanted to spend time with him.

"You intrigued me from the first moment I met you," Leo murmured, stroking her palm with his thumb where their hands were joined as they passed a butterfly bush in full bloom.

"Really? I don't recall you falling at my feet to impress me." She fought to keep her voice steady, even as her pulse throttled up at his touch. "In fact, quite the opposite."

"I remember quite well our first meeting at Lily Belle's."

"You spilled your ice cream cone down the front of my dress."

"Someone bumped me from behind," he protested, but she heard the laughter in his voice.

"You grabbed a bunch of napkins and were ready to help me wipe off before I stopped you."

"Yeah, putting my hands on your chest might have been a bit much for a first meeting."

Nell chuckled. From the start, there had been a spark that had drawn her in, even when it would have been safer to keep her distance. "Did you know I campaigned for you?"

"You're joking."

"I didn't do flyers or go door to door, but I did tell everyone I knew that I thought you were the best choice for mayor."

"You never mentioned that to me before."

"It was before we met." She shrugged. "I checked out your stance on issues and did some searching into your background. There was some stuff about Heather, but not much."

"The breakup occurred so close to the accident that my broken engagement was barely a blip on anyone's radar." His expression sobered, and he heaved a heavy breath. "I still miss Kit and Dani."

"I wish I could have known them."

"You'd have liked them." He gave her hand a squeeze. "And they'd have liked you. Especially Kit. I think you'd have been good friends."

Knowing how he felt about his sister, that was high praise.

"Promise me something, Nell."

The serious edge to his tone had her stopping on the sidewalk to face him. "What?"

"Don't shut me out. I can't support you if I don't know what's going on in your head." His gaze searched her face. "I'll always be here for you. Remember, there's no shame in asking for help. We all need someone in our corner."

Nell tilted her head back and stared into his eyes. "You're a good man, Leo Pomeroy. You deserve only the best."

He shot her a wink. "That's why I have you."

"Good. I'm not the last one."

Nell turned to see Matt striding up the sidewalk toward them.

"We're not late," Leo told his brother.

"Mom told me she wanted everyone at the cottage by seven."

Nell exchanged a glance with Leo. He appeared as puzzled as she was.

"She didn't give us any set time." Leo glanced at the cottage as if he'd somehow find the answer on the deserted front porch.

"What she told me was she'd invited Lilian and was planning to bring out the food at seven." Suspicion filled Matt's eyes. "I bet the party really starts at eight. She probably told me seven because she thinks I'm always late."

"You *are* always late." Leo glanced at his watch. "Eight o'clock on the nose. It appears the ploy worked."

"You go first." Nell smiled. "That way, we can be the last to arrive, not you."

Matt made a sweeping gesture toward the porch. "You go ahead. I don't want to spoil my record."

Although Nell didn't know Mathis well, she liked Leo's brother's irreverence and sarcastic wit. He reminded her of her own brother.

The door opened before they reached it.

Marty stepped out onto the porch. She gave Leo a hug and a kiss on the cheek, then wrapped her arms around Nell. "I'm so happy you could join us for dinner."

"Thank you for inviting me." Nell found herself touched by the warm welcome.

"Hey, what about me?" Matt pointed a hand to himself. "Middle son? Your favorite?"

A laugh bubbled out of Marty's throat.

"I get it," Matt continued. "You decided to save the best for last."

Her middle son's teasing tone had Marty flinging her arms around him in a dramatic gesture. "Oh, my dear, sweet Mathis. I've missed you so."

Nell stepped into the living room and realized the Pomeroy family had been in the middle of a board game. A card table had been set up.

"We can put the game away." Tim rose to his feet to greet Nell and Leo.

Wells did the same.

"I want to finish," Sophie whined. "We're almost done."

"Go ahead." Leo waved a hand. "Nell and I will check out the food."

His mother hesitated, obviously torn between her grand-daughter's wishes and her desire to be a good hostess.

"Seriously," Nell said. "We're fine."

"Sit by me, Uncle Matt," Sophie called out. "I'm winning."

Matt grinned and pulled a chair up next to his niece. "You're the luckiest kid I know."

Leo took Nell's arm. "Let's see what's for dinner."

Leaving shrieks of laughter behind, they ambled into the dining area where mountains of food covered the large rectangular table.

So much food for so few people, Nell thought.

There were several jumbo pizzas, a large pan of lasagna—still covered in foil—as well as breadsticks and a heaping bowl of salad.

"Dixon and I could have eaten for several weeks on this spread."

Nell didn't realize she'd spoken aloud until Leo touched her arm and she saw the question in his eyes.

"I was ten the first time Gloria left me and Dixon alone." Nell touched the box containing one of the pizzas, her fingers traveling nervously over the top. "She'd jetted off for a week in Vegas with her latest boyfriend."

"She left you without any adult supervision?" Leo frowned. "You were younger than Sophie."

"I was ten, and Dixon was six." Her lips quirked up in a humorless smile. "The refrigerator was empty, and we could only find a few dollars in change."

"Did you go to neighbors for help?"

"I knew better. Gloria threatened us with bodily harm if we spoke to anyone outside the house." Nell opened the box and stared at the large pie topped with pepperoni. She shut the box. "Everyone in the neighborhood hated Gloria. I didn't blame them. My mother made enemies wherever she went."

"Surely your neighbors wouldn't have held the actions of your mother against her children."

Nell lifted a shoulder, let it drop.

"How did you survive?"." Leo kept his voice even, but she heard the concern.

"I stole food from the grocery store." She lifted the top of the other pizza box. Hamburger topped this one. And, if she wasn't mistaken, extra cheese. "I couldn't let my brother starve. But I didn't take him with me. I could have used him to distract nosy clerks, but I didn't want the responsibility of starting him on a life of crime."

Gloria would see to that part of his education. There was nothing Nell could have done to stop her.

"You were ten years old."

"I was proud I didn't get caught. I thought my mother would praise my efforts when she got home."

"Did she?"

Nell lifted a breadstick and absently took a bite. "No. In her mind, I'd simply done what was necessary."

"She shouldn't have ever had children."

"No argument here." The breadstick felt like a leaden weight in the pit of her stomach.

"Nell?"

She looked up and found Leo staring at her with a curious expression. Before he could speak, Tim appeared in the archway.

"Is the game over already?" Leo asked.

"Sophie won." Tim chuckled. "That girl is a fierce competitor."

"When we were little," Leo told Nell, "Kit always won."

A shadow of sadness stole over Tim's face, but he quickly rallied. "Soph is following in her aunt's footsteps."

Marty began unboxing the pizzas, and Nell automatically moved to help her.

"I'm glad you joined us this evening." Tim took the foil off the lasagna, his gaze on Nell. "It'll give us an opportunity to get better acquainted."

Leo, who'd started toward the other room as if to help his siblings put away the card table and chairs, paused. "We're not playing twenty questions tonight, Dad. That never goes well."

"Sometimes better than other times," Marty admitted with a smile.

Nell cocked her head. "This sounds intriguing."

"The first time it happened, I was a sophomore in high school. I'd spent weeks trying to impress Tenley Phillips and had finally convinced her to give me a chance. Things were going well." Leo shot a piercing gaze at his father. "Then I made the mistake of bringing her home."

"I was simply attempting to get to know the girl," Tim protested.

"Tim means well, but he can be a bit overzealous." Marty cast a fond look in her husband's direction.

Matt appeared in the archway. "He interrogated Tenley. I was there. I heard every question."

"Wells," Tim motioned to his eldest son, "tell them I didn't interrogate Tenley Phillips."

"You interrogated every girl we brought home." A smile lifted Wells's lips. "I was worried how Dani would take the inquisition, but she adored you."

"We adored her, too." Tim's voice sounded rusty, and he cleared his throat.

A voice from the living room called out, "I'm here. I hope I'm not too late."

Lilian stepped into the room with all the aplomb of an actress making her stage entrance, and the subject of interrogation was forgotten.

The evening chugged along like a train on well-oiled tracks. They ate and talked about inconsequential things. Nell enjoyed visiting with Marty and Lilian and demonstrating her braiding skills on Sophie's hair.

The conversation remained easy and focused on Hazel Green events until it was nearly time to leave.

It was Lilian who brought up the elephant in the room. "How are things going for Steve?"

Nell was on the sofa next to Leo, his arm slung over her shoulders. She felt the arm behind her head tense.

"Nothing new on that front." Tim kept his tone light. "The press coverage had settled to a dull roar before Stanley Britten started stirring things up."

Gloria had once hit her with a board in her stomach and knocked all the air from her lungs. Nell remembered that feeling. She felt that same way now.

"I don't recognize that name." Lilian frowned. "Is he another senator?"

"Stan is a lobbyist," Wells answered. "One who's had a lot of contact with Steve. He even helped him draft some legislation."

"Why is this guy stirring things up?" Matt asked.

The same question was burning a hole in Nell's tongue.

"I'm not sure." Tim's voice turned grim. "But he's doing everything he can to somehow imply that I had direct involvement in taking the bribes."

Leo met his father's gaze. "Do you think he's trying to divert attention from himself?"

"The thought has crossed my mind," Tim admitted.

Nell forced herself to breathe. In and out. In and out.

She'd never done a search to see what Stanley Britten was up to all these years later. The truth was, she hadn't wanted to know how her actions might have influenced the course of his life.

The man causing trouble for Tim could be someone who just happened to have the same name. Somehow, Nell didn't think she'd be so lucky.

"Forget about Stanley." Tim shifted his gaze to Nell. "I'd like to spend some time this evening getting to know Nell better."

"Be afraid," Matt uttered in a ghoulish voice. "Be very afraid."

Everyone laughed.

Nell slanted a glance at Leo, and the look in his eye was as steady as the hand he settled on her shoulder.

He had her back.

She had nothing to fear.

CHAPTER FOURTEEN

Leo waited until they were nearly to Nell's apartment to bring up his father. The truth was, he was still reeling from everything Nell had told him today.

The fact that she had felt she could share such painful, private memories deeply touched him. She certainly didn't deserve to be interrogated by his father. "Sorry about my dad."

He didn't know what to think when Nell chuckled. "He was fine. His choice of questions surprised me."

"The fact that they steered more toward business than personal?"

"Yes. I'd expected the opposite."

It had surprised Leo, too, but listening to Nell talk with such passion about her child-advocacy work had told his father a lot about who she was as a person.

"He's a nice man." Nell made a face. "I hate it that someone is trying to stir up more trouble for him."

"Stan Britten is an ass."

Surprise skittered across her face. "You know the guy?"

"I met him one time when I was in DC. My dad and I were going to lunch, and Stan stopped by for a meeting with Steve when we were on our way out the door." Leo paused, as if searching for the right words. "He was arrogant and full of his own self-importance. Even though our encounter only lasted a few minutes, that came through loud and clear."

"Do you think he's involved in the bribery stuff?"

"It wouldn't surprise me." Leo took her hand and gave it a swing. "Thanks for coming with me tonight."

"You have a lovely family."

"They like you." The thought made him happy. He was close to his parents and brothers. If Nell was going to be a permanent part of his life—

The thought slapped him upside the head.

A permanent part of his life.

He realized he'd started to think of Nell in those terms. The realization was both exciting and a bit frightening.

"—Hazel's diary."

Leo pulled his thoughts back to the conversation. "The diary you got at auction."

"I've been reading bits of it every night. It's fascinating." A smile lifted Nell's lips. "The entry I read most recently was written when Jasper Pomeroy first introduced her to Richard Green."

He slanted a sideways glance. "Was it love at first sight, the way everyone in town believes?"

"I'm not sure if it was instant love, but it seemed as if there was definite interest from the start on both sides."

"I wonder how long it took Hazel to sleep with Richard," Leo mused.

"I'm not sure she did. At the turn of the twentieth century, sex between unmarried couples was frowned upon."

"Hazel was a stage performer when Richard met her," he reminded her.

"I know, but a Chautauqua speaker wasn't the same as, say,

someone on the vaudeville stage." Nell's brows pulled together. "I'm not sure why she saw herself as unsuitable for him."

"She thought she was unsuitable?"

"That's what she said. Hopefully as I read on, I'll know more."

"At least we already know that their story ended happily."

"Yes, from everything I've read, they were very well-suited and extremely happy, despite her fears."

"Which only goes to show that sometimes we worry about nothing." Unable to keep from touching Nell, Leo slid a hand down her arm. She was so soft, yet so tough. "In the end, love prevails and everything works out."

"I think it can." She met his gaze. "With the right person."

It was him.

Nell stared at her computer screen at the images of the boy she'd known all those years ago. Stanley Britten, the lobbyist who was causing all sorts of trouble for Leo's dad, was the same geeky high school junior she'd played for a fool.

The second Leo had left her apartment, Nell had done a search. Stan hadn't been difficult to find. In addition to a successful career, she discovered he was married and had a couple of kids.

She exhaled a shaky breath. She hadn't destroyed his life, after all. It appeared the episode that had loomed so large in her head the past fifteen years had been merely a blip to him.

It was just that Stanley had been so intense. He had been one of those boys who'd taken any little slight to heart.

His parents, wonderful people, would have been angry and disappointed in him. Not that she thought he'd confess his inadvertent role in the robbery and arson, but they'd have known someone had to give the thief the combination to the safe. The Britten home had been protected by a top-rated security system.

Police had determined that whoever had broken in had had the code.

When Nell, her mother and brother had simply left town shortly after the burglary and arson, Stanley had to have realized that the girl he'd trusted and considered a friend had played him.

Nell dropped her head into her hands.

When she'd told Leo some of her secrets, he hadn't run screaming into the night. But anyone could sympathize with a child who'd been abused, or a ten-year-old who'd done whatever was necessary to feed herself and her little brother.

But a seventeen-year-old was almost a woman, nearly an adult. At that age, a girl knew right from wrong. Yet, Nell had continued to do her mother's bidding. She'd lied, cheated and stolen.

The scams and cons had been exciting, like a game. Until they hadn't been.

Would Leo understand her behavior, her desire to please her crazy mother, when she didn't fully understand it herself? Would he question her character? Would he feel she'd played him by not being completely honest from the very beginning?

He'd been puzzled that she hadn't told him Dixon was her brother.

No matter how painful, or how much he insisted she didn't need to tell him everything, she had to do it before they got any closer. Nell reassured herself that she hadn't crossed any invisible lines tonight or gone down any roads she couldn't exit.

She hadn't proclaimed undying love. She'd merely told Leo she *liked* him.

Like was really such an innocuous word. Friends liked each other. You could like someone whom you only recently met. It didn't mean anything, really.

What had he said? *Sometimes we worry about nothing.*

She hoped she was wrong. But she feared that once he had all the facts, he would see that continuing their relationship would put his political aspirations at risk.

Nell sighed, closed the laptop and picked up Hazel's diary. Just holding the leather-bound book steadied her. Reading another woman's intimate thoughts was a privilege, one that Nell didn't take lightly.

Nell had done extensive research on the woman. She admired Hazel, and the last thing she wanted was for the woman's diary to fall into the wrong hands.

No matter how decent and honorable the person, Nell firmly believed that everyone had done things they regretted or had had unkind thoughts toward others. So far, nothing in the passages she'd read had jumped out at her. But Nell had no doubt she'd discover things Hazel would have preferred to keep hidden.

Hazel could count on Nell's discretion. If anyone knew how to keep secrets, it was her.

Nell opened the diary.

Chautauqua, New York 1900

On this night I once again brought Abraham Lincoln to life. He is a man much admired, and each time I speak the words he once spoke, I strive to do justice to him. No matter how many times I say the words, "All men are created equal," it always fills me with a sense of melancholy. As it was in 1863 when Lincoln gave the Gettysburg Address, equality for people of color and for women remains a pipe dream in the distance.

I like knowing President Lincoln rose from humble beginnings to the highest office in the land. He not only made a difference in the lives of those around him, but for many he would never meet.

I strive to make a difference, to uplift those in the audience with my impersonations of great people, both men and women.

This life is a solitary one, but we often meet interesting people. There was a man in the audience with whom I am casually acquainted. Jasper Pomeroy is a successful businessman who frequently attends performances. This evening, he brought a friend and made the introductions after my performance.

Richard Green is the man's name, and if Jasper is to be believed, Mr. Green is a world-renowned architect. He seemed a genial fellow and appeared truly interested in my performances. We conversed for the longest time, until Jasper reminded Mr. Green that they had an event to attend.

I was startled when Mr. Green brought my hand to his lips for a kiss and promised to return for another performance. When he lifted his head, his eyes met mine for a moment, and something passed between us.

It is odd how a simple look from a stranger could set my heart aflutter. He is a charming fellow and very handsome indeed with dark hair and beautiful brown eyes that hold a twinkle.

I find myself hoping that he will return, though I'm not sure why. Not only do Mr. Green and I live in far different worlds, my humble past would make me unacceptable for a man of his standing.

Yet, despite all this, I hope he will come again.

H.

Nell reread the sentence, *My humble past would make me unacceptable for a man of his standing.*

Still, Richard and Hazel had married and had a long and happy life together. Which meant that whatever had happened in her past either wasn't as horrible as she'd believed, or she never told her husband.

Was it possible, Nell wondered, for a woman to find happiness while keeping a secret past from her husband? Closing the diary, Nell set the book aside. There was only one course of action she could embrace.

She needed to tell Leo everything about her past…including her connection to Stanley Britten.

If she lost Leo, there would be only one person to blame.

Herself.

～

Monday morning, Nell leaned back in her desk chair and stared out the window. She loved summer in Hazel Green, with the large leafy green trees and the colorful flowers. Today, a bright blue cloudless sky and a brilliant sun sweetened the picture.

Her court case this morning, an adoption of a foster child into a loving home, had been momentarily satisfying. But as soon as she'd returned to her office, her mood had turned somber.

Nell had yet to reopen Hazel's diary to read about the progression of her romance with the prominent architect.

Hazel had been confident enough to join her life to a man with a past so different from hers. Not that Nell had to follow in Hazel's footsteps. She charted her own course. She always had, always would.

But each time she thought about confessing all to Leo, panic clawed at her throat. That pissed her off.

The intercom on her desk buzzed, and she jumped.

"Ms. Ambrose, Toby Gillenford is here."

Nell swiveled in the chair and expelled a breath. "Send him in."

She was around the desk and standing when the gawky teen entered the room.

Seventeen-year-old Toby was tall—nearly six-two—and skinny. His reddish-brown hair, wiry as a Brillo Pad, looked as if he'd cut it himself. His glasses, with unremarkable brown frames, were also nondescript. Blemishes dotted his cheeks.

The eyes that met hers as he crossed the room held a sharp intelligence. Nell had liked the boy from the moment he'd shown up unannounced at her office door. She admired his courage in coming forth and trying to work through the system, rather than simply running away.

"Have a seat, Toby." Nell gestured to the chairs she'd grouped for conversation, although it was best to speak with some clients from behind the desk.

This wasn't one of those times. She didn't want any more distance between her and the boy. Especially when she had difficult news to discuss.

When the boy lowered his lanky frame into one of the chairs, she sat in the other.

"What's the verdict?"

This was another thing she liked about Toby. Good or bad, he wanted the news straight.

"I approached your mother again about the emancipation."

"It's not happening." There was a hint of defeat in Toby's voice that hadn't been there the previous times they'd talked. While he had to know this would be the likely outcome, the boy had remained remarkably upbeat.

There wasn't anything Toby could have done differently. He worked full time as a dishwasher at Matilda's and had the income to support himself, though certainly not on any grand scale. A couple of older friends who'd graduated from high school last year had offered him the sofa in their apartment at a price he could afford.

Despite all the hours he worked, he'd kept his grades up and was on track to graduate with his class next May.

"She absolutely will not give her consent," Nell admitted.

"The thing is, I don't know how much more I can take." Toby met Nell's gaze. "You know what she's like. What would you do?"

"I'd keep the job. I know it's a lot with school, but the less you're in the house, the better."

He nodded agreement.

Nell tapped a finger against her lips and thought for a second. "Does she still wait up for you?"

Toby nodded and blew out a breath. "I try to sneak in, but she always hears me. I could stay with Jake and Ty."

Jake and Ty were his friends who had the apartment with the sofa bed.

"You know what will happen if you do."

"Just like the other times, she'll call the cops and say I ran away."

"You don't want to go into detention." Nell had been in one of those youth facilities for a couple of days. She'd been fifteen, and her mother had wanted to teach her a lesson.

"I can't stay with her." Toby surged to his feet and began to pace. "Dad sees what she's like, but he won't interfere."

Nell understood. The men in her mother's life had never lifted a finger to help her. She and Toby had talked about having child protective services intervene, but he didn't trust the system to protect him from his mother's psychological torture.

"The problem is, she appears normal in her outside life. She has a good job at the bank, and people think she's wonderful. It's only at home that the crazy comes out." His half laugh held only despair. "Her friends and coworkers think I'm this ungrateful, horrible son, because that's what she tells them."

Nell tapped the pen she hadn't realized she still held against her skirt.

"You know what she did last night? While I was at work, she went into my room and trashed it. When I got home, she told me we needed to have a talk about me respecting my things." Toby's expression turned bleak. "I know if I said anything to anyone, they'd believe her, not me."

"Why do you think she trashed your room?"

Toby paused his pacing and dropped back into the chair. He raked a hand through his bushy mop of hair. "Because she can. Because she's pissed about this emancipation thing, even though she got her way. She thinks it makes her look bad that I went to an attorney."

"You didn't argue with her."

"No." He shook his head. "I think she honestly believes I

trashed my own room. She's very convincing. Heck, sometimes she can almost make me believe it. I know that doesn't make sense."

"It does." Gloria had been the same way. "I knew someone like that, a family member."

This was the first time Nell had mentioned that fact, and his eyes lit up. "What did you do?"

"I don't have anything to do with her now."

"I've been thinking of leaving." Toby's gaze dropped to his hands. "I've got money saved. That may have been what she was looking for."

"Possibly," Nell agreed. "Did she find it?"

He snorted. "As if I'd be stupid enough to stash the money in my room."

"You're right. That would have been foolish. If you did leave, where would you go?"

"I don't know." His shoulders slumped.

"Let's think of some better alternatives. You'll be eighteen in January, which is the age of majority in Illinois."

"I can leave then, and she can't stop me."

"Have you given any thought to graduating mid-term?" Nell inclined her head. "Would you have enough credits?"

Toby thought for moment, then nodded. "I should."

"That's a possibility, then. You'd turn eighteen and have your high school diploma." Nell continued in the same reasonable tone. "You could support yourself and probably qualify for grants to help with college. If you wanted to stay in contact with your parents, you could. Or not. Your choice."

Choice had always been a big thing for Nell when she was that age. For a long time, she'd seen no way out. Her mother was the type to track her down. And just like Toby's mother had trashed his room, Gloria would have trashed Nell's life when she'd found her, for no other reason than she could. Thankfully, the penal system would now be keeping her mother very busy.

"January is still six months from now," Toby said.

Nell pulled her thoughts back to the conversation at hand. "Sometimes, having that end date makes it easier to stick. There's something about knowing that on that particular date you'll never have to walk through the fun-house doors again."

Toby rubbed his chin, his expression doubtful. "Last night when I was asleep, she flung open the door to my room, then stood there and screamed how worthless I am and how she wishes I'd never been born."

"I could speak with someone from CPS." This wasn't the first time she'd made the offer. But Toby was right. At this point it would be her word against his. The boy's previous attempts to record her verbal abuse and video her behavior had failed miserably.

He shook his head.

"You're in a difficult situation." Nell's heart ached for the boy. She knew what he was going through and knew that his life was likely ten times worse than he'd told her. Her gaze met his. "You're strong, smart and determined. You're a hard worker. You and I both know that she's the one who is messed up, not you."

Toby closed his eyes for a moment. "Sometimes, it's hard to keep that in mind."

"From what you've told me, this behavior has been going on for years."

"As far back as I can remember."

"Think of yourself as being in the final sprint of a race. In six months, you'll be free and able to live life on your own terms."

"If we could have gotten the emancipation, I'd be free now."

"We didn't." Nell kept all sympathy from her voice, knowing that wasn't what Toby needed from her. "Now you move on to plan B, which is getting your diploma and surviving until your birthday. Do you think you can make it that long?"

Toby slowly nodded and pushed to his feet. Then he surprised her by extending a hand. "Thanks for trying to help."

"I suggest you don't mention you plan to leave in January. Let that be your secret."

"You really do understand."

Nell placed a hand on his shoulder and resisted the urge to sigh. "You have no idea."

CHAPTER FIFTEEN

"At the moment, I've several young men courting me." Lilian's eyes twinkled as she raised her glass of sherry to her lips. "It's a heady experience."

After a wonderful meal of succulent grilled lamb served with a minted couscous summer salad, Leo had retired to Wells's living room with his family and Lilian for glasses of port and sherry.

Mathis, always the good uncle, had gone upstairs to sing karaoke with Sophie. Leo wondered, not for the first time, if Wells regretted getting his daughter the karaoke machine for Christmas.

Tim smiled at Lilian. While she wasn't a blood relative, the woman had been a close friend of Tim's parents when they'd lived in Hazel Green. When they relocated to Arizona, Lilian had become a de facto member of the Pomeroy family. "Who are these young men?" Tim arched a brow and glanced at Wells. "Anyone we know?"

Though his father's tone was easy and almost teasing, Leo wasn't fooled. The Pomeroy men were protective of their own, and Lilian was one of them.

Leo and his brothers had all been willing to lend their investment expertise to Lilian, but so far she'd refused to take them up on their offer.

"I'm not certain which ones are still in the running for your affections." Wells's smile didn't quite reach his eyes. "You've had so many buzzing around."

Lilian laughed, the sound reminding Leo of Nell when something delighted her.

Leo resisted the urge to glance at the clock on the mantel. The day had been busy, with lots of unexpected interruptions. By the time he'd had a few minutes to call Nell, it had been time for dinner.

"Marc Koenig is one." Lilian's gaze turned speculative.

"He's been dating Rachel Grabinski for the past year," Wells told his father. "You knew her parents."

Tim nodded. "Sad thing that car accident. All those children left without parents."

"From everything I've heard, Rachel did a fine job raising her brothers and sisters." Marty chewed on her bottom lip. "Doesn't Rachel work for the food bank now?"

"She's the volunteer coordinator." Leo sipped his drink. "I like Rachel. The jury is still out on Marc."

"Why?" Tim asked.

"Just a feeling."

"I have some reservations," Lilian admitted. "He seems a little slick. But he's got some interesting ideas where I can invest my money."

"You know, Lil, Tim and I have a financial consultant we really trust in DC. I'd be happy to give you her name."

"Thank you, Marty, but I prefer to deal with local talent, so to speak."

"Who else are you considering working with?" Tim asked.

His father was digging. It might not be obvious to Lilian, but his dad—and Wells, too—were very protective of the older woman.

It probably wasn't a bad idea. Even a smart, savvy woman could be seduced into making bad investments by a sweet-talking man.

For some reason, Nell popped into his head. She was smart and savvy, but it would take more than a sweet-talking man to seduce her.

"There are several others." Lilian waved a hand as if these others were of no consequence. "The one I've grown increasingly fond of is Dixon Carlyle."

Tim frowned. "I don't believe I know him."

"He's new in town." Wells's brows pulled together. "The guy showed up last year out of the blue."

"Dixon has an office on Michigan Avenue," Lilian explained. "But he's a small-town boy at heart. That's why he decided to make his home in Hazel Green."

Leo caught his mother casting a worried glance in his father's direction.

"Apparently, he's also been discussing investments with Pastor Schmidt."

All eyes swiveled in Leo's direction. He wished he'd kept his mouth shut. It almost sounded as if he was vouching for Dixon.

"I didn't realize that." A smile blossomed on Lilian's lips. "That's an extra check in Dixon's favor."

Wells narrowed his gaze on Leo. "How do you know he's working with the preacher?"

"Dixon played the piano for Abby and Jonah's wedding when Frank got sick." Leo took another sip of port, resisting the urge to gulp.

"He just came out and said he was working with the pastor on investments?" Marty's brows furrowed. "That seems an odd thing to bring up at a wedding."

If Leo could have thought of a way to redirect the conversation, he'd have done it. But the way everyone was looking at him told him he had no choice but to explain.

"Dixon drove up while Nell and I were speaking with Jackie, Jonah's sister. I was surprised to see Dixon there. That's when he mentioned he'd been going over some financial matters with the pastor when Frank called to say he was sick."

"Dixon plays the piano beautifully." Lilian sighed. "He entertained me with a few classical pieces when he was over the last time."

Wells fixed his gaze on Leo. "Nell and Dixon are close."

Leo smiled, thinking of how he'd been jealous of Nell's relationship with Dixon before he'd known he was her brother. "They know each other from college."

"What college was that?" his father asked.

"Wisconsin at Madison. That's where she got her undergraduate degree."

Tim rubbed his chin. "Interesting."

"What's so interesting about it?"

"That they'd both end up in the same town after all these years." His dad's gaze met his. "You don't find that odd?"

"Not at all." Leo gave a laugh. "This town is progressive with a lot to offer college-educated young singles. You forget that we're at the end of the Metra rail line, so it's easy and convenient for our residents to work in Chicago. They have the benefits of a big-city job but can enjoy life in a more relaxed atmosphere. We're a prime spot for college graduates who want to stay in the Midwest."

"I agree with Leo," Lilian said, sparing Leo the need to go on. "Besides, when you've lived as long as I have, you discover the world is really a small place. I believe in the whole six degrees of separation idea."

"When do you think you'll decide who you'll work with?" Seeming more relaxed, Tim returned his gaze to Lilian.

"By the end of the summer." The older woman smiled. "I have

to admit I'm enjoying all the attention. I'll be sad to see all the fawning come to an end."

Wells shut the door to his home office. When Leo had announced he was leaving, Mathis had walked out with him. Wells had checked on Sophie and found she was sleeping soundly. Lilian and his mother were in the living room, chatting about, well, whatever it was women who hadn't seen each other in a while talked about. That left Wells and his father alone.

"I'm concerned about this situation with Lilian." Tim crossed to the window to gaze into the darkness. After a moment, he turned back to his eldest son.

"She's an intelligent woman who I believe has good instincts. Dick kept her involved in their various business ventures, so it isn't as if making these kinds of decisions is foreign to her."

"Dick's death was unexpected." Wells tightened his fingers around an antique paperweight that Dani had given him for their anniversary. "When someone that close to you is taken unexpectedly, it clouds your judgment. Even when you think you're making good, rational decisions, sometimes you're not."

The sympathy in his father's eyes had Wells putting the paperweight down.

"I wasn't sure her selling off those pieces of real estate was a smart move, but she got a prime price," Wells grudgingly admitted.

Though it was his son's office, Tim sat in the position of power behind the desk. He steepled his fingers. "What can you tell me about these two frontrunners?"

"Marc Koenig is someone I wouldn't trust farther than I could throw him." Wells gritted his teeth. "He's approached me a handful of times about working together on a project. I can't stand people who try to ingratiate themselves by plying you with compliments."

His father frowned. "We get a lot of those in Washington."

"I'm sure you do." Wells couldn't keep the protective note from his voice. While Lilian meant a lot to the entire Pomeroy family, she'd stepped up and been there for him after the accident.

When he'd finally been ready to go through Dani's things, his mother had already returned to DC. Lilian had been the one who encouraged him to pack away things that might mean something to Sophie as she grew older. Lilian had been a source of strength during a time when he'd needed to lean, just a little.

He would not tolerate anyone taking advantage of her kind and generous nature.

Wells tapped a pen against the desktop. "I believe Lilian sees through all the phoniness. I'm not sure why she's leading him on, unless it's because of Rachel. Or she may be actually considering working with him on a limited basis."

"You think the other man, this Dixon Carlyle, is the one we need to be concerned about?"

"Dixon is smooth. On the surface, he seems like an okay guy, but I don't really know him."

The door opened, and Mathis stepped into the room. Without asking if he was interrupting, Matt crossed the room and dropped into a leather chair.

"I thought you left with Leo." Tim softened the words with a smile, but it was obvious to Wells—and undoubtedly to Matt—that their father would have preferred that he'd gone home.

"And yet, here I am." Matt's gaze shifted from his father to brother.

It was apparent Matt wasn't about to leave, not without being ordered from the room, and that wasn't happening. As much as his father and brother clashed, they were family, and this was a family matter.

"We were discussing our concerns about Lilian and her potential investment counselors," Wells informed his brother.

Matt slouched in the chair and crossed his long legs at the ankle. He arched a sardonic brow. "Without her being present?"

"We care about Lilian." Tim's jaw set in a hard line that Matt appeared to find amusing.

"Taking care of the little woman." Matt's sarcastic tone had his father surging to his feet. "Is that why Leo and I weren't invited to this strategy session? Because you knew we'd object?"

"We thought you'd left." Wells shot his father a warning glance. "Though I'm not sure we'd have included Leo."

The comment had Matt straightening. "That's interesting. Normally, I'm the one excluded."

Tim opened his mouth as if to argue the point, but seemed to think better. It was a smart move. That was one argument he couldn't win.

"It's because of Leo's relationship with Cornelia Ambrose."

"How does him dating Nell play into Lilian's investments?" Matt's gaze narrowed. Though he could be obstinate at times, his brother had a talent for getting to the heart of any issue.

Wells cast a glance at his father and received a nod. "Because of Nell's relationship with Dixon."

"Nell is involved with Dixon?" A look of confusion blanketed Matt's face before he frowned. "This is the first I've heard of that. Does Leo know she's dating him?"

"I don't believe they've been on a date." Wells cleared his throat. "I simply noticed Nell and Dixon were laughing and looking pretty cozy at Liz Canfield's backyard barbecue."

"Seriously?" Matt snorted. "Wow, from now on, I'm going to have to watch who I talk to—oh, and for sure who I laugh with—at parties."

"I think I'll have Pete look at both Marc and Dixon. I'll ask him to dig deep." Tim made the pronouncement in a tone that brooked no argument.

"Pete?" Matt asked.

"A private investigator," Wells explained. "Someone Dad trusts. He'll be discreet."

"Too bad you didn't have him investigate Steve."

The flippant remark earned Matt a scowl from both Tim and Wells. Not fazed, Matt continued. "How do you think Lilian is going to feel about you two butting into her business?"

"We're simply gathering information," Wells told his brother.

"Gathering information would be doing an internet search," Matt pointed out. "It's a simple matter to determine if these two men have the appropriate credentials."

Wells acknowledged the truth in Matt's comment, but Lilian was like family. And because of her husband's recent death, she was vulnerable...even if she didn't view herself that way.

"It isn't as if we don't trust Lilian's judgment," Tim explained. "We don't want to interfere."

"You've been in Washington too long," Matt told his father before shifting his focus to Wells. "What's your excuse?"

"Thank you for your opinion." Wells wanted to get this discussion concluded before his mom and Lilian came looking for them. "You think Pete can do this quickly?"

"Absolutely. If there is something to be found, he'll dig it up." Tim picked up a Montblanc pen and tapped it against his thigh.

"Not that my opinion matters, but I'm opposed." Matt lurched to his feet. "I'm warning you now, the shit will hit the fan once Lilian discovers you've been meddling in her personal business."

CHAPTER SIXTEEN

Nell stared at the golden glow of the Chinese lanterns and fought a surge of happiness. The night was warm with just enough of a breeze to keep the bugs at bay.

As she would be herself tonight and not have to give Hazel a second thought, it had been exciting considering what to wear. Though she loved the fashions of the 1920s, she decided to go with something more modern.

The 1960s got the nod. Eschewing preppy for mod, Nell coupled an orange, pink and yellow paisley minidress with yellow fishnet tights and white go-go boots. Oversized pink Lucite earrings in a geometric shape hung from her earlobes. Silky blond hair brushed her shoulders.

The fun and festive outfit buoyed her mood. The best part was, she wouldn't be taking the trip back to the sixties alone. Leo had picked the same decade, and he looked positively groovy.

His mustard-yellow shirt had a large collar and went well with his brown and yellow plaid flared pants. The Cuban-heeled boots added an extra-nice touch.

She and Leo stood off to the side of the primary roadway into

Gingerbread Village. Streets in the area had been closed to motor vehicle traffic from seven to ten p.m.

"I think the stroll is a hit." Nell couldn't keep the pride from her voice. The Illumination Stroll had been her and Abby's suggestion at a Green Machine meeting last year. Now, tonight, it was actually happening.

Though the merchants in Hazel Green dressed in vintage wear year-round, the residents were encouraged to embrace the fun on holidays and special occasions

"It certainly brought in the tourists." Leo's gaze lingered on two women in their twenties dressed in identical shiny blue jumpsuits with tapered legs, batwing sleeves that started at the waist and shoulder pads. "The seventies?"

"Looking at those shoulder pads, more likely the eighties." Nell smiled. "The crimped hair and mile-high bangs confirm that decade."

"I'm surprised you don't dress vintage more often." Leo returned his attention to her. When his gaze slowly traveled down, as if he didn't want to miss a single detail, Nell shivered. "You look amazing in everything."

Before she could respond, he lowered his voice for her ears only. "Best in nothing at all."

Laughing, she gave his arm a swat and shifted her gaze to study the crowd that had gathered for the start of the stroll.

Residents and visitors had been encouraged to dress in period clothing—any decade of their choosing—and stroll through Gingerbread Village at dusk.

Chinese lanterns were hung from the porches of the cottages. A family-friendly tent had been set up near the Pavilion offering cuisine and desserts families could afford and enjoy.

The Pavilion itself was restricted to adults. After giving a twenty-five-dollar donation—that would go toward supporting the arts in Hazel Green—vendors had come together to offer bites of their finest foods, paired with a curated selection of wine, beer and spirits.

Nell pulled her phone from her plastic beaded purse and glanced at the time. "It's seven."

Hank Beaumont, newspaper editor and president of the Green Machine, moved to the bottom of the steps leading to the portable dais.

Tim and Marty were there, chatting with friends. Dressed in the style of Franklin and Eleanor Roosevelt, the couple made an engaging sight in the late evening light. Marty's cheeks were rosy from all the sunshine the past couple of days.

Marty's relaxed posture told Nell that being back in Hazel Green had been good for her. Leo's father, on the other hand, sported additional lines of strain around his eyes. But his ready smile was warm and friendly.

Nell looked around for Matt and Wells, but didn't see either of them.

Hank, along with Tim and Marty, climbed to the dais. Using a handheld microphone, Hank welcomed the senator and his wife to the community and explained how the event would proceed.

After finishing his introduction, he glanced at Leo.

"I'd like to ask our mayor, Leo Pomeroy, and his companion, Cornelia Ambrose, to join the senator and his wife in leading the stroll."

Though Nell kept a smile firmly pasted on her face, her heart flip-flopped. She would be in the spotlight as herself, not Hazel, which was exactly what she'd feared would happen when she'd agreed to be Leo's girlfriend.

She spoke sharply, without turning her head. "Did you know Hank was going to do this?"

"No." Leo waved to the crowd, who'd cheered the announcement, eager for the event to get started.

Not seeing any way out of the predicament, Nell crossed to

the center of the cobblestone street with Leo, where Tim and Marty joined them.

Before Nell could react, Liz stepped out in front of them and snapped several pictures of the foursome just as the four-piece band began a rousing rendition of a Sousa march. She disappeared into the crowd before Nell could stop her.

Nell vowed to make sure the pictures never made it onto the internet. Since she'd left home, Nell had worn her hair short, rather than long as it had been in her teens. When she'd put on the blond wig today and looked in the mirror, she'd been transported back to her high school days.

As she walked, she pulled out her phone and texted Liz.

Don't post any pics of me.

The reply came quickly.

Too late. You look adorable.

Alarm skittered up Nell's spine, but she told herself she was being ridiculous.

"Something wrong?" Leo asked.

"Not at all." Nell shoved her phone into the tiny bag.

Less than five minutes into the stroll, Tim and Marty were engulfed by friends.

Seconds later, Abby and Jonah, wearing matching bowling shirts and shoes, fell into step beside her and Leo.

Another couple of yards saw Rachel and Marc join them. Marc had gone for a sixties preppy look, while Rachel wore a pink and white polka dot minidress.

Thankfully, Marc was too busy looking around to see who'd noticed him at the head of the stroll to do much talking.

"Where's Eva Grace?" Nell asked Abby.

"She wasn't interested in strolling, and neither was Matilda. We'll meet up with them at the tent a little later." Abby cast a knowing glance at Leo. "You two look ready for a good time."

"We're ready to party like it's 1965," Nell said, tongue in cheek.

"It's too bad there isn't a disco ball somewhere," Leo said.

"Wrong decade. Disco balls were popular in the—" Nell's eyes widened.

A deep voice from somewhere in the crowd spoke through a megaphone. "Elvis has entered the village."

Nell recognized her brother immediately.

Dixon wore Elvis's iconic white jumpsuit featuring gold, red and blue stones in an American eagle pattern. The front, cut low, included the classic red scarf. Still, the outfit showed a good amount of Dixon's muscular chest.

Nell wasn't sure whether it was the Elvis tie-in or that manly chest that was creating the stir. What was her brother thinking? He had to know everyone would be snapping pictures and wanting to do selfies with him.

Irritation held hands with fear until she noticed, despite it being dusk, that Dixon wore gold-rimmed aviator sunglasses that covered most of his face. At least he hadn't gone totally off the rails.

She relaxed and turned back to Leo.

Leo held out his arm, and she slipped hers through his. "He's causing quite a stir," he said.

"I don't understand it."

Leo cocked his head.

"Why anyone would want to be the center of attention?"

"You do it every time you step out as Hazel Green."

"That's different." Nell inhaled the sweet scent of flowers mixed with the pungent scent of evergreen. "I'm Hazel Green, or whoever she's impersonating at the time. Nell Ambrose doesn't like being in the spotlight."

"You're so at ease in front of people. And you're in court every day."

"For some reason, I'm addicted to personal privacy."

"I noticed you don't have any social media accounts."

"Have you been checking up on me, Mr. Mayor?" She kept her

tone teasing, doing her best not to sigh. This was what happened when you became part of a couple.

"Actually, yesterday I snapped a picture of the tai chi group down by the lake. I posted it to the official mayor's Instagram account." He smiled. "I was going to follow you, but discovered you don't have an account."

"Hazel has an account," Nell explained, relying on the answer she gave everyone. "Just keeping up as her takes all the spare time I want to devote to online stuff."

"Makes sense."

They'd slowed their steps, which Nell thought was the definition of a stroll, while others surged past.

"Why is everyone in such a rush?" she mused aloud.

"The route circles back to the Pavilion." Abby smiled up at her husband, and Nell saw that the two held hands. "We're hoping to have time to stop there ourselves before we meet up with Matilda and Eva Grace."

"Marc and I are headed there, too," Rachel said eagerly. "We can all go together."

"Sure." Abby's smile never wavered. "That'd be fun."

"We'll catch up to you." Nell gestured to the cottage they were passing. "Leo needs to stop and pick up something for his brother."

"We can wait," Rachel offered.

"You all go ahead." Nell waved an airy hand. "We'll catch up."

Thankfully, Leo caught on quickly. "We'll see you soon."

"Do you have a key?" Nell asked when they stepped onto the porch festooned with lanterns of every size and shape.

Even as Leo reached into his pocket, the door swung open.

Wells sat back in the chair and gazed out the window at the strange parade. As a business owner and eldest son of one of the state's senators, he should be out there strolling with the crowd, putting a positive face on the Pomeroy name. He didn't have it in him today.

That was part of the reason he'd agreed to let Sophie attend this evening's event with her friend. He trusted Shiloh's parents and knew they'd keep a close watch on his child. Having no siblings and no cousins, Sophie spent too much time alone.

If Dani had lived, their lives would be so much different...

The thought was ruthlessly shoved aside. He'd been down this road too many times to travel down it again. Dani was gone, and no amount of wishing could change reality.

If he wasn't going to take part in the stroll, he should head home.

Home to an empty house...

Wells picked up the glass of wine he'd poured and told himself he was pathetic. He had more options than drinking alone in a dark cottage.

Simply stepping outside would bring dozens of people he knew to him. But he didn't want the gaiety or the sidelong glances.

News of the scandal had reached Hazel Green's paper. Hank had written an objective piece, including Steve's history as Tim Pomeroy's legislative director and friend.

Guilty by association.

A trite phrase and certainly not one that Hank had included in the article, but it was how a lot of people thought. Heck, if the man wasn't his father, Wells would wonder about Tim's integrity.

How could anyone be a close friend and work side by side with a person for years and not know—or at least suspect—he was taking bribes?

The sounds of footsteps on the porch had Wells setting down his wineglass, crossing the room in three long strides and jerking open the door.

"Wells." Leo's eyes widened in surprise. "What are you doing here?"

"Sophie and I had dinner with Mom and Dad. They left. I stayed." Wells shifted his gaze to Nell, who looked like she could have been a dancer in one of those Top 40 countdown shows in the 1960s. "Hi, Nell."

She smiled. "It's nice to see you again."

Her hot-pink lipstick was the shade Dani had worn on their first date. He remembered because that was the first time he'd kissed her, and she'd tasted like cotton candy.

But it wasn't Dani's smiling face or warm brown eyes staring back at him, it was Nell's assessing blue ones.

"Can we come in?"

Leo's question made Wells realize that he was blocking the doorway. He stepped back.

The first thing his brother did as he stepped past was to flip on the lights. Leo's gaze turned questioning as he studied the wineglass.

Wells lifted his chin. Granted, sitting in a darkened room was strange, but he hadn't wanted to draw attention to the fact that he was here. It was as simple as that. "I was getting ready to leave."

"I saw Sophie," Nell told him. "She's with a friend."

"You did?" Leo glanced at her. "You didn't say anything."

"I just caught a glimpse of her." Nell lifted one shoulder in a slight shrug. "The girl she was with has red hair, just like her father."

The woman missed nothing. Wells had noticed that about Nell. Not only was she intelligent, she was observant.

"Sophie is with Shiloh and her parents." Wells turned to Leo. "Jim and Cathy. You remember them from church."

Leo nodded.

"What brought you to the cottage?"

"We were tired of listening to Marc brag." Nell rolled her eyes, and Wells couldn't help but chuckle. "Saying we needed to stop off here for a few minutes was a way to politely put him off."

Nell brushed the fingers of one hand against the front of her dress, as if ridding herself of a piece of lint.

When she and Leo exchanged a smile, Wells's heart lurched. It was a look of intimacy. How long had it been since Dani had looked at him like that, as if they shared a private joke?

Sounds of laughter and conversation drifted in through the screens on the open windows. Leo sat beside Nell on the sofa, and Wells found himself fighting back a twinge of envy. Especially when Leo took Nell's hand and entwined his fingers with hers.

"Have you seen Matt?" Leo asked.

"I haven't." Matt's personal life was a mystery to him. Though they worked in the same office and Wells saw Matt daily, they weren't close. The thought brought a wave of sadness.

When Dani was alive, she'd always been able to smooth the rough spots between him and Matt.

Dani was on his mind tonight, and he wasn't sure why. Unless it was seeing Jim and Cathy with their daughter and remembering what his life had been like before the accident.

Even seeing Leo with Nell brought back memories of how it had been with Dani when they'd been falling in love…

Cheers rang out from the street.

"Sing us a song, Elvis," someone shouted.

Wells cocked his head. "Elvis?"

Leo shifted to look out the window.

"It appears Dixon came dressed as Elvis," Leo told him. "He makes a pretty convincing one."

"Someone should have told the guy there's a difference between vintage clothing and a costume party." Wells drank the rest of the wine in his glass. "Before he went and made a fool of himself."

Nell focused those lethal blue eyes on him. "Elvis was part of mid-twentieth-century history, so it's entirely appropriate for Dixon to come as the king of rock 'n' roll."

The intensity with which she defended Dixon gave Wells pause. Offering a silent apology to his brother for what he was about to do, Wells inclined his head. "That's quite the passionate protest. It sounds to me like you have feelings for the guy. Does this mean the rumors I've heard are true?"

~

Nell wasn't sure what game Wells was playing, but she told herself not to engage. One of the first lessons learned at her mother's knee had been to show no emotion even when anger flowed hot through your blood.

Leo, however, showed no such restraint. He surged to his feet. "What the hell, Wells?"

Wells lifted his hands. "Just asking a question."

"Trust me. There's nothing going on between Dixon and Nell."

Nell was suddenly furious and not just with Wells.

Despite her defense of Dixon, Nell didn't understand why her brother had chosen to come to this event as Elvis. Though their mother was in jail, the police might be still looking for him in connection with the Bakersfield incident he'd told her about. Putting himself in the spotlight had been a reckless act.

Yet, as angry and frustrated as she was with Dixon, she would always defend him.

"Nothing to say in your own defense?" Wells baited, a smug smile on his lips.

Don't engage.

Even as the warning flashed again in her brain, Nell pulled to her feet. She couldn't recall the last time she'd been so angry or unsettled.

Instead of running, she lashed out.

"What is it with you, Wells?" Her voice held the same mocking tone she'd heard in his only moments earlier. "Are you so unhappy in your own life that you want to stir things up for everyone else? Your wife died. I get that. I'm sorry it happened."

Two splotches of red slashed across Wells's cheeks. "Don't you talk about Dani. You—"

"Don't *you* talk about me and Dixon with that supercilious smile on your face."

Leo's entire body vibrated with anger as he met his brother's eyes. "What is wrong with you?"

"You have doubts about her and him, too." Despite the stern set to his jaw, Wells's tone was matter-of-fact. "Either that, or you've got your head in the sand. C'mon, admit it."

"You don't know—" Leo began.

"I don't know her?" Wells's lips lifted in a sardonic smile. "Neither do you. She's led you on a merry chase these past few months. If you think about it, your entire relationship has been on her terms. Perhaps that's what kept you interested."

"Shut up, Wells." Leo's voice was deathly calm.

"She's hiding something, Leo. As much as you want to deny it, there's something between your girlfriend and Dixon Carlyle. I see it. I can feel the connection when they're together."

"Trust me. There isn't anything even the least bit romantic between her and Dixon," Leo ground out.

They were sparring as if she wasn't there. From Wells's reddened face and Leo's clenched fists, things were escalating between the brothers. The last thing Nell wanted to do was cause a permanent rift between them.

"How do you know?" Wells pressed. "How can you be sure?"

"He can be sure," Nell spoke calmly into the tense silence, "because Leo knows that Dixon is my brother."

"Your brother?" Wells's mouth dropped open. His gaze shifted to his brother. "Is that true?"

Leo gave a nod, his arm slipping around Nell's waist.

"Why the secrecy?"

It was a good question and one Leo couldn't fully answer.

"Dixon and I have been estranged for many years," Nell explained. "While I love him dearly, when he showed up in Hazel Green, I wasn't sure we'd be able to forge a new relationship."

Wells's gaze narrowed. Nell smiled slightly.

"Now I'm almost certain we will. But," she continued, likely in answer to the question she saw hovering on Wells's lips, "I'm not yet ready to make our relationship public."

"Who else knows?" Wells asked.

"Only Leo."

Wells's accusing gaze settled on his brother. "You never said a word."

"It wasn't my story to tell," Leo said simply, glancing at Nell. "It's hers. And Dixon's."

CHAPTER SEVENTEEN

The Fourth of July week festivities continued on Tuesday when Leo strode into the Great Skate at the edge of town. He wished his father would have let him host a cocktail party at his home instead. But Tim agreed with Wells that another family-friendly event was needed.

Ever since the news of the money in Steve's freezer and the raid on Tim's Senate office, the media had been in a feeding frenzy. Although his father said it went with the territory, Leo could see the toll the critical coverage was taking on both his parents.

Since the local roller-skating rink was normally closed on Tuesdays, Tim had been able to book it at the last minute. Promoted as a family event, the late afternoon party boasted free hot dogs and sodas and a low entry charge for an entire family.

Conceived as a way for Tim to reconnect with his constituents, the creative, think-outside-the-box event appeared to have hit a responsive chord with the public.

His father, dressed casually in jeans and a polo shirt, greeted people at the door. Leo's mother stood at his side, her smile warm and welcoming.

Leo wondered what kind of politician's wife Nell would be. As Hazel Green, she'd certainly had a great deal of experience in the public limelight. He put thoughts of her aside as he reached his parents.

"Nice turnout." Leo shook his father's hand.

"I can't wait to see your father on skates." His mother spoke loudly, then lowered her voice as if conscious of the family behind Leo. "Is Nell coming?"

"She had court this afternoon. But she'll be here."

When Leo stepped inside the recently renovated rink, he was struck first by the noise, then by the number of children.

"It's a good turnout."

Leo stiffened and turned toward Wells. He hadn't spoken to his brother since last night. While his temper had cooled, he was still irritated.

"I'm thinking that having a Green Machine event here would be a good idea." Leo's gaze scanned the large room with the multicolored lights and mirror ball over the highly polished oval rink. "Though we'd have to charge."

"This is more of Dad connecting with his constituents and building his image rather than a fundraiser." Wells paused and narrowed his gaze as Matt strode up. "Where's Sophie?"

"Chill out, Wells." Matt rolled his eyes. "Rachel is giving Soph some tips. She's much better at this whole skating thing than I am."

"Whatever she told Sophie seems to be sticking," Leo remarked, his gaze following the two as they skated around the rink.

"When I asked you to watch her, I expected you to be with her, not pawn her off on someone else."

A muscle in Matt's jaw jumped. "She's safe. She's happy." His voice was as flat as his eyes. "You're welcome."

Without another word, Matt turned and headed toward the concession stand, leaving Leo and Wells alone.

"You seem to be pissing off everyone lately." Leo rocked back on his heels. "Matt gave you good advice. Chill out."

Before Wells could respond, Jackie strode up with Dixon at her side.

"I don't know about you guys, but I haven't skated in years." Jackie flashed both Leo and his brother a bright smile. "Dixon assures me he won't let me fall. I'm not sure I can trust him."

"The not-knowing is part of the fun." Dixon shot Jackie a wink, his smile easy when it shifted to Leo. "No date this evening?"

"Nell had court, but she'll be here." Though at a quick glance, the two didn't look anything alike, now that he knew Nell and Dixon were related, Leo saw the similarities. It was subtle, but the shapes of their eyes and mouths were the same. "I'm glad you could make it tonight."

The warmth in his voice had Dixon's eyes narrowing ever so slightly. Though the man's expression gave nothing away, Dixon obviously sensed something had changed.

The ability to quickly and accurately assess a situation was a skill he and his sister shared.

"C'mon, Dixon." Jackie tugged on his arm. "Let's get our skates."

Leo sensed Wells studying him curiously, but like Dixon had only seconds earlier, he kept his expression impassive. This was not the place to discuss anything private.

The Pomeroy brothers, as much as their father, were under scrutiny this afternoon. After all, he, Wells and Matt lived in this community. Their father might represent Hazel Green in Congress, but it had been a long time since this town had been his home.

Iris Endicott and Rachel stopped to say hello on their way to pick out shoes. Leo wondered why Marc wasn't with Rachel, but didn't ask.

"A skating event was a fabulous idea." Iris gestured with one hand to the crowd. "Most of my students came with their families."

Beau strolled up. "A terrific way for your father to shore up that family-friendly image and combat some of the recent negative press."

"My father's image is who he is deep down," Wells responded stiffly. "This event is simply a way for him to reconnect with his supporters."

"Still a brilliant plan." Beau offered Leo and Wells a mock salute.

Iris gave Beau a cool look, but Rachel greeted the trial consultant with a hug.

It was obvious, at least to Leo, that Iris didn't like Beau. Why? Before the question had a chance to settle, the women went one way and Beau headed in the direction of Liz and her son.

"Arctic chill," Wells remarked.

Leo nodded, his gaze drawn to the door. He resisted the urge to glance at his watch.

"All is good between you and Nell?"

Leo glanced back at his brother. "Very good. We're solid."

For the first time since he and Nell started seeing each other, Leo wasn't concerned about them staying together.

Wells nodded. "I'm happy for you."

Leo saw her then, standing just inside the entrance, her gaze searching the room.

Searching for me, Leo thought with satisfaction.

His irritation with his brother forgotten, Leo wove his way through the people milling around. Trying, he guessed, to decide whether to eat or skate first.

When he reached her, Leo resisted—barely—the urge to kiss her. "You made it."

"I told you I'd be here." She studied Wells, now speaking with a couple Leo recognized as former neighbors. "How are things?"

"Good enough." Leo guessed that was true. "Dixon is here. He's with Jackie."

Surprise skittered across her face. "A skating rink doesn't seem his style." Then she laughed. "Actually, until this moment, I didn't think it was mine. But you know what's crazy?"

He shook his head, enjoying the happy gleam in her eyes.

"I can't wait to put on skates. But first things first." She stepped closer.

His heart gave a solid thump against his chest. Could it be that she wanted to kiss him as much as he wanted to kiss her?

Her lips brushed his ear, and she whispered her desire. "I'm in desperate need of cotton candy."

"It's a Love Thing" by the Whispers might not be the most romantic song Nell had ever heard, but it fit the needs of the crowd.

Kids loved the catchy rhythm and the multicolored laser-light show that pulsated to the beat. Even the mirror ball got in on the action, turning a variety of colors and filling the room with light.

Nell held Leo's hand as they negotiated the crowded oval. Partly because she needed the support. More because she found it hard to be this close and not touch him.

She gazed into his eyes and smiled. He gave her hand a squeeze. Would it be possible for this to continue? For them to be happy together long term?

"Ms. Ambrose."

Nell turned, and there was Toby, holding hands with a girl as tall and skinny as he was.

"How's it going?" Because she didn't want to give any indication he was a client, she kept the question deliberately vague.

"Good." The relief in his voice matched the look on his face. "For now anyway."

"Glad to hear it."

"Well, see you later." Taking his girlfriend's hand, the boy skated off.

"Avery?" was all Leo said.

She gave a nod, knowing he wouldn't press for more.

"Sounds as if things are going well."

"For now." Nell smiled, but she didn't hold out much hope that the good times would continue.

She'd learned the hard way that, when dealing with someone volatile, you never knew what might set them off. A couple of days, even a few weeks of relative normalcy, and a boy—or girl—could be tempted to let down their guard. To start to believe that this time of peace might endure. That the monster had changed. That everything might be okay, after all.

Nell had been down that road too many times to believe the good times would last. Still, as she glanced up at Leo and he smiled down at her, as the music and words of love washed over her, she found herself wishing that this time could be different.

"My parents are having a party for just close friends and family tomorrow night after the fireworks." Leo spoke quickly, as if wanting to get out the question before she came up with some objection. "Very casual. A way to chill out after the big day."

The skating party had ended nearly thirty minutes ago, and Tim and Marty were at the exit saying their final thanks and goodbyes to those leaving.

"Thank you for the offer." Nell smiled up at him as they made their last circuit round the oval. "But I'm not family or part of their inner circle."

"You're wrong."

"I'm rarely wrong."

"You're *my* close friend." He grabbed her hand and brought it to his lips for a kiss before she could stop him.

She laughed. "You're something else."

"Say you'll come."

Nell had been about to utter some flippant remark, but the pleading look in his eyes told her that attending was important to him. "Sure. If you want me there, I'll come."

He gave her hand a squeeze. "Will you come over to Wells's house now? We're going to do a political wrap-up."

"On that, I'll take a pass."

"I know you and Wells haven't gotten off on a good—"

"It's not that, Leo. Honestly. Wells doesn't have a thing to do with my refusal." Nell dipped the toe of one skate to slow her forward motion as they exited the rink. "Between the volunteer work at the cottage and my pro bono work, I'm behind on case prep. I planned to get in a few hours once I got home tonight."

Leo understood obligations. While his position as mayor wasn't as onerous or demanding as being the leader of a large city, he was a hard worker. If a project needed his attention, he gave it the time it deserved.

"Okay. I wish you could come, but I do understand." He waited for her to take a seat on a nearby bench, then sat beside her.

"This was fun." Nell unlaced her skates and slipped them off. "I actually wasn't sure how it would go."

"I know." He chuckled. "I'm surprised, too. You know what it means?"

She smiled up at him.

He tapped her on the nose. "You and I, Ms. Ambrose, need to make a concerted effort to step outside our comfort zone more often."

CHAPTER EIGHTEEN

Other than for a few brief moments earlier this evening, Nell hadn't spoken with her brother since the Illumination Stroll. The skating rink hadn't seemed like the time or the place to let him know she'd blown his cover. Which was why, once she'd gotten home, she'd texted and asked him to come over.

She hadn't received a reply, but when an unannounced knock sounded on her door, Nell knew exactly who was paying her a visit. Dixon was the only person who could show up at her door without being cleared through security.

She glanced through the peephole, but it was only for form. Pulling open the door, she stepped aside to let Dixon enter.

He swaggered into the room. "I was surprised to get the text."

"Did you have fun skating with Jackie?"

"She's nice enough." He glanced around. "Do you have any of that imported beer I like?"

Nell nodded. "I'll join you."

Moments later, they sat on opposite sides of the sofa, bottles of brown ale in hand and the lights of Hazel Green stretched out before them.

Dixon gestured with his hand holding the bottle. "Quite a view you've got here."

"I wanted to tell you something."

He slanted a glance in her direction. "You look guilty. What did you do?"

"Who said I did anything?"

"You forget who you're talking to." His eyes softened. "Did you cheat on lover boy? Rob a bank? Tell the cops where I am?"

She chuckled. "None of the above."

"Then whatever you did, you're forgiven." He brought the bottle to his lips.

"I told Leo and Wells that you're my brother." The words came out in a rush.

Dixon slowly lowered the beer and studied her. "Thanks for letting me know."

"That's all you're going to say? Thanks for letting me know?" Her voice rose.

"I was never into keeping the fact that we're brother and sister a secret." He shrugged. "How did they take it?"

"Fine. They were fine with it."

"Cool."

Would she ever understand this man?

"Is that why I'm here? To confess you let a couple of guys know that we're related?"

Nell shifted under his penetrating gaze.

"I can see that there's something else." He opened his arms. "Okay, lay it on me."

"Why did you dress like Elvis the night of the Illumination Stroll?" Nell frowned. "You brought unnecessary attention to yourself. That isn't like you."

"That's why you wanted to see me tonight." The teasing light disappeared from his eyes. Taking another pull from the bottle, Dixon set it down, then moved to the window. He braced his hands on the sill and stared out into the darkness.

"Sometimes, all those *lessons* she taught us spin around and around in my head—all the dos and don'ts—until I can't take it anymore." He turned abruptly, his face a mask of controlled fury. "The night of the Illumination Stroll, I simply didn't care. I mean, I wore the glasses, but sometimes Gloria gets in my head and I want to do the opposite of what I was taught, just to spite her."

He paused for a long moment. "Which is crazy behavior that makes absolutely no sense."

Nell's phone buzzed. She glanced down. It was a text from Leo. She'd get back to him later.

Dixon spread his hands, and she saw the little boy behind the confident mask he wore. "I don't want to be like her, Suze, but sometimes I fear I am."

"You're nothing like her." Nell wrapped her arms around him. "Neither am I."

Nell couldn't recall the last time she and her brother had hugged. Closing her eyes, she hoped with all her heart that the words she'd just uttered were true, for both of their sakes.

Leo resisted the urge—barely—to text Nell again. It wasn't like her to ignore his texts. For a second, he worried something might have happened to her and considered driving over to make sure she was okay.

Then he recalled why she'd decided not to come with him to his brother's house.

Case prep.

Nell was likely deeply engrossed in what she was doing and not even paying attention to her phone. She might have even shut it off.

Leo refocused on the story his niece was telling him about her adventures at the skating rink. How had he missed that she'd won the limbo contest for her age group? "That's great, Sophie. It isn't easy going under that stick while on skates."

At least, he assumed it wasn't easy. Leo had never tried and had no plans to do so in the near future. Then he thought about what he'd told Nell about stepping outside of their comfort zone and trying new things.

Who knew? Perhaps a limbo contest *was* in his future.

"Dad says it's okay, but he doesn't like me skating." Sophie wrinkled her nose and lowered her voice, even though they were the only ones in the room. "He's afraid I'll fall and hurt myself."

"Your dad loves you very much." Maybe his eldest brother was a bit overprotective. If Leo had lost a beloved wife in a freak helicopter crash, he'd likely be overprotective, too.

He thought of Nell and what it would be like to have her in his life one day, then gone the next. A cold chill traveled up his spine, and he shoved the disturbing thought aside.

"Where did you say your grandma was?"

"Her stomach was upset. It was making these loud sounds." Sophie pursed her lips and made a noise that was between a gurgle and a growl. "She ran upstairs to the bathroom. That was a long time ago. Should I go tell her you're here?"

The girl hopped up, but Leo put a restraining hand on her arm. "She'll come down when she's ready." He offered a reassuring smile. "How about your dad and your grandpa?"

Sophie had launched into her skating adventures the second he'd walked through the door, so he had yet to see anyone.

He'd already surmised that Matt wasn't here when he didn't see his truck parked out front. He hadn't expected him to show. Matt had considered the skating rink somewhat of a command performance. That amount of time at his father's side had probably been more than enough for his brother.

"Oh no." Sophie clapped a hand dramatically over her mouth. "I was supposed to tell Dad and Grandpa the minute I saw your car. But I forgot."

"Where are they?"

"In Daddy's office." Sophie expelled a gusty sigh. "Talking business."

"I'll tell them I'm here."

"No," Sophie wailed, putting a restraining hand on his arm. "That's my job."

Leo had to smile. Though Wells didn't have a dramatic bone in his body, Sophie might have a career on the stage. Or maybe that was just the way girls were. She was the only child he spent any time with, so he had no basis for comparison.

"Wait right here." She pointed to him, her tone brooking no argument.

Then she was off, reminding him of a whirlwind with her skirt twirling around her thin legs, her long hair pulled back in a tail that bounced as she rushed down the hall.

His dad and brother didn't keep him waiting long. Seconds later, they appeared with hearty smiles plastered on their faces.

"What had you two holed up in the study?"

Wells swept a dismissive hand. "Just business."

Leo arched a brow, and his brother flushed.

"It wasn't business in the sense you're thinking, Leo." His father crossed the room, drink in hand, to sit in a burgundy leather chair that had once been his. "I was updating Wells on Steve."

"Is Uncle Steve coming for fireworks?"

Sophie's question had Tim jolting. It was as if he'd forgotten his granddaughter was in the room.

Uncle Steve. Aunt Karen. While the two weren't related to the Pomeroy family, they'd been a part of so many celebrations, Sophie had been calling them aunt and uncle since she'd first learned to talk.

"No, honey." Wells put a hand on his daughter's shoulder. "They won't be coming this year."

Sophie frowned. "I want them to come. Uncle Steve showed

me how to play the ukulele. I've been practicing, and I'm really, really good."

Wells offered his daughter a sympathetic smile, then changed the subject. "Where's your grandmother?"

Leo was about to send his brother a warning look when his mother appeared at the top of the stairs.

"How nice to see all my boys in the same room." She frowned as if noticing one of the boys was missing. "Where's Matt?"

His father took a sip of bourbon. "He had somewhere to be."

"I was so happy to see him at the rink." Marty reached the bottom of the stairs and held out her hand to Sophie. "Time to start getting ready for bed."

"Can we read Nancy Drew?" Sophie asked her grandmother.

"Of course." Marty pulled Sophie to her for a hug, then planted a kiss on the top of her head.

Without any prompting, Sophie rushed to her father for a hug, then moved to Leo and finally to her grandfather.

"I'll check in on you," Wells promised.

Only when the three of them were alone again did Leo cast a questioning glance at his father. "What's the latest?"

"The authorities have discovered Steve has a gambling problem. He got in deep and apparently decided taking bribes was his only way to pay his debts."

Leo swore under his breath. "What would make him think that was his only option?"

"I don't know." Tim heaved a heavy breath. "Honestly, if you had asked me a month ago, before everything came out, I'd have said no way would Steve ever take a bribe. But he did. Not just once. He lied to me every day for months, maybe for years. I trusted his research on legislation and his recommendations."

His father scrubbed a hand across his face. "I feel like such a fool."

"Don't blame yourself." Leo's anger rose. "Steve betrayed your trust. He lied to you. Oh, maybe not outright lies, but lies of omission are just as serious. Each time he didn't give you all the facts or encouraged you to vote for a piece of legislation that wasn't in your constituents' best interests, he betrayed the trust you placed in him and tainted you politically."

"What I hate the most is what this may do to your career." Tim shook his head. "You've got such a promising future ahead of you, Leo. You're a rising star in the political ranks. This scandal may tarnish your reputation to such an extent that you never achieve your full potential."

"Let's just worry about your political future for now, Dad." Wells put a supportive hand on his father's back.

"I agree." The words had barely left Leo's lips when his mother moved to her husband's side.

He watched as she laid her head against his shoulder in a gesture of comfort.

"I'm sorry, Marty." Lines of weariness edged his father's eyes. "I know what your friendship with Karen has meant to you. But until the FBI clears her…"

"I know, Tim." Marty heaved a sigh. "I'll keep my distance. But I still hold out hope that in the end we'll find out that the only thing Karen did wrong was, like you, place her faith in a man who couldn't be trusted."

Like many communities that thrive on tourist dollars, Hazel Green went all out for the Fourth, starting with a huge pancake breakfast put on by the Green Machine.

Nell had offered to help, but the volunteer slots had been filled. Instead, she sat beside Leo at one of the long tables with a platter of pancakes dripping with butter and maple syrup. "I'm surprised your family isn't here."

"They'll be here later." Leo paused, a chunk of pancake dangling from his fork. "My mom wanted to make waffles for

Sophie. Although they'll be in town for a few more days, much of my father's time—and hers—are tied up meeting with people and making appearances."

"She wanted quality time with her granddaughter."

Leo chewed and swallowed. "While this breakfast is prime time to meet his constituents, his entire day is like that. My mom isn't as outgoing as my dad. Back-to-back events exhaust her."

"It's good he understands and they can compromise."

Surprise flickered in Leo's eyes. "You do understand."

"Since he's not here, I assume he not only accepted her decision, but supports it."

"You're right. He—"

"Is there room for one more?" Dixon appeared, plate in hand, at the end of the table.

"Actually, there's plenty of room." Nell motioned for him to sit on the other side of the picnic table. "There was a large family who took up all the seats when we arrived, but they just left."

"Lucky for me." Dixon nodded to Leo. "Good to see you, Mr. Mayor."

"May I join you?" Lilian's plate held a single hotcake and one strip of bacon. In the other hand, she gripped a Styrofoam cup filled with coffee.

"Let me help you with that." Dixon set his food on the table, then took Lilian's plate and placed it beside his. "You're looking festive today."

While Nell had chosen a 1950s day dress in a red gingham with contrasting trim, Lilian could have stepped straight out of the 1940s in her blue A-line skirt and chunky heels. Her red-and-white-vertical-striped blouse added just the right festive touch.

Leo's dark denim jeans had rolled cuffs, and his white T-shirt showed off his broad chest. She and Leo were a match made in 1950s heaven, she thought with a smile.

"Why didn't you dress up, Dixon?" Nell inclined her head. "You live here now."

Dixon broke out in raucous laughter. "Did you even look at me before I sat down, or were you too busy making googly eyes at him?"

Nell flushed. Little brothers could be a pain. Her chin jutted up. "I looked."

"I'm wearing pol-y-ester." Dixon spoke slowly, as if she was having difficulty comprehending. "Can you say vintage 1970?"

"Your shirt—"

"My shirt is a *polyester* golf shirt from the seventies. Take a good long look at the collar if you don't believe me."

His mocking tone set Nell's teeth on edge. She recognized he was teasing her, but she hadn't liked it when she was fifteen, and she didn't like it now.

She opened her mouth, but Lilian spoke first.

"You look so happy today, Dixon. The light in your eyes simply shines through." Lilian shot a wink at Nell. "I daresay not many women will even notice those hideous polyester pants."

Nell expected her brother to laugh, but a softness filled his eyes. "Thank you for the compliment."

Dixon liked Lilian, Nell realized, genuinely liked her. Some of the tension that had gripped her since she'd learned he was courting Lilian's investment business eased.

While their mother would have had no compunction about shafting a friend—in fact, would have loved doing it—Dixon was different. His loyalty was hard to earn, but once gained, well, you could trust him with your life.

"You're coming over to the house after the big fireworks display." Leo might have phrased it as a statement, but there was a question in his eyes when he glanced at Lilian.

"I wouldn't miss it," Lilian said.

Dixon said nothing, simply forked off a bite of pancake. Nell thought about the event at Wells's home tonight. It wouldn't be just family in attendance, close friends of the family would be there, too.

She thought of all the holidays she and Dixon had spent apart. And all the ones they'd spent together perpetuating one scam or another. Gloria always sneered that people let down their guard around the holidays.

Nell wished she could invite Dixon. She wondered if he'd be alone tonight.

"Dixon, my brother is having some people over to his house after the fireworks tonight." Leo's voice broke through her thoughts. "If you don't have plans for later, I'd love to see you there."

Nell met Dixon's questioning gaze. "It should be fun. There'll likely be lots of people you know there."

"No one throws a party like the Pomeroys," Lilian added.

Dixon appeared to consider the offer. "Are you certain your brother won't mind if I crash his party?"

"It's not his party, and I invited you, so you won't be crashing," Leo said firmly.

"Oh, say you'll come, Dixon," Lilian urged. "We need more young people to liven things up. I feel quite certain this will be a night none of us will ever forget."

CHAPTER NINETEEN

Dixon and Lilian were in the middle of a conversation about the upcoming football season when Leo and Nell said their goodbyes.

"Lilian appears genuinely fond of Dixon," Leo said, slanting a glance in Nell's direction. She looked so pretty today, her blonde hair a mass of loose waves that softened the angular lines of her face.

She smiled up at him. "Dixon can be very charming."

"I can be charming, too."

She poked him in the ribs with her elbow. "You're extremely charming, even without trying."

Despite the flippant tone, her words pleased him. When she looked at him, he saw the affection. An affection that went both ways. How had they become so close in such a short time?

The sexual intimacy they'd enjoyed this past year had been a primer for the deeper intimacy that existed between them now that they'd been dating. While most couples dated and then became physically close, he and Nell had done it backward.

The thought made him smile.

"You're looking pretty pleased with yourself."

He lifted her hand and tucked it around his arm. "It's a beautiful day, and I'm spending it with an amazing woman that I'm crazy about. Why wouldn't I be pleased?"

"You're crazy about me?" Her teasing tone lowered the stakes on his answer.

He could be off-the-cuff and defuse the situation or be honest and take a risk.

Leo stopped walking and stared into her intense blue eyes. "Seriously crazy about you."

"Good." She gave a decisive nod. "Because I'm seriously crazy about you."

"Leo. Nell." Abby's voice rang out, and they turned in that direction.

Eva Grace was riding high on Jonah's shoulders.

"I was just saying to Jonah I wondered if you and Leo were here." Abby wore a red, white and blue romper. A romper, like the kind his sister had once wore.

"I saw you," Eve Grace blurted out. "I told Mommy and Daddy, there's Aunt Nell right over there."

Jonah, who reminded Leo of a 1960s hippie with his bell-bottom jeans and fringed shirt, lifted a hand, his fingers forming a peace sign. "Eva Grace has eagle eyes."

The child smiled, revealing a missing front tooth. "I'm wearing culottes. They're like shorts but different."

"I love them." Nell touched the cherry-red fabric.

"Mommy made 'em." Eva Grace smiled down at her mother.

What would Nell be like as a mother? Leo wondered. From the little she'd said of her home life, it hadn't been the best. Yet, she'd still come through the experience as a warm and caring woman. And she was good around children.

Leo had the feeling that not only would Nell make a good politician's wife, she'd be a good mother. He remembered what his father had once said, that when you look at a woman to marry, you need to consider what kind of mother she'd be to your children.

The fact that he could think of the word *marry* in conjunction with Nell without breaking into a cold sweat told Leo his feelings went deep.

"We're headed to the three-legged race." Abby gestured with one hand in the direction of where most of the games were to be set up. "Want to come with us?"

"To watch?" Nell asked cautiously. "Or to participate?"

"We're just going to watch," Abby told her.

The pronouncement earned a moan from Eva Grace.

Jonah gave his daughter's leg a tug. "We signed you up for the sack race and the bean-bag toss."

Eva Grace's entire face brightened. "When can I do the sack race?"

"It's right after the three-legged races." Abby slanted a glance at Nell. "I bet it feels strange not to be Hazel Green today."

"Very strange," Nell admitted. "But nice, too. No speeches to give."

"Now that Abby mentions it, I thought you were speaking today." Leo took her hand as they followed Abby and Jonah.

"I gave up my spot to your father." Nell gave his hand a squeeze. "I get to be me all day. He gets another chance to rally his supporters. Win-win."

"That was generous."

"That's me." She smiled cheekily. "Generous to a fault."

Nell stood between Leo and Abby and waited for the bell to sound on the next heat of the adult three-legged race. They'd already watched the various groupings of children.

No wonder Eva Grace had wanted to participate. The children seemed to be having great fun. Even when they fell over, which was often, they simply laughed and got back up—or tried to get back up.

Leo's arm slipped around her shoulders, and she leaned her head against his arm, feeling utterly relaxed and content. At the moment, she was exactly where she wanted to be.

"Penny for your thoughts," he whispered, his breath warm against her ear.

"I was thinking how happy I am." She lifted her head and gazed into his eyes. "There isn't any other place I'd rather be right now than here with you."

Emotion clouded his eyes. "I feel the same way."

Nell wanted him to kiss her, to hold her tight and never let go.

He didn't, just tightened his arm around her shoulders and returned to watching the race.

Was Dixon right? Could she trust in this new life she'd built? Trust that her past would stay away forever? With the summer sun shining hot and bright overhead and laughter filling the air, she thought that, for the first time, it seemed possible.

Even three weeks ago, she couldn't have seen a happy ending in sight. But she and Leo grew closer every day. He was a decent, honorable man, but one who realized life wasn't always perfect.

On the way to the breakfast this morning, he'd mentioned Karen, the wife of his father's legislative director. Though he had no idea of her guilt or innocence, he held on to hope she'd be shown to be simply a victim of her husband's bad decisions, just as Leo's father was a victim.

Nell wondered if that's how he would view her and Dixon. Would he see them as victims of their mother's machinations? Or as willing participants and therefore criminals?

Sophie was on the field, and his gaze was focused on her. A slight smile lifted his lips as he watched his niece and her friend position themselves at the starting line.

"I wish I could be in the race," Eva Grace said, her lips forming a pout.

"Next year," her mother said reassuringly.

Would Nell be standing beside Abby next summer and cheering on Eva Grace? Or, once she told Leo everything, would she see no other option but to start fresh in a new community?

"Go, Sophie, go!" Leo yelled as his niece and her friend wobbled their way down the field.

He shifted his gaze to Nell and grinned.

The sight of his happiness was nearly her undoing. But in that moment, Nell knew she had to tell him everything. Secrets festered. Small lies multiplied and promoted distrust. If she didn't tell him, their relationship wouldn't have a chance of going the distance.

She would tell him.

And she would do it tonight.

Leo spread the blanket out on the grass. He and Nell had scored this prime spot on top of a small incline surrounding Spring Lake, thanks to Liz and the rest of Nell's friends who'd arrived early and claimed the area.

All of their friends were here. Liz, with her mother and son. Jonah, Abby and Eva Grace sat with Matilda barely a foot from his and Nell's blanket. Iris had arrived, then moved to the other side when Beau had arrived.

As usual, Iris avoided the trial consultant. Beau, on the other hand, appeared intrigued by the schoolteacher. Right now, he'd claimed a spot beside Rachel and Marc.

Most of the phones were set to a local radio station playing patriotic music. Once the fireworks began, music that had been mixed to accompany the display would play.

"This has been a wonderful day." Nell breathed the words.

"You make it sound like it's already over." He trailed a finger down her arm. "We still have the fireworks, then the after party at Wells's home."

She slanted a glance in his direction. "And then the after-after party at your place."

The heat in her eyes told Leo exactly what kind of party she had in mind. Saving the best for last, he thought, with a wry smile.

A nearly overwhelming urge to kiss Nell's sweet lips stole over Leo. The way her lips parted and her breathing quickened told him she wanted him, too.

He gripped the blanket in his fists and reminded himself he was the mayor and this was a community event. He settled for bringing her hand to his mouth and placing a kiss in her palm.

"Tonight." Nell leaned close, and the vanilla scent of her shampoo teased and tantalized. "I don't want there to be anything between us."

He cocked his head, unsure of what she was saying. But he didn't have a chance to ask, because the music on his phone changed, signaling the show was about to begin.

Leo slipped his arm around Nell, and when she leaned against him, all was right in his world.

The woman he loved was in his arms. He was surrounded by friends, and tonight he'd be around family. The job he held allowed him to give back to the community he loved.

Yes, he was a lucky man.

In the backyard of the house that had once been the family home, Tim fully relaxed for the first time since he'd hopped out of bed at six a.m. His boys were all here, as well as his precious granddaughter. The only others in attendance were close family friends whom either he or his sons had invited.

Marty stood beside him, a smile on her face. For several

minutes, they watched Sophie play badminton with Lilian and Dixon. Dixon—who'd arrived as Lilian's escort—played the role of the clown to perfection. Each time he swung wildly and missed the birdie, he let out an anguished sound that had Sophie dissolving into uncontrollable giggles.

"Look. Leo is showing Nell how to play croquet." Marty sounded pleased.

Tim obligingly turned in the direction of the croquet game. Sure enough, Leo had his arms around Nell as he demonstrated the proper way to hold the mallet. While they watched, she looked up at Leo, and he kissed her gently on the mouth.

Marty exhaled a sigh. "Remember when we were that age, Tim? You'd just been elected to the Senate, the youngest to be elected from the state of Illinois."

"I was older than Leo, but not by much." Though it had been difficult being so young and inexperienced, Tim had learned quickly. It had helped that he'd had his friend by his side.

Steve.

His best friend since boyhood and the one man he'd thought would never betray his trust.

The man who'd stood beside him when he married Marty.

The man who was Wells's godfather.

Karen had been a part of his—and Marty's—life nearly as long.

"I remember Karen and I learning to navigate the Metro together." Marty's eyes grew soft with memories. "We exchanged parenting tips and babysat each other's kids."

Tim heard the emotion in his wife's voice and knew she was near tears. He wrapped his arms around her, pulling her close. "I know it's been hard for you. It's hard for me, too. I miss Karen. Heck, I even miss Steve."

A muscle in Tim's jaw jumped, and he forced himself to relax. "But I can't go through life being pissed off."

"This whole thing makes me angry, too," Marty said with a heavy sigh. "And sad."

"If Steve had come to me, said he had debts he was having difficulty paying, I'd have moved heaven and earth to figure out a way to help him." Tim blew out a harsh breath. "Instead, he put his future—and mine—on the line with his lies and deceit."

"Steve's father was an alcoholic, remember?"

Tim frowned. "What does that have to do with anything?"

"I've been doing some reading on addictions since all this happened."

Just the way she spoke brought back memories of those days early in their marriage when Marty supported him through law school with her social work degree. Tim liked seeing the light back in his wife's eyes.

Out of the corner of his eye, Tim saw Nell's ball go through the last wicket and hit the stake.

Leo let out a war whoop and spun her around.

"Anyway, pathological gambling is regarded as an addiction. Research seems to show pathological gamblers have a lot in common with drug addicts," Marty continued, appearing to warm to the topic. Tim wondered if Marty ever regretted giving up her career to support his. "As time goes by, gamblers, like drug addicts, need stronger hits to get high. Which for Steve translated into riskier acts."

"Playing for higher stakes."

"Until it all came crashing down." Marty's gaze turned distant.

"Steve made his choice when he took bribes, when he put not only his career but my perceived integrity at risk. I hope he gets the help he needs, I really do. But right now, he's on his own. He'll have to accept the consequences of his actions." Tim found his gaze drawn once again to his youngest son.

Marty followed his gaze. Her lips curved. "Leo has been so happy lately."

"I haven't seen him this interested in a woman since Heather," Tim agreed.

"He's happier with Nell. More himself with her than he was with Heather."

Tim didn't dispute her assertion. He was too busy watching his middle son slip out the back gate. "Where's Matt going?"

Marty glanced around the yard. "He's here somewhere. I just saw him a few minutes ago."

"I just saw him leave by the back gate."

"He probably went to get something from his truck."

Tim pressed his lips together. "I can't figure that boy out."

"He's trying to find where he fits in the world."

"He's in his thirties. It's high time he figured it out."

"He will."

"Look at Wells. He's never deviated from his course in life."

Marty glanced over to where their eldest son stood talking with Lilian. "Wells needs more in his life than work. I know he has Sophie and he's a terrific father, but he's become more solitary since Dani died."

Tim watched Lilian grab Nell's hand and pull her toward the badminton net.

"I'll get the ball and gloves," Leo called to Sophie and headed toward the garage.

"I'll show you where they are," Wells's voice boomed after him.

Wells expelled a melodramatic sigh when he reached his parents, but his smile was easy. "I should have anticipated someone might want to play catch."

"You can't think of every contingency." Marty put a hand on Wells's arm. "This is a lovely party. So relaxing. Thank you for hosting this at your home."

"The house was your home before it was mine," he reminded her.

"Thank you," Marty repeated, brushing a kiss across her son's cheek. "Your dad and I are having a wonderful time."

"We were talking about Leo and Nell." Marty's eyes turned dreamy. "Seeing them together reminds me of when your dad and I were young and in love."

"They seem like a good match." Wells shrugged. "I guess time will tell if they have what it takes to go the distance."

CHAPTER TWENTY

Liz opened the gate, her gaze searching the yard.

The birdie Lilian hit sailed to the right of Nell's badminton racquet and dropped to the grass.

Dixon paused and offered the reporter a friendly wave, but she didn't respond. Liz's gaze remained focused on Nell.

As she drew close, Nell saw that Liz's brows were furrowed in worry, and her face was pale.

Nell's hands turned sweaty on the racquet, and her heart picked up speed. Had something happened to Abby? Or to Eva Grace?

Oh no, not the little princess who'd already been through so much.

Nell hurried toward Liz. "Is it Abby? Or Eva Grace?"

"No. No. They're both fine. I wanted—" Liz stopped, as if suddenly realizing they weren't alone. All eyes—and ears—were focused on her and Nell.

"Is everything okay?" Tim strode over, the picture of a man in charge.

Leo, bat and glove in hand, appeared at Nell's side. "What's going on?"

"Everything is fine." Liz offered the kind of bright smile a teenage girl might give a parent when she'd been caught with a boy in her room. "I simply need a quick word with Nell. Nothing important, really."

"Important enough to bring you over here." Tim's friendly smile never wavered, but his gaze sharpened.

Whatever it was, Nell knew it had to be serious for Liz to show up looking for her. "Not really. Just time sensitive. Liz and I are working together on a project that's nearing completion, and you know how it is sometimes, every second counts."

Nell hadn't lied so blatantly in years, but all those early years of practice came in handy now.

"Right now?" Leo asked. "It can't wait until tomorrow?"

"Liz is here." Nell crooked her arm through the reporter's. "Why wait?"

For a second, Nell thought she might end up dragging Liz across the yard. But Liz's feet began to move, as if she realized Nell was giving her a way out.

"I'm sorry," Liz whispered. "I didn't think about how this would look. I should have texted."

"This is better. My phone's in the house, so I wouldn't have seen your text until later."

"It's important," Liz continued in a low voice.

"I know."

Liz's gaze sharpened. "How do you know?"

"You wouldn't be here if it weren't."

Before she could say more, Leo jogged up. "Can I help?"

"You're so sweet to offer." Without stopping to think, Nell leaned close, cupped his cheek with her hand and kissed him. "I won't be long."

When Nell turned away, she saw the puzzled look in his eyes. Had the kiss felt to him like she was saying goodbye, too?

Perhaps she was worrying for nothing, but Nell had the

feeling whatever Liz had to say would impact her relationship with Leo.

Neither she nor Liz said anything until they were out the gate and at the front of the house. Though the sidewalk was deserted and nobody was in sight, Nell went around to the passenger side of Liz's car.

"Let's talk in here," Nell told her friend. "That way we're assured no one will overhear."

Liz opened her car door and slipped behind the wheel. The car sat in shadows, the only light coming from the streetlight.

"What's going on, Liz?"

"I know who you are."

Everything inside Nell turned to ice, but she still managed a little laugh. "Of course you know who I am. We've been friends since I moved to Hazel Green."

"I know your real name is Susannah Lamphere."

The sudden certainty that her past had caught up with her, punched like a fist. Nell drew her tongue over suddenly dry lips but played it cool. She inclined her head. "Where did you hear that name?"

"It's true, isn't it? That's your real name."

"Yes. It's true. Though I've been Cornelia Ambrose for nearly as many years as I was Susannah." Nell shifted in her seat and fixed her gaze on Liz. "Tell me what you know."

"Hank called me. He said there was a message on his voice mail from a man out of DC asking for background information on Cornelia Ambrose for a story he was writing." Liz studied Nell's face as if seeing her for the first time. "Hank's home sick with the flu, so he asked me to call the guy back."

"What did he say?"

A muscle in Liz's jaw jumped. "When I reached him, the guy told me this crazy story about a robbery and a house burning down. Apparently, the family blames you. They've been looking for you for years, but said you went by the name Susannah Lamphere back then."

"How did they find me? Did he say?"

Liz paused, then slowly pulled a notepad from her bag. "Is it true?"

Nell didn't have time for questions. "Tell me what you know."

"Is it true?" Liz repeated.

"Yes."

Liz expelled a shaky breath. "The guy's name is Stan Britten. Supposedly, he's a lobbyist in DC. He said he's been closely following Senator Pomeroy's situation. Apparently, he saw the picture I took the night of the Illumination Stroll that I put on Instagram and posted to the town's website. I'm sorry, Nell."

"It's not your fault." Nell forced a reassurance into her voice she didn't feel. "What did you tell him?"

"Nothing."

Nell cocked her head. "He didn't press?"

"Of course he pressed." Liz's lips lifted in a smirk. "But he was satisfied when I promised that you and I would meet with him at eleven tomorrow at Matilda's."

"You *promised* him?"

"Promises can be broken. Unless you're interested in meeting with him?" Liz's tone might have been lighthearted, but her expression turned serious. "What's this all about?"

"Did Stan tell you what he wants from me?" Nell knew there had never been enough evidence to charge her mother. Besides, the statutes of limitation for both a criminal trial and civil suit had long since expired.

"He didn't say, but I got the feeling that he doesn't hold Senator Pomeroy in high regard. He said something about you better not be counting on the senator to help you, because he doesn't have any loyalty."

"I wouldn't expect the senator to vouch for me. I barely know him."

"You're close to his son."

Nell wanted to weep. Instead, she lifted her chin. "Stan better be careful. I'm sure the senator wouldn't take kindly to anyone slandering his character."

"My take is Mr. Britten is obsessed with you. Do you think he's dangerous?"

Letting her mind drift back for a second, Nell considered the question. "No. I don't believe he's dangerous."

"What are you going to do?"

"I don't know yet, but thanks to you, I have time to decide."

"You have friends in this town." Liz's gaze was steady on hers. "Friends who will stand by you, no matter if your name is Nell or Hazel or Susannah. I want you to remember that as you're deciding what to do."

"Thanks." Nell opened the car door. "Don't worry about taking time off to meet with him. If I keep the appointment, I'll go alone."

Nell didn't want to return to the party, but she knew it'd look suspicious if she left with Liz and didn't return.

She was walking up the drive when a man stepped from the shadows. Her heart gave a wild leap, then settled when she recognized him. "Dixon."

"What did she want?"

In a clipped tone, Nell gave him the pertinent details.

"Stanley Britten was a whiny weasel back then. Sounds like nothing has changed."

"Once this hits the papers, my career is over." Nell closed her eyes for a second. "I went to college and law school under a name that isn't my own. I never went through the courts and legally changed it. I was always afraid that having a name change on record would lead Gloria to my doorstep."

"That's why you went to college in Madison. Remember, consistent and continuous use makes a name your own in Wisconsin. You *are* Cornelia Ambrose."

"I thought you were coming back to the party." Leo's appearance took them both by surprise. His gaze shifted from Nell to Dixon. "Where's Liz?"

"She left." Nell forced an easy smile. "Then Dixon showed up, and we got to talking and—"

"Nell received some disturbing news tonight that she wants to share with you." Dixon ignored her hiss of protest. "He has a right to know everything."

How could Dixon expect her to talk to Leo about what she planned to do when she didn't know herself what her next step would be?

She was still fuming when her brother did something totally unexpected. He enfolded her in his arms and held her close.

"Begin anew," he whispered in her ear. "It's always possible."

The quote about starting over from wherever you were in life had been their childhood mantra, buoying their hopes that one day they'd slip from Gloria's clutches and start over.

Which was what Nell had done. Now, the new life she'd worked to build was threatened. Heck, who was she kidding? It was over.

She'd have no choice but to *begin anew*. Again.

Her gaze shifted to Leo, to this fine, upstanding man she loved. When he offered a tentative smile, Nell realized she *did* know what her next step would be, what it had to be. She would not let Leo or his family suffer because of her past.

She moved from Dixon's arms, more shaken than she'd realized. Just as he'd appeared from the shadows, her brother disappeared into them, leaving her alone with Leo.

"What's going on, Nell?" Leo's gaze met hers. "Are you in trouble?"

"Yes, I am." She offered him a wobbly smile. "I'm in big trouble."

CHAPTER TWENTY-ONE

An hour later, Nell sat in a chair in Wells's living room. She'd considered packing up and leaving town tonight. Until she realized she'd be leaving Leo and his family, not to mention her friends, to handle the fallout.

She'd insisted Dixon leave. He hadn't wanted to go, but he understood that this was between her and Leo...and his family.

Once Dixon and Lilian left and Sophie was in bed, Leo called a family meeting.

She knew Leo had been surprised when she insisted that what she had to say was best spoken with his entire family present. Instead of sitting on the sofa and taking the chance that Leo would sit beside her, Nell grabbed a floral wingback.

This was her battle, and she needed to fight it alone. She didn't want his family to think she was going to drag him—or them—into this mess. Any further than she could help, that was. She hoped that once Leo heard her story, he would see the wisdom in distancing himself from her.

Gloria's hijinks had made a splash in the press more than once in the past, and Nell knew tabloid reporters liked nothing better than a juicy story, especially one where someone got bloodied.

By the time they finished with Nell, her reputation would be in tatters. She would never be able to stay in Hazel Green without screwing up Leo's life and the lives of everyone she held dear.

She might have already done irreparable harm to Leo's career, and the thought made her want to weep.

"Would anyone like a glass of wine before we get started?" Wells asked. "Or a brandy?"

"I'll take a brandy," Tim said.

"None for me." Leo remained standing, his hands resting on the top of her chair. "I've had enough alcohol tonight."

"I made coffee," Marty said with a hopeful smile.

Nell certainly didn't need any caffeine, but then, she wasn't going to sleep tonight anyway. Besides, a mug would give her something to do with her hands.

"Thank you, Marty." Nell summoned a smile. "Coffee would be nice. I can help."

When she started to rise, Leo waved her down. "I'll get some for us. Black, right?"

For us. As if wanting to make sure the family knew he had her back. *Oh, Leo.*

"You know me so well." It was a thoughtless remark, one she regretted uttering practically from the moment it left her lips.

He squeezed her shoulders, then headed into the kitchen, returning less than a minute later with two steaming mugs.

After setting one in front of her, he finally took a seat on the sofa when his mother sat and patted a spot beside her.

Wells handed his father a brandy, then picked up the mug of coffee his mother had brought him. "What's this about?" he asked Nell.

The two men remained standing behind the sofa where Marty sat with Leo.

"Liz informed me that someone from my past will be in town tomorrow. He wants to speak with me. I'll meet with him at Matilda's." Nell wrapped her hands around her mug and glanced around the room. "This situation will provide a lot of fodder for the gossip pigs. I have no doubts that this man will serve me up to them on a silver platter."

Wells exchanged a puzzled glance with Tim.

Concern blanketed Leo's face. "If it has to do with our relationship, there's nothing sensational about—"

"It has to do with my past. A lobbyist—Stanley Britten—saw a picture that was taken of you and me with your parents at the Illumination Stroll. He recognized me." Nell expelled a breath. "Stanley mentioned to Liz he's been looking for me for a long time."

"Why do you believe Stan Britten is out to get you?" Tim's brows drew together. "What's his connection?"

"Stanley and I went to the same high school, back when my name was Susannah Lamphere."

Wells's fingers tightened around his cup.

Leo rounded the chair to stand in front of her. "What do you mean when your name was Susannah?"

"Cornelia Ambrose isn't my real name." Nell took a deep breath and let it out. "My given name is Susannah Lamphere."

"I didn't even know your real name." His handsome face looked as if it had been chiseled in stone. "You should have told me."

"Yes. I should have."

Leo stepped back. Though it was only a few feet, it felt like miles. He crossed his arms across his chest. "Go on."

"I was raised in an unconventional household by my mother, Gloria." Nell lifted the mug from the table in front of her, needing the warmth of the cup. Simply saying the woman's name had everything inside her going to ice. "Gloria is a charismatic sociopath and a compulsive liar. She's also very beautiful. Most people who meet her are initially charmed."

Nell set down the mug, realizing the heat couldn't begin to touch the coldness inside her. "Gloria has been arrested several times and interviewed by the police numerous times for crimes she's committed. But she's smart and savvy and always manages to land on her feet."

"Couldn't have been much of a childhood." Sympathy filled Marty's voice. "Having someone like that for a mother."

"It wasn't a childhood." Nell's laugh held no humor. "By the time I was Sophie's age, I was picking pockets, shoplifting and being her decoy."

Marty's hand rose to her throat. "You poor thing."

Leo said nothing. He just continued to stare at her with unblinking blue eyes.

Oh, how Nell wished she'd told him everything. But that train had already left the station. She blew out a breath.

"When I was ten, Gloria started setting fires. Sometimes, she did it to cover up a job or simply out of spite. Sometimes, just for fun. It was always someone else's home or business. Except once, when she needed the insurance money, it was a house she recently purchased."

"Was she ever charged with arson?" The question came from Wells.

"She was under suspicion by the police plenty of times. No matter how hard they tried, they were never able to pin anything on her. The funny thing was, she would deny she'd done any of the crimes and truly seemed to believe she hadn't." Nell forced herself to stay seated. Just thinking of Gloria made her twitchy. "As I grew older, I realized if I stayed much longer, I'd end up in jail. Or worse, turn out just like her."

"Did you ever speak with a school counselor?" Wells asked. "Or with a pastor?"

"Saying anything to anyone would have brought severe repercussions." Nell licked her lips. "My brother and I were beaten for simple infractions, or for nothing at all. We feared she'd kill us if we ever betrayed her."

Nell slanted a glance at Leo. Her heart lurched. Same stony expression.

"How does Stanley Britten factor into all of this? Why do you believe he has it out for you?"

Had the questions come from Wells? Or his father? Did it really matter?

"I was seventeen and a senior in high school when my mother ordered me to get friendly with a junior named Stanley Britten."

"Did you sleep with him?" Wells's question earned him a sideways look from Leo.

"No, I didn't have sex with him. I became his friend. It wasn't hard. I was popular. He wasn't. Being seen with me upped his status at school." Nell took a moment, remembering back. "He was a loner, and I was lonely on the inside, so we connected. I never took friends home. My mother was unpredictable. The lives other girls my age talked about were foreign to me."

"You were telling us about Stan." Tim's gaze remained riveted on her face.

"Stanley was smart. I was smart. Our conversations revolved around topics most high school students had no interest in."

Marty offered an encouraging smile. "You became his friend."

"I did. I spent time at his house, got to know his family. His dog, Daisy, adored me. She was a Maltese." Nell paused, then added, "Gloria wouldn't let Dixon and me have a pet."

Now, Nell realized that had been for the best. When Gloria got angry, her first impulse was to strike out. A puppy wouldn't have stood a chance.

"If you and Stanley were such good friends, why do you think he wants to hurt you now?" Leo asked quietly.

"After our friendship was solidified to Gloria's satisfaction..." Nell paused and shifted her focus to Wells. "I let Gloria believe I slept with him. In her mind, a friendship with a man was always about sex. Anyway, Gloria ordered me to get the code to the Brittens' safe that was in the parents' bedroom closet."

"How did your mother know about the safe?" Marty asked.

"Mr. Britten bragged about it at a party my mother crashed." Nell shook her head. "The safe they had was known for its thicker, stronger metal. My mother didn't want to go to a lot of work to get the money and jewels inside. She wanted the combination."

Silence filled the living room. Nell understood. They were a nice Midwestern family. What she was saying sounded like it came straight out of the script of a soap opera.

Nell took a sip of lukewarm coffee. "I stalled for as long as I could, but Gloria became impatient."

"How did you get it out of him?" Leo asked.

"Through casual, everyday conversation. We talked a lot about current events and school gossip. Stanley was fond of discussing history, especially World War II." These discussions had been the best parts of her time with Stanley. Though he could be snarky, he had a curious mind. "Remember, he considered me a friend. We were always discussing computer passwords and lamenting the need to change them frequently. This was before the days of password-manager apps."

"Why does he have it in for you?" Leo impatiently circled a hand.

"Don't rush her," Tim snapped. "These details may be important."

"It's okay." Nell expelled a breath. "Stan had told me many times that his dad had trouble recalling his passwords, so he kept them all the same. Mr. Britten used his wife's name and year of birth."

"A password isn't the same as a safe combination," Wells pointed out.

"No. It isn't." Nell tightened her grip on the mug. Until that fateful day, Stan hadn't even mentioned the safe. "Stanley was in high spirits the day he gave me the combination. He'd aced his calculus final. We started talking numbers again, and he brought up his dad. It bugged him that his father was so tech challenged. He repeated what I already knew about his mother's name and her year of birth. I asked what his dad did about combinations, and he told me the sequence on the safe."

"Did he realize the significance of what he'd divulged?" Leo's expression remained unreadable.

"Not until later. Gloria broke into their house that night and took all the money and jewels from the safe. On her way out, she lit a fire." Though the cup was still in her hands, the coffee had gone cold. Nell drank anyway. "The family was at the symphony at the time. Daisy was the only one home."

"The Maltese," she clarified when she caught Marty's questioning look. "Daisy nearly died of smoke inhalation. The picture of the firefighters resuscitating her made the front page of the newspaper."

"Stanley knew it was you."

Nell heard the question beneath Leo's comment.

"When they found the open safe, the police assumed the burglary and arson were connected. For reasons too numerous to mention, my mother was their number one suspect. I was her alibi. I told the detectives she was home with me all evening."

"Stanley knew it was you," Leo repeated. "He knew you'd played him. You lied to him, made him care, then stabbed him in the back."

Tears stung the backs of Nell's eyes, but she blinked them back before anyone could notice. She deserved every bit of Leo's censure. He'd trusted her, and she'd lied to him.

"Stanley was on his knees in the picture that made the front page. He was crouched over Daisy while the firefighters worked to save her life. The family had arrived home shortly after the firetrucks rolled up. The photographer captured his expression of anguish." Nell cleared her throat. "Anguish was the word used in the article, but I saw guilt. Shortly before we left town, Stanley attempted suicide."

A wave of nausea washed over Nell. The guilt over knowing she'd caused a boy so much pain that he hadn't wanted to live, had been the impetus she'd needed to make the break with Gloria and leave home.

Nell kept her gaze focused straight ahead as the silence stretched and extended. She swallowed past the lump in her throat. She did not want this family to be hurt because of her.

"You need this information to protect yourselves. I believe Stanley wants payback. He's going to want to bring to light all the ugliness of my past and make me suffer." Nell gave a humorless chuckle. "If I stay, Gloria's legal difficulties—she's being held without bond —will become mine. Her life and escapades will become mine. Stanley's vendetta against me will bleed onto all of you. Knowledge is power."

Tim gave a curt nod. "First, Leo needs to distance himself from you."

"That would be best," Nell agreed, resisting the urge to glance in Leo's direction.

"I'll speak with Anissa, my PR person, to see if we can get some talking points for the family." Tim stroked his chin. "That way, if Stanley goes public, we're already prepared."

"You were just a child." Marty's eyes were soft with sympathy.

"She broke the law. She lied to the police to give her mother an alibi," Wells reminded his mother. "Nell was seventeen at the time. That's old enough to know right from wrong."

Nell glanced at Leo, saw him scrub his hands across his face. She surged to her feet. "Please know that the last thing I wanted to do was cause problems in your family."

Leo cleared his throat. "We wouldn't be having to scramble at the last minute to figure out how to deal with this if you'd been honest from the beginning."

"You're right." She licked her lips, her heart pounding an erratic rhythm in her chest. "I should have told you everything."

"Yes, you should have." Leo cocked his head. "Why didn't you?"

"I was afraid of losing you." Nell lifted one hand as if to reach out and somehow bridge the chasm between them. But his eyes were dark and unreadable, and she let her hand drop. "Now it seems I've lost you anyway."

Leo said nothing, but the flicker of pain she caught in his eyes was worse than if he'd screamed at her.

"I'm truly sorry I let you all down." Nell cleared her throat and glanced around the room. "My meeting with Stanley is at eleven."

She turned to go, but when she stepped past Leo, she gave in to impulse. Flinging her arms around him, she gave him a fierce hug.

He didn't pull away or tell her she was holding him too tight, but neither did he wrap his arms around her. He simply stood there, his body stiff and unyielding.

That's when she knew it was truly over.

Burying her head against Leo's shirtfront, she savored the sensation, holding it tight to her heart so that she could recall his scent, the feel of his body next to hers in the years to come when she was alone.

Tim touched her arm, his voice soft. "Nell, you need to let go."

"Yes." She dropped her arms to her sides and expelled a ragged breath. "It's time to let go."

CHAPTER TWENTY-TWO

"What's the plan?" Wells swirled the brandy in his snifter and glanced at his father, who was pacing the living room. "You told Mom before she went to bed that we would support Nell. Did you mean it?"

"Of course I meant it. I don't make a habit of lying to your mother." The tight edge to Tim's voice had Wells lifting a brow.

"Sorry." Tim raked a hand through his two-hundred-dollar haircut. "This is a cluster. First, Steve. Now, Nell."

Wells finished off the last of his brandy. "Leo loves her. He's angry with her right now—and hurt—but he loves her."

Tim nodded. A muscle in his jaw jumped. "We don't have much time, so let's get down to business. Stanley Britten."

"We already know he's considered one of the top lobbyists for the gaming industry and has worked with Steve on legislation." Wells tapped a finger against his thigh. "He's also married with a couple of kids in private schools."

"He and Steve worked closely on several important pieces of legislation." Tim frowned.

"Do you think he could have slipped money to Steve under the table for a vote on the gaming legislation?" Leo asked.

"It's a distinct possibility. Heck, he could even be the one who gave Steve the money that was found in his freezer." Tim expelled a breath. "I wish I knew if Stan was on the FBI's list. Either way, we need to keep our distance."

Wells rubbed his chin. "I'm not sure we're going to be able to keep Leo from that lunch meeting."

"You're going to have to sit on him. Keep assuring him that staying away is what's best for Nell." Tim pressed his lips together. "It sure as hell is best for his career."

"If this was Mom or Dani, you'd never keep us away."

His father speared him with a glance. "Nell isn't your mother or Dani."

"I'm just saying."

"And I'm telling you to sit on him. Recruit Matt if you think you'll need extra hands."

"If I can find Matt." Wells shook his head. "What about you? What will you be doing?"

Tim expelled a breath. "I called Pete. I've got him searching for dirt on Britten."

"You're really going to try to help Nell?"

"Don't sound so surprised." Tim's gaze grew distant. "I remember when your sister was seventeen. Kit thought she was a grown-up, but she was still very much a child. Nell may have been more street savvy, but that doesn't change the fact that seventeen is still a kid."

Wells nodded in agreement.

"Besides, you know Stanley Britten has been on my blacklist ever since he implied to the media the FBI thought I might have a role in the bribery." A sardonic grin spread across Tim's face. "The maraschino cherry atop this very ugly sundae is that I may get to take down Britten in the process."

～

As soon as Nell stepped into her apartment, she started packing. She'd do what she could to defuse the Stanley situation, then she would leave Hazel Green forever. Hopefully, her absence would save Leo, his family and her friends from the full impact of Stanley's wrath.

The years she'd lived with her mother had taught her how to pack at a moment's notice. Nell had just snapped a suitcase shut when she sensed someone in the room. Grabbing a hairbrush, she whirled.

"Dixon." His name came out on a whoosh of air. "What are you doing here?"

He stepped around her and sat on the bed. "It took you long enough to get home."

"What are you doing here?" she repeated.

His gaze shifted to the suitcase. "It appears I'm just in time to say goodbye. Funny, you didn't mention you were taking a trip."

She waved the hairbrush in the air. "It's a last-minute kind of thing."

"Did you forget about your lunch appointment tomorrow with our old friend, Stanley?" Dixon wagged his finger. "Don't tell me you're standing him up."

"I'm not standing him up." She heaved a heavy breath and plopped down on the bed beside her brother. "I'm leaving town right after I meet with him."

"Getting the hell out of Dodge, eh?" Dixon's light tone didn't match the serious look in his eyes. "You must be anticipating a less-than-positive outcome."

"I certainly don't believe Stanley is coming all this way to renew our friendship." Nell sighed again, weary all the way to her core. "I'm hoping when I meet with him that he'll unload all his pent-up anger and frustration on me. Later, when he discovers I've left town, he'll most certainly come after me. Everyone I care about in Hazel Green will no longer be of interest to him."

"It could work." Dixon tapped two fingers against his lips. "Odds are it won't, but hey, long shots come in every day."

"Thanks for the encouraging words." Nell pushed to her feet. "I'll be in touch."

He stood, his gaze locking on hers. "I'll do whatever I can to help."

She knew all he was offering and was touched. "Thank you."

Dixon stood. "How did Leo react to the news that you're leaving?"

"He doesn't know." Nell's heart rose to her throat, and she made a sound that fell somewhere between a laugh and a sob. "But at this point, I don't think he'd care. He's so angry with me. Oh, and let's not forget disappointed and hurt."

The grave expression on Dixon's face told her he understood. This was the reason they'd both kept any interactions with the opposite sex free and easy. Still, her brother knew how much Leo meant to her. "You—"

"I could what? Stay and try to convince him to give me another chance? Or maybe stay and let Stanley make Leo's life and the lives of his family miserable?" Nell shook her head violently. "If I did that, I'd be as bad as Gloria. Except, unlike her, knowing I was hurting those I care about would tear me apart."

"I think you're underestimating the people who love you." Dixon stared at her for several long seconds. "I'm going to miss you, Suze. This time, keep in touch."

When she heard the door click shut behind him, Nell expelled a ragged breath. It seemed ironic that just when she and Dixon had found each other again, they'd had to say goodbye.

Tomorrow, she'd be leaving not only her brother, but every-thing—and everyone—she held dear...including the only man she would ever love.

≈

The next morning, after leaving a message for her secretary to cancel her appointments for the rest of the week, Nell texted Abby.

Need to talk. Urgent.

The reply came right away. *My house? Or ???*

Your house. See you in thirty.

Nell strode up the steps to the massive front porch in twenty-five. The large yellow Victorian enclosed by a black wrought-iron fence had a homey feel.

Abby opened the door before she knocked. The jeans, sleeve-less tee and bare feet told Nell her friend had been relaxing at home.

"I didn't mean to disrupt your morning. But I—"

"You didn't disrupt anything except me enjoying a moment of solitude with my coffee and scone. Jonah left for the station over an hour ago, and Eva Grace is still asleep." Abby tugged Nell to a room at the back of the house filled with plants and an abundance of sunshine.

A carafe of what Nell assumed was coffee sat on a white distressed-wood table. Yellow gingham placemats sat beneath blue mugs and plates holding scones.

Though Nell told herself she couldn't possibly be hungry, her stomach growled.

Abby smiled. Though the dark hair pulled back in a jaunty tail made her look much younger than thirty, this was no hothouse flower. Abby knew the pain that came with difficult decisions.

"You're probably wondering why I'm here."

"I'm curious, especially about the urgent part." Abby filled a cup for Nell from the carafe, and the rich aroma of coffee filled the air.

Before Nell could respond, a large golden retriever entered the room.

"Ginger is here to make sure you didn't bring a treat for her."

Abby motioned with one hand. "No treats today. Sit on the rug, girl."

Instead of obeying, the retriever moved to Nell's side.

The dog pressed her body against Nell's thigh in what felt like a gesture of comfort. Nell didn't push her away. Couldn't push her away.

Nell swallowed the lump trying to lodge in her throat.

"Tell me what's so urgent." Abby closed her hand over hers and gave it a squeeze.

"I'll be leaving town later today. I came to say goodbye."

"Leaving?" Abby cocked her head. "I didn't know you had a trip planned. How long will you be gone?"

"Forever." Nell tried for a matter-of-fact tone, but she could hear the emotion in her voice. "I won't be returning to Hazel Green."

"Bu-but why?" Abby sputtered.

Keep it simple, Nell told herself. "It's complicated. But trust me, it's for the best."

"There's no way you leaving is for the best." Her friend's brows pulled together. "What about Leo? What does he think about this plan?"

"I have an ugly past, Abby. One you know nothing about. Last night, I confessed all to Leo and his family. Leo had no idea. I should have told him everything before, but I was a coward. I let him believe that he knew me, that he could trust me." Nell's insides quivered, but her fingers were steady as she broke off a piece of scone. "He's angry and disappointed."

Compassion filled Abby's dark eyes. "He'll get over it."

Nell shook her head. "He'll be glad to see me gone."

"I don't believe—" Abby stopped herself, then began again. "Don't you think you should tell him anyway?"

"No. It's best I go and go quickly. The person I'm meeting today will try to trash Leo and his family and create a media circus. Partly because of our past association."

Abby narrowed her gaze. "Who is this person?"

"His name is Stanley Britten. We were friends of sorts when I was seventeen." Nell hesitated, aware Abby's husband was the chief of police.

"Is he an old boyfriend?"

"No. He was never my boyfriend." Nell considered how much to say. "Stanley blames me for something that happened a long time ago."

"Why are you being so secretive?" Frustration filled Abby's voice. "I'm your friend. I want to help. But I can't if I don't know what's going on."

"There isn't anything you can do to help." Nell's hand closed over Abby's. "I simply came to say goodbye. You're my best friend. If Stanley comes to you and asks what you know about my past or if you know where I went, I want you to be able to be honest and say you have no idea."

"I don't understand—"

"He'll likely take great delight in sharing some things I did when I was younger. Details that will make you wonder if you ever truly knew me."

"Why would he do that to you? I mean, you said at one time you were friends."

"We were, but if Stanley even *thought* that you had slighted him, he had it out for you." Nell thought of Mr. Jenks, a popular history teacher at their high school. "I remember when Stan didn't get picked to represent our school in an all-city History Day competition. He did whatever he could to get the teacher who hadn't chosen him, fired. And he was sneaky about it."

There was no doubt in Nell's mind that Stan was out for payback.

As if sensing her distress, Ginger rested her head on Nell's lap. The sweet gesture had Nell fighting back tears. Or perhaps it was the thought of leaving Abby and her other friends behind.

"What could you have done at seventeen that was so horrible? You were a child."

"I was never a child." Nell pushed back her chair and stood. "Trust me, I did plenty of bad things."

Ginger scrambled to her feet.

"Don't go." Abby's voice was tremulous but firm. "Whatever it is, we can work through it together. Jonah will help."

Nell leaned over and gave Ginger one last rub. "Please tell the others I love them and I'm sorry I deceived them."

"Deceived?" Abby flung up her hands. "How did you deceive us, Nell?"

"Nell isn't even my real name." Her voice rose, then broke.

"What do you mean it's not your name?" Abby tossed her napkin to her plate and stood. "Okay. No more questions. I don't care what your real name is or why you changed it. I only care that you're planning to leave me and everyone else who loves you."

"I love you, Abby." Nell forced a calm she didn't feel. "Thank you for being such a wonderful friend."

Abby threw herself at Nell, enfolding her in a tight hug. "I'm here for you. Always."

Nell blinked back tears and stepped back. "Do me one last favor?"

Abby wiped her eyes. "Anything."

"Let Matilda know I have a special lunch meeting planned with Mr. Britten at eleven? Perhaps she can set aside a table that's more private."

Abby didn't ask why Nell didn't make the call herself, and Nell was grateful.

"Should I have Jonah stop by? You know, just in case this man who hates you gets out of control?"

"I appreciate the offer." Nell's lips quirked in a humorless smile. "But I think Stanley would see the chief of police as *his* friend, not mine."

CHAPTER TWENTY-THREE

Nell arrived at Matilda's dressed in a blue suit and heels. Looking professional always made her more confident.

Matilda was at the check stand, wearing a navy 1940s dress that flattered her figure with its fitted waist and knee-length A-line skirt. A perfectly tied bow of the same fabric rested just below her chin.

"I saw the sign on the door," Nell told Matilda. "I didn't realize you were closed for lunch today."

"Once your appointment arrived," Matilda gestured with her head toward a man in a dark suit at a far table, "I put up the sign. Abby told me a little about what's going on and that you need privacy. This way, you won't be disturbed."

"Thank you, but it's not necessary for you to close your restaurant." Nell touched Matilda's arm. "Think of all the revenue you'll be losing."

"A friend's welfare is always more important than money." Matilda shot a sharp glance in Stanley's direction before refocusing on Nell. "If you need anything, I'm here for you."

I'm here for you.

It was the same sentiment that Dixon and Abby had intoned.

Nell had made good friends in Hazel Green, built a satisfying life here and fallen in love with a wonderful man. Now, Stanley, this boy-turned-man who couldn't let go of the past, had tracked her down and seemed determined to make her pay.

Nell thought of the suitcase in her car, thought of all she'd be leaving behind when she ran again, like that scared girl of seventeen.

Skipping town. One step away from disaster. Just like Gloria.

Was her plan to leave the right choice? Or would it only make things worse for those she loved?

She would feel Stanley out, see what he was like after all these years, find out what he wanted from her.

Then she would decide her next step.

The closer the clock ticked toward eleven, the more agitated Leo became. Under his brother's watchful gaze, Leo paced his office like a caged animal.

"You're worried about Nell and her meeting with Stanley," Wells commented, obviously feeling compelled to fill the pulsating silence.

"I'm curious." Leo resisted the urge to slant another look at the mantel clock he'd glanced at only seconds before. "I don't understand why she thinks she needs to protect us."

Wells shrugged.

"She thinks Stanley Britten may make trouble. I wish I knew more about him." Last night, when he'd gotten home, Leo had scoured the internet for anything he could find on the man. There had been nothing that could be used as leverage.

"Dad thinks it's possible Stan and Steve were co-conspirators." Wells glanced at the clock. "Pete should have a report for Dad this afternoon."

"A PI won't find that information, especially not on short

notice." Leo continued to pace. "You'd have to go to the source for that."

His brother's gaze turned sharp and assessing. "Are you suggesting we ask Steve to give him up?"

Leo shook his head. "Steve is off-limits because of the indictment. But Karen may know something. Or she could find out."

"I'll call Dad." Wells pulled out his phone. "He'll get right on it."

"It might still be too late."

Wells lifted a brow.

"I think Nell plans to leave Hazel Green after the meeting."

"If that's the case, I know what I'd do."

Leo cocked his head.

"If it were Dani in that restaurant, you couldn't keep me away." His brother rose and moved to the window. "You know, I'd give up everything for one more day with her. For another chance to tell her how much I love her."

Though it wasn't the same situation he faced, Leo could relate to the sentiment.

"I'd tell her how sorry I was for pushing her. If I'd paid attention to her concerns, we'd never have gotten on that helicopter, and she'd still be—" Wells's voice broke. He quickly brought it under control. "If Nell means half as much to you as Dani meant to me, don't let her go. Accept her for who she is, past baggage and all."

What had appeared murky became suddenly clear.

"I'm going to make sure Stanley Britten knows that Nell isn't alone in this fight. He screws with her, he better be prepared to deal with me."

"Just as long as you realize this scandal, if that's what it ends up being, could be the end of your political career."

"I'd give it up in a heartbeat for Nell."

"That kind of says it all."

He was nearly out the door when he heard Wells call out, "Good luck."

Leo smiled. Stan Britten was the one who was going to need the luck.

~

Stanley didn't get up when Nell reached his table next to the window. Nell knew how he'd been raised and the position he held in DC. Rising to one's feet was common courtesy. Staying seated was a backhanded slap.

The second his gaze met hers, Nell saw that he had the same cold, dead eyes as her mother. In that moment she knew reason wouldn't work with him, and neither would trying to get him to empathize with her situation.

"Stanley." Nell paused, resisting the urge to extend her hand. Another common business courtesy that he would likely ignore.

"Sit." Stan gestured with his head toward the chair adjacent to his at the four-top. Instead of taking the one he indicated, she rounded the table so her back would be to the window.

Nell considered herself to be an expert at quickly sizing up a person. From the tips of his burnished calfskin Ferragamos to his Maybach tortoise-shell eyewear, Stan appeared determined to show he was a man of power.

The nerdy, science geek she remembered was nowhere to be seen. That didn't mean he wasn't there, simply that he wasn't going to let her see that part of his nature, at least for now.

Nell sat down and placed the linen napkin on her lap.

Matilda appeared tableside, her smile easy, her gaze watchful. "Would you care for a cocktail?"

While eleven in the morning seemed early for a drink, Nell glanced at the glass in front of Stan.

"The gentleman is having a gin martini."

Ah, a serious drink for a serious discussion. Nell hid a smile. "Scotch, neat."

"Right away." Matilda cast a glance at Stan's stoic expression and hurried off.

"This place doesn't appear to do much business."

Nell guessed that was as good of an opening gambit as he was going to give.

"Matilda is a friend. She closed her restaurant so we could be assured of privacy."

Surprise flickered for an instant in his brown eyes before the shutter dropped.

Matilda reappeared and set the faceted whiskey glass in front of Nell. "Do you have any questions about the menu?"

Stan handed his to her. "I'm not interested."

Matilda's eyes cooled, but the smile remained on her lips. "Let me know if you change your mind."

"Thanks, Matilda." Nell turned to Stan and fired the opening salvo. "Tell me why you wanted to see me."

"I've been searching for you for years." Stan's gaze flicked dismissively over her. "A small-town attorney. I almost laughed. You were the golden girl, and I was the geek that everyone dismissed as nothing. We can see now who came out on top."

"Are you happy, Stan?"

Once again, she'd surprised him. His eyes widened, and he took a gulp of his drink. "I'm very successful."

"You didn't answer my question." Nell inclined her head and studied him. "I know you're married with a couple of children."

"I'm in the process of a divorce. Not that it's any of your business. The ungrateful bitch is trying to take me for everything I have."

"You realize what happened between us was a lifetime ago." Nell lifted the tumbler to her lips and took a sip. "Ever hear the saying, 'Holding on to anger is like drinking poison and expecting the other person to die'?"

"You might not die, but you're going to pay. I'll make sure of it."

"I'm sorry to hear you feel that way." She kept her tone even and her expression merely curious.

"You acted like you were my friend, when all you wanted was the combination to the safe." A flush stained his cheeks, and a muscle in his jaw jumped. "You made a fool out of me."

"I liked you, Stan. The boy that you were back then anyway." Nell kept her tone matter-of-fact. "We had so many common interests, like Harry Potter. Remember when we spent a whole weekend sorting ourselves and our classmates into appropriate Hogwarts houses?"

Stan's eyes narrowed. "You thought I was a Slytherin."

"You told me I was crazy." Nell recalled the conversation vividly. "But even back then, you were ambitious and achievement-oriented."

"Slytherins are also shrewd and cunning." His eyes glittered. "And goal-oriented. I've never stopped looking for you."

Accepting that the trip down memory lane had been a bust, Nell tried to redirect the conversation. "You've done really well for yourself despite the events back then."

She saw no reason to bring up that insurance had covered his parents' losses.

It was one of the arguments Gloria had often used as Nell got older and began to question her actions. According to Gloria, the people they stole from could afford it. Insurance reimbursed them for their losses. No harm.

The explanation had made a certain amount of sense to a teenager. Until people started getting hurt. Until Nell realized that sentimental things couldn't be replaced.

"I was glad Daisy made it out okay."

"I don't care about the stupid dog." Stan clenched his glass so tightly his knuckles went white. "My parents were furious. It didn't take them long to figure out who'd given out the combination. Especially when the police started sniffing around your mother. I had to feign a suicide attempt to get my parents off my back."

Relief flooded her at the knowledge he hadn't been suicidal, after all. A heavy weight that she'd been carrying all these years slipped off her shoulders to pool at her feet.

Nell said nothing, merely took a sip of Scotch. Stan reminded her of a runaway locomotive, picking up steam as he continued down the track.

"They made me go to counseling for a year. I played that psychologist like a violin." Stan sneered. "Twelve months of my life messed up, all because of you. I tried to tell them you forced it out of me. My father got this pitying look on his face and said something about 'being fooled by a pretty face.'"

Nell studied Stan for a long moment and, for the first time, saw what she had somehow failed to see all those years ago. This man possessed many of the same characteristics as Gloria.

While he appeared to have it all—a loving mother and father, a quick and agile mind and now a successful career, the perfect façade held cracks.

How had she missed the signs?

She thought back and remembered how he'd never take the blame for his actions. If he didn't do well on a test, it was the teacher's fault for not pointing out the important content. He'd once smashed the robot he'd spent weeks building when another kid had taken first in a science competition.

Nell had chalked up his actions to immaturity. Just like his snide comments that someone Nell considered a casual friend had *absolutely* nothing going for her.

And he'd spent much of the time they were together talking about himself. At the time, she'd appreciated that fact, knowing it was through conversation that she'd learn his secrets.

Which was why Nell knew that today wasn't about the theft, the fire or even Daisy nearly dying. This was about him losing face with his family and having what he saw as his imperfections exposed.

For that, he was determined to make her pay. If he could take down people she cared about in the process, all the better.

Nell had to know what he had planned. Which meant she needed to respond to him as she would her mother. "You're a smart man, Stanley. And a successful one."

He studied her through hooded eyes. "You fooled me once with that act. It won't work again."

"What is it exactly you want?"

"To make you bleed."

The comment took her by such surprise, Nell flinched.

He laughed. "Oh, not literally. You're not worth going to prison over. Though I should have screwed you back in high school when I had the chance. You'd have done anything for that combination. We both know it."

He was wrong about that, Nell thought. Even back then, she'd had limits on how far she'd go to please her mother.

"I wonder what you would do now to ensure that I keep my mouth shut about your criminal past?"

"I don't have a criminal past." Nell sipped her Scotch. "I've never been charged with a crime. If you'd done your research, you'd know that."

"I have done my research, you stupid bitch. I'm sitting here, aren't I? And when I snapped my fingers, you came running." Stan gave a harsh laugh, his eyes taking on that crazy gleam she'd seen all too often in her mother's. "You changed your name and did an okay job of covering your tracks. Yet, I still found you."

Stan leaned forward across the table, his eyes glowing with malevolent glee. "I'm going to make you suffer. I'm going to make your friends, including the mayor and his family, wish they'd never met you."

Nell thought about how weak she'd been back then and how scared she'd been of what Gloria might do to her. That's why she'd done as she was told until she'd eventually run away. But she wasn't scared anymore, not of Gloria nor of Stan.

She now had friends who loved her and who would be there for her. Knowing that gave her a strength she hadn't had back then.

Today, she wasn't going to run. She was going to stay and fight for those she loved to her dying breath.

She'd been a girl when she left home, wise far beyond her years in many ways, but still a child. She was a woman now, strong and capable of dealing with anything life threw at her. If the police wanted to question her, bring 'em on.

If the bar association decided to yank her license for not divulging those episodes as a minor, she'd find some other way to support herself. What she wouldn't tolerate was letting this man harm the Pomeroy family or her friends.

She would find a way to stop Stanley. She just had to figure out how.

"I might be persuaded to be merciful." The lascivious look in his eyes wasn't lust as much as it was the need to control. "You spread your legs for me and I might go easy on your friends."

Nell lifted a mocking brow. Common sense said you didn't poke a bear. In Stan's case, she'd make an exception. "If you think I'm going to sleep with you, Stan, you're not as smart as I thought. I would never have slept with you then, and I won't now."

Stan's eyes took on an even more menacing gleam. "You still think you're better than me? You're not prepared to handle what I'm going to do to you, you bi—"

"Nell is capable of handling anything. She's smart, she's strong and she's surrounded by friends who love her."

Nell glanced up, and Leo kissed her lightly on the mouth, then took a seat at the table and pinned Stan with his blue eyes. "I'm Leo Pomeroy, and I'm going to tell you exactly how this is going to go down."

CHAPTER TWENTY-FOUR

It took every ounce of Leo's self-control not to haul the guy up by the lapels of his hand-tailored suit. He'd dealt with people of this ilk before and knew how they operated. Instead, he smiled and allowed several beats of silence to descend over the table.

"I know who you are," Stan began, "and before I'm done, your reputation will be as trashed as Senator Pomeroy's."

"Did I hear someone mention my name?" Tim crossed the room with the confident strides of a man who knew his place in the world.

A smile, or rather the semblance of a smile, lifted Stan's lips. In the light streaming through the lace curtains, his eyes held a feral gleam.

Nell glanced at Leo.

Leo lifted a shoulder in a barely perceptible shrug. He was as surprised as she was by his father's appearance.

Tim took a seat at the table. "Britten. It's fortuitous that I've run into you here. I was thinking about Franklin this morning. How's he doing?"

"Franklin?" Leo asked before Stan could respond.

"Franklin Kunz. He's head of the lobbying group Stan works

for." Tim lifted a staying hand as Matilda approached the table. "Franklin and I were fraternity brothers. I don't know if you realized we had that connection, Stan."

"I didn't know, but it doesn't matter."

"It could matter." Tim's hand hovered above Nell's water glass. "Mind?"

Nell shook her head. "Not at all."

Tim lifted the crystal tumbler and took a drink.

Stan sneered. "If you think I'm going to back down just because you threaten me—"

Tim's eyes were cool, even as the easy smile remained on his lips. "I didn't threaten you." Tim glanced at Leo and Nell. "Did you hear me threaten Stan?"

"Of course, your son and his whore would side with you."

"I didn't hear the senator threaten you." Matilda, Leo realized, had stayed on this side of the room. "I heard him ask how your boss is doing."

Leo knew with absolute certainty that his father had requested she stay close. Smart move.

"Do you know Cornelia Ambrose isn't her real name?" Stan jerked his head toward Nell. "Are you aware her mother is a con artist being held without bond in Palm Springs?"

"Old news." Tim took another sip of water. "But I have some new information for you that you might find interesting. You remember Steve, my legislative director."

"I always knew he was dirty."

"Really? You were aware illegal activities were going on, but you didn't report them?"

"I suspected," Stan backpedaled. "I didn't know."

"Anyway, I was visiting with Steve this morning by phone. He says to tell you hello."

Leo fought to hide his surprise. His father speaking to his former friend was news to him, too. He wondered if the FBI had been in on the call.

While Nell's expression remained impassive, she was likely wondering where this strange conversation was heading. For now, she appeared content to let his father take the lead.

"I don't communicate with criminals." Stan looked at Nell and added, "The last time I did left a bad taste."

Stan's sanctimonious smugness scraped against Leo's last nerve.

"Next time I speak with him, I'll mention that." Tim's pleasant expression never wavered. "He had some interesting things to say about you."

Tiny beads of perspiration sprouted on Stan's forehead. "What kind of things?"

"Well," Tim took another long drink of water, "he mentioned that you offered him money in exchange for securing my vote on certain bills of interest to you."

"That's a lie," Stan shouted and jerked up from the table, nearly upending it.

"Sit down." The command in Tim's voice had Stan stiffening. Then the senator's voice turned conversational again. "I feel certain you'll want to know everything Steve said. I know I would if he was talking about me to the FBI."

Clearly stunned, Stan sat. "I admit I am curious about the lies he's spreading."

"A paper trail is difficult to dispute." Tim slanted a glance at Nell. "As an attorney, I'm sure you agree with that statement."

"Evidence, especially in written form, is very difficult to fight."

Nell, Leo saw, was trying not to smile.

"What kind of evidence does Steve have against Stan?" Leo asked, relaxing against the back of his chair.

"He doesn't have anything, because there isn't any evidence." Stan's tone reminded Leo of a belligerent child.

As his father had raised three strong-willed boys, Tim Pomeroy knew just how to deal with a belligerent child.

"What were you thinking, Stan, putting offers of bribes in an email?" Tim shook his head. "Granted, you were smart enough to not send the emails to his work account, but still, you should have been more careful."

"That was a huge error," Leo agreed.

Stan's face had gone bone-white.

"Did Steve have any other evidence?" Nell asked, her tone conversational.

"Actually, yes. Steve was meticulous about record-keeping. Each time he met with Stan, he not only wrote down the date and time they met, he noted what they discussed and included actual quotes of what Stan said. The FBI does the same when they meet with someone they don't quite trust."

Stan leaned forward. "He gave these notes to the FBI?"

"As well as the emails. He wanted to be thorough."

Stan's hands balled into fists. His face reddened. "So, what are you saying? If I leave you alone, you can make this go away? You're fooling yourself if you think this is going to stop me."

"I've said no such thing nor made any such claim, Stan. I've been cooperating with the authorities fully in every aspect of their investigation. Steve was one of my oldest friends, and even for him, I didn't try to escape the law. I certainly wouldn't do so for a man like you."

Stan made a broad sweep with one hand, encompassing everyone at the table. A smug little smile lifted his lips. "I'm going to bury you all."

"You might try," Tim said. "But I doubt you'll succeed. I seem to recall you're quite a history buff. If so, you might remember that a two-front war was Germany's downfall in World War II. I'd say you've got more than enough of a fight on your hands with the FBI."

"Steve didn't take the money I offered," Stan insisted. "There was no crime."

"Look up the statutes, Stan." Nell gave him a pitying glance.

"You'll find the corrupt gift, the offer and the promise all are defined as acts of bribery and provide the same punishment."

Leo leaned back in his chair and studied Stan. "It makes me wonder that since you attempted to bribe Steve, maybe you targeted others as well."

Tim nodded approvingly. "You're thinking like an FBI agent now, son."

Stan shoved back his chair and jerked to his feet. "You haven't seen the last of me."

"Three words, Stan." Tim held up a hand and counted off. "Two. Front. War."

Several seconds later, the front door of the inn slammed shut.

"Do you think we'll hear from him again?" Leo asked.

Tim shot Nell a wink. "I think the FBI is going to be keeping him plenty busy."

Nell was still trying to process everything that had just occurred when Tim rose.

"I'm sure the two of you have a lot to talk about, so I'm heading home." Tim's lips curved. "This ended up being quite enjoyable."

"Why did you do this?" Nell asked before Tim could step away. "Why did you help me?"

"You've built a life you can be proud of here in Hazel Green. You were forced into situations beyond your control as a child. You didn't choose any of that for yourself. And once you could make your own choices, you've made good ones." Tim's tone gentled. "Besides, Leo loves you. That makes you part of the family."

"I may have made something of myself, but along the way, I made some mistakes."

Understanding flickered deep in Tim's eyes, along with

another emotion—regret, maybe—that she couldn't quite identify. "Life is one game you cannot play without making mistakes."

"Thanks, Dad." Leo was on his feet now and holding out his hand.

Instead of taking it, Tim gave his son a one-armed hug. "You've got a good woman there. The fact that you came to be with her for this meeting tells me I raised you right."

Nell's gaze fell on Leo. "I told you to stay away."

Tim chuckled. "He wouldn't be the man I admire if he'd let the woman he loves face that maniac alone."

"Did you really speak with Steve?" Leo asked. "Or was that all a bluff?"

"I did speak with him. It isn't easy reaching someone in federal custody, but I pulled a few strings." Tim's voice wavered for just a second. "Steve was glad to hear from me. Your mom will be dropping by to see Karen when we get back to DC."

Leo's gaze turned speculative. "What happened to the need to keep your distance?"

"It's still a good political and legal strategy, but I've come to realize that there are more important things than retaining a Senate seat."

Leo and Nell exchanged a glance.

"Steve sincerely apologized and admitted to his gambling and money issues. He acknowledged that's no excuse, but he never would have betrayed our friendship if he'd been thinking clearly." Tim cleared his throat. "He's cooperating fully with the feds and has made it perfectly clear to everyone who'll listen that it was all him and I knew nothing."

"Glad to hear it," Leo murmured.

Well, that about sums it up." Tim clapped Leo on the back and nodded to Nell. "I'll see you both later."

Leo moved to her side as Tim strode out of the restaurant.

"He doesn't have anything to worry about."

Nell turned and realized Matilda still stood in the same spot she was in when they'd all been at the table.

"Worry about?" Nell asked.

"About being reelected." Matilda smiled widely. "Illinois voters love an honest man who stands by his friends."

∾

"It's so lovely." Nell gazed out over Spring Lake, which appeared to be the same blue as the sky. The land surrounding it had been recently mowed and now looked like an endless carpet of green. Flowers and strategically planted bushes only added to the beauty of the vista.

A group of Scouts and their leader were floating boats that appeared to be made out of items found in the area—twigs, pinecones and bird feathers. Farther inland, the tai chi group practiced their moves.

"Yes." Leo took a step closer and brushed his lips against her hair. "You are so beautiful."

When Leo's arms slid around her waist, pulling her close, Nell didn't resist. Instead, she dropped her head against his shoulder and breathed in the citrusy scent of his cologne.

"I'm glad you came to Matilda's," she said finally. "I wasn't sure what to think when you just showed up."

He tucked a strand of hair behind her ear. "You were a little pissed."

"No—"

"C'mon, tell it straight."

"Okay, so maybe I was a little irritated. I felt like I could handle Stanley on my own." She blew out a breath. "He was different today. He reminded me of my mother."

"That can't be a good thing," Leo murmured, playing with her hair.

"But mostly I was upset that you'd come because I didn't want him to take his anger at me out on you. He could have ruined your career. He still might try."

"Even if he does, all that matters to me is having you in my life. Before I ran for mayor, I helped run a successful real estate development company. If Stanley somehow managed to turn the voters of Hazel Green against me, I'd happily go back to working with my brothers."

She turned in his arms to face him. "But you love being mayor, and you're good at it."

"I do. But I could give it up." His eyes locked on hers. "There's only one thing I couldn't give up, and that's you. I love you, Nell. I can't do without you."

"I come with a lot of baggage," she reminded him.

"Have you seen the size of my house?"

Nell laughed and flung her arms around his neck. How had she gotten so lucky? "What am I going to do with you?"

"I've got some ideas."

"What are they?"

"Let's just say they involve a ring and a promise and a lifetime together."

As his mouth closed over hers, Nell thought that sounded like a pretty good plan.

Illinois 1900

Richard and I were married six weeks after we first met. Some people you know their entire lives and they remain strangers. Some, your heart recognizes immediately. Richard's family is lovely. They have accepted me as one of their own, simply because their son loves me. What a wondrous thing it is to not only have a husband, but a big family as well.

Is it possible to be too happy? From the moment I set foot in this new community, I felt as if I'd found my true home. My husband, this man I love with my entire heart, told me as we watched our first sunset together, that this was going to be my town.

I am reminded of a saying about expecting nothing but getting everything.

I have everything.

H.

∼

From Cindy Kirk:

Thanks so much for spending time with Leo and Nell and their friends and family in Hazel Green. The character of Nell came alive for me when the idea of Gloria sprang into my head. I wondered what it would be like to be raised by a charismatic sociopath. And, if you did get away and rebuild your life, what would happen when the past came calling?

I hope you enjoyed reading One Step Away as much as I enjoyed writing it.

The story continues with Dixon's book, ONE & ONLY YOU. This book is another personal favorite and I hope you'll find yourself sighing with relief (and happiness) when Dixon and Rachel find their own happily ever after.

Pick up your copy of One & Only You today (or keep reading for a sneak peek)

Rachel Grabinski stood outside the Chicago hotel room and wiped sweaty palms against the skirt of her summer dress. She wasn't an impulsive person, and taking the train into the city to surprise her boyfriend at a conference was out of character for her.

Not to mention, Marc Koenig, her boyfriend of the past year, didn't like surprises. He'd made that clear when she'd popped by his apartment one evening. She felt her heart pound an erratic rhythm just remembering the look on his face.

Yet, he'd also told her many times this past week how disappointed he was that she couldn't get off work to meet him for an early dinner tonight. It had felt to her like their relationship was stumbling, but she wasn't sure how to right it.

She wondered if he'd have been more understanding if she had a different job. Marc didn't approve of her position as the volunteer coordinator at the Hazel Green Food Bank. According to him, working for a nonprofit meant she'd decided to toss aside any hope of a decent career.

Rachel pushed that discussion from her head. Not the time, she reminded herself. A gas leak down the street from the food bank had had everyone leaving early. This was her chance to enjoy a beautiful summer evening with her boyfriend.

This time, she let her knuckles fall against the door. She considered calling out to Marc, but wanted—really wanted—to see the surprised pleasure on his face when he saw her.

On the fourth knock, she heard him yell, "I'm coming. Just wait a damn minute."

Rachel dropped her hand to her side and touched her tongue to her lips, tasting the cherry flavor of the lip balm that she had applied during the ride up in the elevator. She resisted the urge to reach up to straighten her glasses.

The tortoiseshell frames sat just fine on her nose. Adjusting them was a nervous habit she was determined to break.

She widened her eyes as the door flung open.

Her smile turned tentative when she saw the towel he held around his waist. His hair and skin were dry, so obviously she'd caught him just as he was about to step into the shower.

"Rachel." Surprise had him nearly releasing the towel. "I thought you were room service. What are you doing here?"

She'd started to step forward, but he blocked her.

"There was a gas leak just down the block from the food bank. They evacuated everyone, so I got off early." She lifted her hands. "Surprise."

"It was about time they brought up the champagne and strawberries." The sultry voice came from inside the room before Marc could respond.

Rachel shoved him aside and stepped into the suite.

The brunette wasn't a supermodel, but she was pretty, with a mass of tousled dark hair. She'd carelessly tossed on one of the hotel robes, letting the front gap to show an impressive amount of cleavage. Her feet were bare, and her toenails were candy-apple red.

The woman's dark brows slammed together. "You're not room service."

Rachel shifted her gaze from the woman to Marc. "You explain it to her."

He grabbed her arm in a firm grip as she pushed past him out of the room. "It isn't like it looks."

"Tell your lies to someone who'll believe them." She jerked her arm free. "Don't call me ever again. We're done."

"Rachel," he called out, but she strode down the hall without looking back.

Just as she reached the elevator, the ornate silver doors slid open, and a couple holding hands exited. She watched the man lean over and brush his companion's lips with his.

Rachel pressed her cherry-red lips together and punched the button that would take her to the lobby.

Dixon Carlyle considered himself a social creature. One with a talent for reading clients and responding in a way that made them trust him. The talent had come in handy when he was growing up. Only then, he'd needed to read marks. He'd quickly learned that saying one wrong thing could have disastrous consequences.

Those games were in the past. Now, he was a respected financial consultant with a growing list of clients, whom he did right by. The fact that most were pleased with his investment advice and the returns they'd been enjoying guaranteed his business would only continue to grow.

He'd attended the seminar at Palmer House in Chicago this morning on "Understanding the impact of erosion through inflation and taxation." While he listened to the experts, Dixon had been in text communication with a potential client. The twentysomething entrepreneur had hit it big last year and was searching for someone he trusted.

They'd met several times, and Dixon liked the kid's sharp eyes and quick wit. Various strategies for investing the young man's millions had been explored. Now, they were in final negotiations.

Like many Millennials, Raj Agarwal preferred texting over phone calls or face-to-face meetings. Today, while Dixon listened to the presentation at the front of the large ballroom, Raj had confirmed his desire to chart a certain course.

It was the course Dixon had recommended early on...but the boy had wanted to explore all options. Dixon was aware Raj had been consulting with other financial planners, but he hadn't worried. The kid was smart. He would realize Dixon was the best.

Dixon texted his sister. *Finalized deal.*

There was no need to say more.

Congratulations! We need to celebrate.

He added a thumbs-up to the comment, knowing any celebration would wait until all the papers were signed. Their mother had impressed upon both her children that you didn't count on anything, especially not when something seemed like a done deal.

As memories of Gloria threatened to dim his sunny mood, Dixon shoved the thoughts of her aside. The presentations had wrapped for the day, and the gala didn't start until eight.

More than enough time to stroll down Michigan Avenue and enjoy the beautiful day. Many conference attendees must have had the same idea, as hordes of smartly dressed men and women headed for the exits in the main lobby.

Shoved against someone, Dixon turned with an apology already on his lips. The woman, wearing a flirty summer dress covered in large poppies, stood out like a breath of fresh air.

"I'm sorry—" he began, then he realized he knew her. "Rachel?"

She shifted her gaze for a second, just long enough for him to see her reddened eyes. The determined set to her jaw and shoulders was at odds with the evidence of tears. "I need to get out of here."

Dixon, never at a loss for words, hesitated. Rachel was a good friend of his sister. They'd been at many parties together since he'd moved to Hazel Green. Every contact he'd had with her had been brief.

Not only was she dating Marc Koenig, but she was just so… good. Not a single ounce of sass or snark in her.

Still, he narrowed his gaze as he followed her out the front doors of the hotel. The woman had backbone, and something had happened to bring it out in full force.

Even as he told himself to keep to his original plan, Dixon fell into step beside her. She continued to be a good friend to Nell, which meant he needed to at least try to see if he could help.

He was still trying to figure out how to broach the subject of the tears when she stopped in the middle of the glittery sidewalk and whirled. "I don't need you. I don't need any man."

Now they were getting somewhere. Rachel and Marc had obviously had a fight. Something he knew Nell would firmly applaud. Dixon shared his sister's low opinion of Rachel's boyfriend.

"We are mostly scum," he agreed. "You look hungry. I was going to grab something to eat. Will you join me?"

Confusion furrowed her brow. "Why would you want to have dinner with me? We barely know each other."

"You're one of my sister's closest friends." He flashed a smile. "That makes you practically family."

It was lame. Surely he could have thought of something better to address her concerns.

"I am hungry." She expelled a shuddering breath, then appeared to notice his dark suit, crisp white shirt and perfectly knotted red tie. "I'm not really dressed for anyplace fancy."

Since it was barely five, he hadn't planned on going anywhere *fancy*. "What kind of food do you like?"

"Wherever you want to go is fine."

Dixon didn't have any trouble taking the lead, and from

Rachel's response, she would go along with whatever he suggested. He swallowed the words on his lips when he recalled Nell telling him of her frustration that Rachel let Marc run the show. Instead of standing up for what she wanted, she let him decide.

Was that what had happened today? Had Marc broken it off?

Dixon stopped himself from making assumptions. Hadn't he been taught from a young age to gather information before drawing conclusions?

"Tell me what kind of food you like." He placed his hand on her elbow when the mass of people around them threatened to push them apart.

"I like Italian," she said after a long moment. "And Thai. But I really like anything, so—"

He cut her off before she could offer once again to go wherever he wanted. "Both sound good to me. Maggiano's isn't far."

When she hesitated, he added, "Italian is a favorite of mine."

"Okay."

Once they were seated at a table and their orders taken, Dixon could almost see Rachel relax. It wasn't hard. The atmosphere at Maggiano's practically begged patrons to breathe in the scent of fresh bread, garlic and cheese and enjoy.

Dixon had finalized many business deals at the tables covered in red-and-white-checkered oilcloths. The restaurant was a popular place for families, couples and tourists to enjoy a good Italian meal.

When he caught Rachel eyeing the Italian sangria at a neighboring table, he ordered them a pitcher as well as a plate of antipasti.

She picked up a piece of salami and nibbled. Her small, almost delicate hands had nails painted a pale pink.

Dixon ate a roasted pepper, then lifted his glass for a toast.

Tentatively, Rachel lifted her own. "What are we toasting?"

"You."

She flushed, her cheeks turning a bright pink. "Me?"

"Nell mentioned the idea for the field-to-food-bank initiative was yours." Dixon clinked his glass against hers. "To Rachel, for improving the nutrition of struggling families through fresh produce."

"I was just doing my job," she protested, but he saw that the haunted look had left her eyes.

"Now," he set his glass on the table and leaned forward, giving her his full attention, "tell me what brought you to Palmer House."

Grab your copy of One & Only You to see how this story ends.

ALSO BY CINDY KIRK

Good Hope Series

The Good Hope series is a must-read for those who love stories that uplift and bring a smile to your face.

Check out the entire Good Hope series here

Hazel Green Series

Readers say "Much like the author's series of Good Hope books, the reader learns about a town, its people, places and stories that enrich the overall experience. It's a journey worth taking."

Check out the entire Hazel Green series here

Holly Pointe Series

Readers say "If you are looking for a festive, romantic read this Christmas, these are the books for you."

Check out the entire Holly Pointe series here

Jackson Hole Series

Heartwarming and uplifting stories set in beautiful Jackson Hole, Wyoming.

Check out the entire Jackson Hole series here

Silver Creek Series

Engaging and heartfelt romances centered around two powerful families whose fortunes were forged in the Colorado silver mines.

Check out the entire Silver Creek series here

·

Made in the USA
Monee, IL
18 March 2023

30133535R00138